interest level grades 4-8
AR points: 3.0
ATOS Book Level: 3.7

DRAGON
GAMES

Also by P. W. Catanese

The Books of Umber
Book 1: Happenstance Found
Book 2: Dragon Games

The Thief and the Beanstalk

The Brave Apprentice

The Eye of the Warlock

The Mirror's Tale

The Riddle of the Gnome

P. W. CATANESE
THE BOOKS OF UMBER

DRAGON
GAMES

ALADDIN

NEW YORK   LONDON   TORONTO   SYDNEY

ALADDIN

An imprint of Simon & Schuster Children's Publishing Division

1230 Avenue of the Americas, New York, NY 10020

First Aladdin hardcover edition January 2010

Copyright © 2010 by P. W. Catanese

For information about special discounts for bulk purchases, please contact Simon & Schuster Special Sales at 1-866-506-1949 or business@simonandschuster.com.

The Simon & Schuster Speakers Bureau can bring authors to your live event. For more information or to book an event, contact the Simon & Schuster Speakers Bureau at 1-866-248-3049 or visit our website at www.simonspeakers.com.

Designed by Mike Rosamilia

The text of this book was set in Bembo.

Manufactured in the United States of America

1209 MTN

2 4 6 8 10 9 7 5 3 1

Library of Congress Cataloging-in-Publication Data

Catanese, P. W.

Dragon games / by P. W. Catanese. — First Aladdin hardcover ed.

p. cm. — (The books of Umber ; bk. 2)

Summary: Having learned more about his mysterious past, Happenstance accompanies Lord Umber on a daring journey that could affect the future of Kuraharen.

ISBN 978-1-4169-7521-2

[1. Adventure and adventurers—Fiction. 2. Fantasy.] I. Title.

PZ7.C268783Dr 2010

[Fic]—dc22

2009018743

ISBN 978-1-4169-9868-6 (eBook)

FOR MY AGENT,
PETER RUBIE

DRAGON GAMES

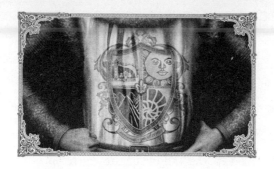

CHAPTER
I

The boy gripped the railing tight.
He watched the leviathan's enormous tail rise from the brine until it almost broke the surface and then sweep down again in a powerful and dreamlike rhythm that propelled the barge through a rolling black sea. The port city of Kurahaven, storm-battered but still glorious, was far behind, and the sun's fire had been doused hours before on the horizon ahead.

Happenstance eyed the dark waves uneasily. He'd hoped his dread of water might fade as he spent more hours plying its surface. *But it's as bad as ever,* Hap thought, with a little twist at the corner of his mouth. His shoulders rose toward his ears.

There was an open hatch on the deck of the barge, with stairs leading down to the spacious central cabin. A giddy sound drifted up the stairs and into the night. Hap recognized the particular laugh of his guardian. Lord Umber was in his usual high spirits, which were always at their loftiest after a satisfying meal and a hot mug of his beloved coffee, and with the prospect of some thrilling discovery ahead.

Hap walked to the railing at the square prow to see what might lie before them. His extraordinary eyes pierced the darkness and found Nima, the barge's captain, sitting cross-legged on the back of the leviathan, Boroon. Perhaps sensing that someone was watching, she turned to look back at the barge that was strapped to Boroon's immense back.

"Hello, Nima," Hap called. He wasn't sure that Nima could see him in the gloom of night, with tatters of cloud shrouding the moon, but she waved. She stood, walked across the bony plates of the leviathan's back, and climbed the stairs to stand beside Hap.

Nima was clad in black sealskin. As she ran her hands through her long hair, Hap stole a glance at the translucent skin that bridged the space between her knuckles. He pulled his gaze away in an instant; he knew better than most how it felt to have someone stare at a physical oddity.

"Why aren't you below with the others, Happenstance?" she asked.

Hap shrugged. "I felt like coming up here." That was hardly

true. What he'd really felt like was not setting out on this adventure at all. He wished Umber could be content to stay home in the Aerie. It was a fine place to dwell, with wonders and mysteries galore inside its crammed archives. Those were the kind he preferred: adventures in ink, which couldn't crush you in their jaws or under their feet. But, sadly, Umber liked the real thing. And to make matters worse, running off to a new land always exposed Hap to more strangers who would point and gawk at his strange green eyes.

"I'm glad to find you here alone," Nima said. "There's something I've been meaning to give you." There was a silver chain around her neck. She lifted it over her head, and Hap saw a fat locket dangling, shaped like halves of a seashell. She held it out, and Hap opened a hand to accept it.

"It's beautiful," Hap said. "But . . ."

"Why am I giving it to you? Because I heard how you risked your life to save Umber. And Umber is my friend. You have spared me an ocean of grief."

Hap clamped his jaw as he thought back to that terrifying night when he'd climbed a crumbling tower to confront the awful, eye-stealing creature that had taken Umber hostage. "It wasn't just me who saved Umber," he said.

"I know that. But Hap, you haven't seen the true gift yet. Open it."

Hap brought the locket closer to his eyes and saw a tiny clasp at the seam of the two shells. He pried it open with a fingernail, and the shells parted. Inside was an enormous pearl. It was as round and lustrous as the moon, which chose that moment to emerge from hiding and shine down on its little cousin. Hap goggled at the orb. He'd seen pearls in the jewelers' tents in the marketplace at Kurahaven, but none so large or stunning. "How can I accept this? It's too much!"

"You land folk value pearls more than I do. And do you really think it is so hard for me to find such a thing?" Nima asked. Hap supposed it wasn't. Nima was amphibious, and she could breathe under the waves as easily as above them. Of course she could dive down and bring up all manner of wonders. Balfour had told him once that the leviathan barge was built and paid for by the fortunes she'd found in sunken ships.

"It may be useful in a difficult spot someday," Nima said. "Or it might help a friend in need. Your heart will tell you when to use it."

Hap snapped the locket shut and put the chain around his neck. "It's wonderful. Thank you."

"It was Boroon's idea, in fact," Nima said.

Hap stared at the leviathan's broad head, cutting the waves before them. "Really? Boroon?" He knew that Nima communicated with the leviathan, but he had no idea that they discussed matters so . . . specific. "Would you thank him for me, please?"

Nima nodded.

A minute passed, silent except for the hiss of water along the leviathan's side. "Where are we going?" Hap asked.

Nima smiled. "Umber wanted it to be a secret. You know how he is about these things."

Hap sighed. If he could change one thing about Umber— besides his constant need for the thrill of exploration—it would be his obsession with secrets and surprises.

Before long everyone else was asleep, even the great leviathan, who bobbed in the water like a breathing island. Hap kept watch for the others, because he needed no sleep. That was another one of the great mysteries about him, the boy with no memory of who he was or where he'd come from.

Boroon's fins swirled in the water, holding the barge in place an arrow's flight from the coast. Hap, like the others, shielded his eyes from the rising sun, staring at the spot where Nima pointed. He looked at Oates, who frowned and shrugged.

Umber thumped the railing with both hands and laughed. "I can see why nobody's discovered this before! Why would any ship come close? It's just a craggy sea cliff, unremarkable

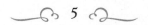

and uninviting. Still, Nima, I don't see the opening you mentioned."

"Watch when the wave hits the shore," Nima said. "There."

A crest of water rolled toward the cliff. Hap watched, expecting it to slam against the rock and throw up an explosion of foam. But something else happened: The wave collapsed, as if its foundation had vanished.

"I see it now!" Umber cried. "A cave, under the surface! But how can we get inside?"

"Boroon can take us," Nima said.

Umber's eyes gleamed. "It's *that* big in there? And we won't . . . you know . . . disturb them?"

Nima nodded. "It's large enough. And I have done it once before."

"I'm so glad you discovered this!" Umber cried, with his knees wiggling.

"It was Boroon who saw the cave from underwater. He is a curious soul," Nima replied quietly. "But sometimes I feel I never should have told you about it."

"Hold on, Umber," said Oates, raising a thick hand. "What did you mean, 'disturb them'?"

"Let's not wait another second!" cried Umber, ignoring the big man. "Do we need to douse the fires?"

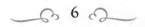

Nima shook her head. "We'll be under for only a moment," she said.

Under, Hap thought. *Not again.* He crossed his arms to suppress the shivers that ran through his body.

Umber rubbed his hands together and laughed. "Everybody, down the hatch. Boroon is going to dive!"

Hap followed the others down the stairs into the central cabin. Only Nima, who was in no danger of drowning, stayed above. Oates pulled the hatch shut behind him and sealed it, then came muttering down the stairs. He held on to one of the beams in the middle of the room and stared at the ceiling as the barge lurched forward.

This was the second time Hap had been aboard when Boroon took the craft underwater, and it terrified him as much as the first. He sat beside Balfour, Umber's elderly friend and trusted servant, at the dining table that was anchored to the floor, his bloodless fingers clamped on the table's edge. Sophie—the girl who was just a few years older than Hap and was valued for her skill as both artist and archer—was across from him, and she gave him a reassuring smile despite her own obvious nerves. There were round windows of thick glass in the walls, and the water rose past them as Hap watched. The light changed from pale daylight to the dim, shimmering green of the sea and then vanished as they passed into a space where little sun could reach. He felt the squeeze of pressure deep inside his ears, and when he worked his jaw, his eardrums popped.

Umber stood at the bottom of the stairs, bouncing in place and humming. "Listen, everyone—it should be safe to go up in a moment, but I think we should keep as quiet as we can."

"You make more noise than anyone," Oates pointed out.

"Do I?" Umber asked, narrowing one eye.

"With all your squealing and clapping."

Umber glared. "Nothing wrong with a little enthusiasm."

Balfour cleared his throat. "Umber, would you mind telling us why we need to be quiet?"

Umber raised a hand, palm out. "Patience, my friends! We're almost there!" The barge's bow tilted upward again. Boroon brought them to the surface, but the ascent was slow, as if the leviathan was trying to be as stealthy as such an enormous creature could be.

"It's so much better if you see for yourselves," Umber said. Hap could measure his guardian's excitement by the diameter of his eyes, and they looked now like a pair of dinner plates. Umber dashed up the stairs and threw the hatch open. "Bring the lamps," he called in a half whisper. "And walk softly!"

Hap waited for Oates, Balfour, and Sophie to ascend before him. When he followed, he heard Umber telling them: "Give your eyes time to adjust to the dark." But Hap, of course, needed no time.

Boroon had swum into a great cave that must have been bored out over eons by the endless undermining of ocean waves. The entrance was behind them and underwater. Hap could see a glimmer of dim sunlight filtering through, as if passing under the threshold of a door.

The sea cave was immense. The ceiling of stone was a hundred feet above the top of the barge, and Boroon fit easily in the pool of water that washed up against a broad stone ledge in the interior. When Hap saw the monstrous things that occupied the ledge, his breath was snared inside his throat. For a moment he thought they were toppled statues or mummified creatures—anything but living beings. But then he heard the air rushing in and out of enormous mouths and nostrils, and he saw the subtle rise and fall of the vast chests.

They all stared, grasping the rail. Even the leviathan raised his head from the water to eye the five slumbering things.

Boroon was still the largest creature Hap had ever seen, but these titans were not far behind. A grown man could disappear under one of their feet. Two might have been female, but it was hard to tell with faces so monstrous: warty and craggy, with blunt horns sprouting from chins, cheeks, and foreheads. Their filthy hair had the coarse texture of a horse's tail. The skin on their limbs was etched with countless lines as deep as the bark of ancient trees. Hap noticed, with some alarm, that their ragged garments seemed to have been made from the hide of a beast much like Boroon.

The creatures were sprawled on the ledge in almost drunken poses. Two slumped against the wall of the cave with legs splayed. One lay flat on her stomach with a hand dangling over the ledge and fingers in the water. Two more curled on their sides like babies.

"What are they?" asked Sophie, almost too quietly to hear.

The answer suddenly came to Hap. He'd read about them in Umber's books. "Sea-giants!" he said, hissing the words. More than two hundred years before, the sea-giants had invaded the great city of Kurahaven and smashed it into ruins. The sorceress Turiana had somehow driven them away, and the sea-giants had stalked into the sea, vanishing under the waves, never to be seen again. *Until this day,* Hap thought.

Umber's giddy smile was so wide it threatened to divide his head. "Exactly! We've found their den. Their resting place."

"Resting place! Are you a crazy man, bringing us here?" cried Oates. "What if they wake up?"

"Kindly lower your voice," Umber said, patting the air with his hands. He gestured for the others to gather close, and spoke in a hush. "I don't think we have to worry about waking them."

"We don't?" Balfour asked quietly. "Why is that?"

"I think they're waiting for something," Umber said.

"Waiting? What kind of nonsense is that?" scoffed Oates.

Umber could barely keep still. He rubbed his hands together and shifted his weight from foot to foot. "Do you know why they came to Kurahaven, all those years ago?"

"To crush and plunder," Balfour replied.

Umber shook his head. "They didn't come to crush the city. They came to crush the hubris of its king."

"That must have hurt," Oates said.

Umber pinched the bridge of his nose. "Hubris means arrogance, you great buffoon. Now listen carefully, Sophie and Hap—I don't think you know the entire legend."

Hap and Sophie stepped closer so Umber could keep his voice low. "These days the kingdom of Celador is a peaceable place, friendly to neighbors and interested mainly in trade. But in that age the kings were growing in power and bent on conquest. They declared themselves the lords of the sea, and their pride grew as fast as their fortunes. They made Kurahaven the wonder of its age, with the greatest fleet ever seen. Then came King Brinn, the fiercest and most ambitious ruler of them all. No ordinary castle was enough for him. And so in the harbor he built Petraportus, the ultimate symbol of his kingdom's might and mastery of the sea: a castle so grand that a ship could sail through its gates and into the man-made harbor in its great hall. Petraportus was quite a statement— so loud that it finally reached the ears of those who did not appreciate man's challenge to their dominion." Umber jutted his chin toward the sleeping giants. "And so the sea-giants roused themselves and put an end to Brinn, his fleet, his city, and his castle. Not to mention his hubris."

Umber's face lost its color for a moment. His gaze wandered to some distant, imaginary point. "It was a message to all humanity, come to think of it: Don't get too big for your britches. There are always forces bigger than you can imagine, ready to put you in your place. If your ambition burns too hot, they'll snuff you out."

For a moment Umber looked ready to plummet into one of his episodes of despair. "But Lord Umber," Hap asked quickly, "how do you know these are the same sea-giants?"

Umber gave his head a shake, and his eyes came back into focus. His smile was resurrected. "Why, I believe that's the famous Bulrock, right there. Hap, do you remember the story of Brinn's leap?"

"He jumped from the top of Petraportus, swinging his ax, and cut off Bulrock's nose," Hap said. Beside him

Sophie, who had brought a pad of paper and charcoal, began to sketch the amazing scene. But she suddenly gasped and pointed at the largest of the giants, who was leaning against the wall of the cave. The tip of his nose was clearly missing.

"Nima," Umber quietly called, "do you think you could have Boroon paddle us a little closer to the ledge?"

Hap looked down. At the moment just fifteen or twenty yards of water separated them from the rocky shelf where the giants slumbered. The idea of getting nearer seemed like madness.

He wasn't the only one who felt so. Sophie's eyes looked like they might pop out and fall onto the deck. Balfour said, "I'm not sure that's a good idea, Lord Umber."

"I agree," Nima said, folding her arms. "It would invite disaster."

Umber waved a hand. "Come now, my friends. They won't be roused easily—they've hibernated for centuries. I'd love to get a closer look. Touch one, if I can."

Oates glared at Umber. "You *are* a crazy man," he said.

"Because I'm not afraid of my own shadow?" Umber said. "Come on, Hap, you'll join me, won't you?"

Hap shifted his weight from foot to foot. "But . . . Lord Umber . . . if they awaken . . . you know what they could do. We could all get killed. And what if they went back to Kurahaven?"

Umber glowered and worked his jaw from side to side. "What's the matter with all of you? You're as meek as mice." He lifted his feet, one after another, and hopped as he pried off his boots. When they fell to the deck, it sounded like thunder. "Stay here if you like. I'll swim over. Be back in a minute or two, that's all."

"For heaven's sake, Umber," Balfour said. He fired a look at Oates, and Oates nodded back. Just as Umber hooked a leg over the railing, the big man stepped closer and wrapped a powerful arm around Umber's waist.

"What's this?" Umber cried, thrashing in Oates's grip. "I'll decide what I can and can't do! Let go of me, you insolent, muscled mor—" He froze abruptly with his mouth hanging open, staring across the water. Hap turned to look, and his blood turned to cold sludge in his veins.

One of Bulrock's eyes was open.

CHAPTER
2

For a moment none of them moved,
not even to breathe. Oates held Umber suspended in the air.
The giant's single eye gleamed, catching the yellow glow of
the lanterns. *How big is that eye?* Hap asked himself, and then
answered: *As big as my head.*

"Get below, all of you," Nima whispered. "Softly now.
Take the lamps. Seal the hatch."

Oates lowered Umber to the deck and released him. Umber
didn't struggle or try to climb over the railing again, but the
angry expression hadn't left his face. He backed toward the
open hatch, still watching the sea-giant.

Hap's legs quaked as he made his way to the stairs. A tear
ran from the corner of Sophie's eye, and sweat beaded Balfour's

brow. Hap wasn't sure that Bulrock was truly awake—not yet, anyway. The eye didn't turn to follow them, and it never blinked. It simply gleamed, as vacantly as the moon. *Don't wake up,* Hap said inwardly, over and over again, as if repeating the words would cast a spell.

They descended the stairs to the lower deck. Umber stopped to look back one more time, until Oates seized him by the back of the collar and pulled him down. Nima had run onto Boroon's back to tell him to dive, and she would cling to the leviathan's back when he submerged.

Oates closed the hatch, and a moment later the barge tilted. Hap heard water hiss up the sides and a dull roar as the sea engulfed the top deck. The vessel turned and surged forward before rising again, outside the vast cave, into the light of day.

Umber sat on the bottom step. He scowled and hammered his knees with his fists, darting angry glares at the rest of them. When he heard water rushing off the barge, he threw the hatch open again and raced out, leaning far over the rear rail and staring at the cliff. The others followed, and Hap watched, praying that the giants would not suddenly rise up and wade after them in pursuit.

"They must still be asleep," Balfour said at last, letting out a long breath. "Thank the stars for that." He pulled a white handkerchief from his pocket and dabbed his brow.

Umber slapped the railing and whirled to confront the others. "What was *that* all about? How dare you restrain me, after all I've done for the lot of you!"

Hap dropped his gaze, unable to meet Umber's fiery stare.

"Umber . . . what you tried to do . . . It was . . . ," Balfour began, before his voice trailed off.

"It was *what*?" cried Umber. "Out with it, Balfour! What, do you think I'm dangerous? Do you think I'm mad?"

Balfour's jaw worked up and down, until words finally eked out. "Umber, you know how much I esteem and respect you. All of us do."

"Ha!" spat Umber. "Respect, you say? Is that what you call what you did?" Umber spun toward Sophie. "Tell me, Sophie: Do I frighten you? Do you think I'm crazy?"

"No, my lord," Sophie said in a quaking voice. She covered her mouth with her only hand and turned away.

Umber crossed his arms and scowled. "And you, Hap! You know how our fates are intertwined. Are you afraid of me as well, to follow me wherever I go?"

Hap felt a thousand hot pinpricks across his face. "It's—it's not that you frighten me—" he began, before Umber cut him off.

"Cowards!" he snapped. "Will none of you speak honestly? Wait a minute—where's that bloody Oates? Oates, come back here!"

Oates had been quietly edging his way across the deck and down the stairs, trying to escape from sight. His shoulders slumped when he heard his name called, and he trudged back to stand before Umber.

"At least I know *you'll* be honest," Umber said.

"Don't do this to me," Oates muttered.

Hap felt sorry for the big fellow. Because of a mysterious curse Oates was compelled to speak the truth at all times. This candor had offended many and earned Oates countless slaps in the face. But because of it Umber knew he could trust Oates completely.

"Tell me, Oates: Is that what you think of me? Am I mad? Am I a hazard?"

Oates sighed. "You're reckless. You can't find a beehive without wanting to stick your hand inside. You want to discover things, and you don't care if you risk our lives along the way. I think one of these days you'll get one of us killed."

Umber snorted like a bull and stamped a foot on the deck. But then his fierce expression softened. He turned his back to them, staring at the sea. "But . . . I would never want . . ." He hung his head till his chin touched his chest. After a moment his shoulders began to bob.

Balfour looked at the others with mournful eyes. He stepped forward and put a hand on Umber's shoulder. "We know you mean us no harm. But still . . . that was something to see, wasn't it? Think of it, Umber: the sea-giants!"

Umber turned around. He was crying, but not from guilt or despair. The tears flowed past a mouth that had spread into a broad, elated smile. "Amazing! Astonishing! One of the things I wanted to see most in this world, and now I've seen it. Weren't they incredible? Bigger than I ever imagined. Sure, I'd have liked to get closer, but that wasn't prudent under the circumstances, I'll grant you that. But I *saw* them. Sophie, tell me you got a good look! Do you think you can draw them well enough? Should we go back?"

"No!" cried Sophie, in a tone louder than Hap was accustomed to from her. "I—I saw enough, Lord Umber. I promise."

"Wonderful! Wonderful!" Umber shouted, laughing. Behind his back Balfour looked at Hap and shook his head. Hap knew what he was thinking: Umber's moods shifted so quickly it made a person dizzy.

...veries are chronicled in those boo...

But I also feel the need to record, separately and secretly, the thoughts that I cannot express openly. Because if I did speak of these things, the people of this world would think I am crazier than they do already. But really, Balfour, my first friend in this new life, I write this journal for you. Some— day I may even let you read it. And if anything happens to me, and you are reading this, it is because you found it in the pla... that I told you about, along with instructions on how to di...

...t that w...

CHAPTER
3

Umber preferred not to disrupt the bustling harbor of Kurahaven by riding in on the back of a gargantuan sea-beast. Miles from the city they met with the *Bounder*, a ship from Umber's merchant fleet—dashing vessels of daring design that could outsail anything the world had known. The *Bounder* was captained by Sandar, half brother to Nima. From that rendezvous it was only a few hours' sail into Kurahaven. A savage storm had caused great destruction just a few weeks before, smashing the wharf into splinters and driving ships into the streets. Every vessel in the harbor had been damaged in the tempest, but the *Bounder* had been on a journey of commerce when it struck, and so was spared.

Dozens of boats of all sizes were usually cutting across the bay at all times, but when the *Bounder* sailed in, she was among a lonely three. Things were far busier on the shore, where thousands of people were occupied with repairs to the city and waterfront. Kurahaven was the wealthy capital of a prosperous country and so possessed the resources to rebuild its glory. Craftsmen who'd journeyed to Kurahaven from a hundred miles around hammered on the walls and roofs of the buildings; they pulled the pieces off damaged ships, cannibalizing the useful planks, beams, cords, and sails; they constructed new docks, which reached even farther into the waves. On the long hill beyond the city Hap saw rolling wagons laden with lumber and bricks. Even a half mile away he could hear saws and hammers and smell paint and sawdust.

The *Bounder* sidled up to one of the few surviving berths, scraping past a similar vessel that lay half sunk on its side. "Poor *Swift*," Sandar said, bowing his head. The *Swift* was his usual command, but the sleek ship had fallen prey to the storm.

Once Sandar's men had secured the *Bounder* to the dock, an anxious Umber scurried down the plank, waving for the others to hurry after him. A carriage waited. "Hoyle is hunting for you," the driver called to Umber. It was Dodd, one of Umber's servants and guards.

"I know—I saw her coming!" Umber cried. "Who knew

she could move that fast? Get in, everyone!" Even the rickety Balfour practically broke into a sprint, and they piled into the carriage, with Oates climbing atop beside Dodd. Hap exhaled deeply as the carriage lurched into motion. Like the others he had no desire to be in the vicinity when Hoyle unleashed her wrath on Umber.

Hoyle was the short, squat, iron-willed woman who ran Umber's business ventures. While she in theory worked for Lord Umber, it never seemed that way in practice: She was quick to scold him in a loud and unpleasant tone on the wastefulness of his pursuits of all things magical and monstrous. "I'm still walking on air after seeing the giants," Umber said, slumping out of sight below the carriage window. "I refuse to be brought to earth by one of Hoyle's tirades right now. She'll find me soon enough, though."

That's true, Hap thought. Even he knew why Hoyle would be furious: Umber had commandeered the leviathan barge at a time when many of their merchant vessels were ruined by the storm. To Hoyle a lost business opportunity was more lamentable than the loss of a leg.

The carriage tilted as the muscular horses hauled it up the causeway that led to the Aerie, the remarkable tower of hollow stone where Umber and his trusted friends lived. Hap felt as if tight bands of iron were springing loose from around his chest.

It was good to be away from the sea and back to the place he'd come to call home. If it were up to him, he'd never leave.

Lady Truden, the tall, silver-haired woman who ran the household of the Aerie, stood beside the open door with her hands clasped at her waist. "Welcome home, Lord Umber," she said. Her smile settled into a thin horizontal line as she nodded to the others, and Hap thought one of her eyes twitched at the corner when she looked at him.

They stepped onto the water-driven lift, which rattled and creaked toward the upper floors of the Aerie: the grand hall, the living quarters, and Umber's rooftop tower.

"I'm going to bed," Oates announced through a yawn.

"Of course you are, because you have the sleep habits of a cave bear," Umber said. "But Sophie, my dear, please get to the studio while the images are fresh in your mind and commit them to paper. And Balfour, do you know what I could use?"

"An ounce of common sense," Oates suggested.

Balfour dared a guess. "A pot of coffee?"

Umber clapped his hands and stepped off the lift at the grand hall, where the kitchen lay ahead. "Just the thing!"

Hap kicked off his boots and flopped onto the small bed in his little room at the upper corner of the Aerie. It was a satisfying

thing, he decided, to lie down in your own bed after a journey—even if sleep was not your intent. He wrinkled his nose. The air in his room smelled stale, because the room had been kept shut in his absence. So he stood and opened the pair of windows that looked over Kurahaven and its harbor. The windows were like eyes in the truest sense, because they were set under the brow of a great face that was carved in the Aerie's outer wall.

As soon as he opened the window that faced the city, he heard the clatter of hooves and rumble of wheels on the causeway. He stuck his head into the breeze and saw a carriage. There was gilding on the wheels, and the driver wore the four-part coat of arms of the kingdom of Celador: the crown, the sun, the mountains, and a shell for the sea. Hap assumed it was a royal messenger until he saw a familiar head bob unsteadily out the window to gaze at the towering Aerie. It was Galbus, the middle prince.

Hap sighed, knowing that he would have to stand by while Umber spoke to Prince Galbus. Umber was determined to keep Hap involved in any significant development; if Hap didn't go of his own accord, Umber would summon him. *It could be worse,* Hap thought. Of the three princes he preferred by far the company of this one. The eldest, Argent, was dull and severe. And the youngest, Loden, while outwardly charming, filled Hap with unease.

When Hap came down the steps to the grand hall, Galbus was gazing wide-eyed at the curiosities that filled the shelves. A figurine slipped from his hand, and he slowed its fall with the toe of his boot. He giggled, hiccuped, and fumbled it back on the shelf. Umber entered through the kitchen doors and smiled at his visitor.

"Galbus, my friend! How good to see you! May I offer you some coffee?"

Galbus returned the smile but wrinkled his nose. "You and your coffee, Umber—I don't know how you can bear that bitter stuff. It's wine for me, if you have it." A silent belch inflated his cheeks.

Balfour emerged from the kitchen with a goblet before Umber could turn to call for it. Galbus drained half in a gulp. When he wiped his mouth, he saw Hap lurking by the stairs. "Happenstance! Come here, you mysterious imp. Let me get a look at those eyes!"

The prince was a fun-loving fellow, but he had a tendency to treat Hap like some adorable but exotic pet. As he watched Hap approach, he looked a little disappointed that Hap didn't arrive with one of the fantastic leaps of which he was capable. Nevertheless, Hap forced a smile and turned his face up for inspection as Galbus tousled his hair.

"This visit is most welcome," Umber said, coming to Hap's rescue. "How can I serve you, my prince?"

"Actually, I'm here with an invitation. My brothers are going on a hunt, and your company has been requested."

"A hunt, Your Highness?" Umber inhaled sharply between his teeth. "Forgive me, but I've never been fond of—"

"I know, I know, you don't have the heart for the kill," Galbus said, twirling his hands in the air. "But you'll be interested in this hunt, because the prey is exotic."

Umber's mouth puckered. "Is that so?"

"Oh, yes!" Galbus said, tipping the goblet for another long sip. "A creature they call the *death-boar* has apparently been seen in the mountains. The folk are terrified. Wooo!" He waggled his fingers in the air in mock fear. "Loden asked Argent and me to hunt the creature with him, as we used to hunt together in our youth." Galbus hiccuped again, and wiped the corner of his mouth with his sleeve. "But it was not Loden's idea that you come along. Argent has some things to discuss with you—serious matters, I presume," Galbus added, with a look of disgust on his face.

"And will you be joining us, Galbus?"

Galbus snickered over the lip of the goblet. "Really, Umber. Everyone knows I am foolish and lazy. Do you expect me to risk that reputation? No, I will take ill tomorrow morning when it is time to depart. After all, there are games to play and parties to plan."

Hap closed his eyes and sighed. He knew already that he would be dragged along on this unwelcome adventure; his future was written in the smile forming on Umber's broad, toothy mouth.

"This is tasty stuff," Galbus said, tapping the goblet to shake the last drop into his mouth. "Do you have any more?"

At night, while the others slept, Hap wandered about the dark rooms of the Aerie. This was his time to explore the strange artifacts on its shelves and read the volumes of books that Umber had gathered from around the world. In the peaceful silence he liked to imagine that it was his domain.

He picked up an item that was said to be a dragon's claw. It was a piece of hollow bone the size and shape of a cow's horn. As he ran his finger over its curved surface, he heard a small voice calling from below.

"What, will you be down here every night now?" It was Thimble, the reclusive fellow who stood only a few inches high and dwelled inside the cracks and nooks of the Aerie. Thimble had no patience for "big folk," as he called them, so Hap felt somewhat honored that the little fellow had actually spoken to him. Thimble scowled up at Hap while leaning on his long spear, which had a glossy beetle impaled on its point.

Hap smiled. "Does it bother you if I am?"

"More than a little," Thimble replied, jutting his jaw. The beetle twitched, and its legs began to scramble. "Thought you were dead," the little hunter complained. He flipped the spear, pinning the insect to the ground, and put his little boot on its belly. Then he lifted the spear and plunged it down again, into the poor thing's head. The twitching ceased at once.

Hap wrinkled his nose. "You don't eat those, do you?"

"What if I do?" Thimble asked, sneering back.

A sour taste bubbled up Hap's throat. "There's better stuff in the kitchen. Balfour made berry pies today. . . ."

"I *know* that," Thimble said. "I can get some if I want."

"I'm sure you can, but wouldn't it be easier if I got it for you? Wait here," Hap said. He jogged to the kitchen and brought back a heaping slice for himself and a spoonful for Thimble. It was a surprise to find Thimble still there when he got back, but he tried not to let it show. The little fellow fascinated him, and Hap wanted to keep this encounter going as long as he could. He sat on the floor with his legs crossed and put the spoon between them.

Thimble dug a hand into the spoonful and broke off a piece of berry-stained crust.

"Good, isn't it?" Hap said.

"It's all right," Thimble replied, cramming as much into his mouth as he could fit. He swallowed and wiped his mouth with his sleeve. "You and I have something in common."

"We do?"

"We're both weird. Me 'cause I'm small. You 'cause . . . you're just strange in so many ways."

Hap couldn't deny it. Whose story was as odd as his? He'd awoken weeks before in an underground city far away, with no memory of his previous life. The only clue to his identity was a note from the man who had left Hap for Umber to find. The note, signed with the initials WN, instructed Umber to take Hap with him on his adventures, and said that certain "skills" would arise. Those skills included the ability to see mysterious filaments of light that might someday allow him to steer the course of fate. For the moment, though, Hap had caught only fleeting glimpses of those threads and had no idea how to use them. This unusual power suggested that he belonged to a race of magical people called Meddlers—elusive beings who dabbled in human events for their own mysterious reasons.

"What's with you?" Thimble snapped.

Hap realized he'd fallen silent for a while, and that his face had settled into a deep frown under a furrowed brow. "Nothing," he said quietly. Then he remembered which way his thoughts had been headed. "Except . . . well, there's something I'm supposed to do someday. For Umber. And I don't know if I'll ever be able to do it."

"Save that other world, you mean?" Thimble asked. "The one Umber thinks he came from?"

Hap's head rocked back. He'd forgotten what an accomplished spy Thimble was, lurking in the crevices of the Aerie and listening to conversations nobody was supposed to hear. He cleared his throat. "Maybe."

Thimble gathered as many crumbs as he could carry and stuffed them into his shirt. He pried the beetle off the point of his spear and kicked it away, no longer hungry. "Well, if it helps to know, I'm not sure you'll be able to do it either." He walked off with his shirt bulging and vanished in the crack of the wall that he called home.

"It doesn't help at all, you little monster," Hap finally replied, resting his chin on one hand.

CHAPTER
4

The rays of dawn pierced the narrow windows of the Aerie. Hap munched on buttered toast and fruit while Umber closed his eyes and smiled into his mug. His eyes opened again and rolled sideways as Dodd stepped into the grand hall.

"Lord Umber?"

Umber grinned at him. "Morning, Dodd."

"Don't know if it's worth mentioning or not, but a young man just wandered up the causeway. Not from around here, I think. He asked if we'd allow him to go over to the old castle across the breakwater." Dodd looked down at the floor, not the usual cheerful fellow who liked to rattle off a poem he'd composed on the spot.

Umber waggled an eyebrow. "So he wanted to see Petraportus. Did you tell him it's falling apart, and he could get killed?"

Dodd tried to smile, but it wouldn't hold. "I said as much, but he was determined. I think he'd have swum over if we hadn't let him by."

Hap felt something like a feather teasing the back of his neck. He and Umber had nearly met their doom in the ruins of Petraportus. "But why does he need to see it so badly?"

"That's the strange thing, Master Hap," Dodd replied. "He thinks the old fisherman and his wife might have been his parents. He came looking for them . . . but of course I had to tell him what happened. How they were murdered and all, by that monster, only a few weeks back. The news hit him pretty hard. But he still wanted to see where . . . you know."

Umber looked at Hap with his lower lip thrust to one side. Hap blinked back at him. His heart ached in sympathy.

"I know you always wondered about that pair, Lord Umber," Dodd said. "And it was nice, what you did after they died. So I figured . . ."

"Yes," Umber said. "Thank you for letting me know. Do me a favor, Dodd? When this young man comes back, invite him in. I'd like to meet him."

As Dodd trudged down the stairs, Hap went to the tall,

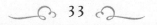

slender window that overlooked Petraportus, and watched. An hour later a young man emerged from the ruins and picked his way across the bridge of rubble that connected the old castle to the foot of the Aerie. The fellow was twenty or a little older, with brown hair braided in the back in the style of sailors.

"He's coming now, Lord Umber," Hap said.

"Would you mind asking Balfour to whip something up to eat?" Umber replied.

Hap was still in the kitchen with Balfour when he heard Umber talking to the stranger. The kitchen door was ajar, and he peeked at the fellow as Umber sat him at the table. The stranger's face was marked by sorrow, with a mouth that tugged down at the corners and dark circles under his eyes. He lifted his head to take in the surroundings, and his brown eyes widened. Hap remembered how amazed he'd been the first time he stepped inside this splendid place, hollowed from a great pillar of stone.

"What's your name, friend?" Umber said, taking the opposite seat. There were goblets on the table. Umber filled them with wine from a pitcher and handed one to the stranger.

"Eldon Penny," the young man answered, almost grunting the words. Hap frowned. Most people treated Umber with deference, but Eldon's manner was blunt. He hadn't even thanked Umber for the wine, or called him "my lord," for that matter. Even if Eldon didn't know that his host was a lord of the kingdom, the grandeur of the Aerie should have hinted at Umber's stature. But the grim, lost expression reminded Hap why Eldon was behaving so: Hoping to find his parents, he had come instead to a pair of graves.

"Welcome, Eldon," Umber said. "Forgive me for asking, but Dodd tells me you think the hermits who occupied the old castle might have been your parents?"

"Hermits, you say?" Eldon asked, wrapping his fist tight around the stem of the goblet. His mood was fragile, Hap realized. The sadness could turn to anger in a flash.

"They can't have been hermits," interrupted Oates, who'd just come down the stairs.

"What's that?" said Umber, cringing a little at Oates's entrance.

"A hermit lives alone, right? So you can't have *two* hermits who live together. It doesn't make sense." Oates puffed his chest.

"You make a good point at a bad time, Oates," Umber said, rubbing his temple. "Would you mind exercising your intellect in some other room?"

"Fine," muttered Oates, and Hap heard his heavy feet trudging back up the stairs. Eldon looked from Oates to Umber with a strange expression, both irritated and confused.

"I was about to say, I meant no offense," Umber said, raising his palms. "It's just that they kept to themselves and shunned company. I tried to talk to them a few times, even sent some food and clothes their way. But they refused to speak. I finally decided to stop bothering them."

"Ah." Eldon raised the goblet and sipped. "Well. The truth is that they were my mum and dad. Horace and Alma Penny were their names. I'm certain it was them. I found some of their belongings that I recognized." Eldon breathed deep and looked at the ceiling. "Was it you, then, who had them buried so nicely?"

Umber nodded. Hap thought about the two handsome stone caskets that Umber had brought to Petraportus, and the slab of marble with the engraving: *May they find the peace they sought together.*

"Then I am grateful to you, sir," Eldon said. "That is a noble resting place. More than simple folk like us would ever dream for." The words were polite, but the voice was bitter. He stared into his cup and swirled the wine.

"Tell me, Eldon," Umber said. "Do you know why your parents came here? And how did you find them? If you don't mind telling, that is."

In the kitchen Balfour nudged Hap in the back with a tray and whispered, "Go on out and join them, Hap. Umber would want you there. Besides, I've got to bring this food out, and you're in my way."

As Hap pushed the door open, Eldon heard the noise and looked up to see who was coming. He had begun to answer Umber's question, but the words caught in his throat when he saw Hap. He made a choking sound, and the goblet fell from his hand.

"Eldon?" Umber said, rising.

As the young man tried to stand, his eyes rolled up, and he crumpled to the floor.

Umber and Balfour sat Eldon up. His eyes fluttered open, crossed, and focused, and then his gaze darted about until it found Hap again. Hap's throat twisted itself into a knot.

"It . . . can't be so," Eldon whispered, gaping. "*Julian?*"

Hap took an awkward step back. "Who? Me?"

Eldon rubbed his eyes with his fingertips. "No . . . impossible. Sorry. You can't be Julian."

Umber's eyes blazed. "Eldon, who is Julian?"

Eldon took his shaking hands away from his face. "My brother."

"Come on, my friend," Umber said, tugging Eldon's arm. "We can't have our guest sitting on the floor. Let's get you back in your chair and fill that goblet again." As he helped

Eldon up, Umber looked at Balfour. Balfour grimaced back and shrugged.

"Eldon, this is my ward, Happenstance," Umber said. "Hap, why don't you join us at the table?"

Hap was torn between curiosity and the urge to run. Umber met his gaze and flicked both eyebrows upward. *Play along,* the gesture said, and so Hap lowered himself uneasily into the chair opposite Eldon. "How do you do?"

Eldon blinked at him and took a deep breath. "Happenstance, was it? Please understand. I thought I'd forgotten what Julian looked like. But seeing you . . . it's like seeing his ghost."

A tingle ran down Hap's arms, all the way to the fingers.

Eldon leaned closer and looked Hap up and down. "Of course you aren't him. Julian would be a man by now, almost twenty. Not a boy like you. And his eyes were brown like mine. Your eyes . . . I've only seen one other set like those." His gaze narrowed as if a dark memory shadowed his thoughts. His expression teetered between wonder and loathing.

Hap looked down at the table, unable to bear the look. "Who was it? Who had eyes like mine?"

Eldon sniffed and wiped his cuff across the corner of his eyes. "The man who made Julian die."

Hap jolted upright. "D-die? How did he die?"

"He fell through the ice and drowned in the river."

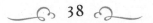

The world dimmed for a moment, and Hap saw sparks. There was a hand on his shoulder. It was Balfour's. He saw Umber staring at him with his lips pressed tight together, willing Hap not to lose control.

It's true, he thought. *I am that boy. I was Julian Penny.* His thoughts reeled, as things that had been merely hints and clues finally asserted their meaning: Someone had once taunted him by telling him he was dead. *Of course, because I died.* He feared water more than anything. *Of course, because I drowned.*

"Well, as you told us, this can't be Julian," Umber said, a little too loudly. "But please, Eldon, I'd like to hear your story if you're willing to share. And have something to eat, will you? It will do you some good."

Hap struggled to stay upright and not to cry out. A headache pierced his temple, and the sound of his own heartbeat within his ears muffled everything. He was dimly aware of Umber pushing a plate of food in front of Eldon. Eldon must have been starving, because he spent a few minutes joylessly wolfing down the cheese and bread and sweets that Balfour had prepared. Hap could barely pay attention to the conversation that followed. But at some point Eldon must have started to tell them his story.

". . . a family of fisherman," Eldon was saying. "We had a farm on the river. It was just our parents and us, and it was a good life. We didn't need anything but one another. I was the older brother by three years. Julian was . . ." Eldon paused, and his eyes went to Hap, as they did every time he spoke of his brother. "He was a special child. Different. Simple, I guess you'd call him. He didn't talk much, and he couldn't learn the way other boys did. But he was sweet as honey. Not a wicked bone in his body, and always a smile on his face. And my mum and dad . . . well, they adored Julian. He was everything to them. And they blamed me when it happened." Eldon let out a deep, deflating breath.

There was an uncomfortable silence. Hap's fingernails dug into the surface of the table.

"What happened, Eldon?" Umber finally prodded.

Eldon rubbed his temple with one hand. "It was winter's end. How many years ago—seven? I went to check some traps I'd set for rabbits. Julian wanted to come along. Mum dressed him in a heavy cloak and told me to watch out for him. She always said something like that when we went off together, with Julian so simple. You know how mothers are. We walked down to the river—it was still frozen, though the days were getting warmer. And then we saw him."

They waited. Glances careened among Umber, Balfour, and Hap. Balfour chewed his bottom lip.

"There was a man by the river, sitting on a stump," Eldon

continued. "Like he was waiting for us. He was dressed oddly—not warmly enough, for one thing. His hair was strange too. White, sort of, but there were colors inside the white. But the first thing you noticed was his eyes. Green eyes that shined, even sparkled." Eldon stared at Hap, and another painful silence fell.

Umber interjected. "What did this green-eyed man do, Eldon?"

Eldon's hands curled into fists. "He ignored me, as if I wasn't there. Told Julian there was something he should see, out on the ice." Eldon's lips trembled, and he pressed them together for a moment.

Hap felt dizzy. He closed his eyes and recalled, with perfect clarity, the vision he'd had weeks before, when in an attempt to restore his memory Umber had hypnotized him. *He took me back to the beginning of my memory,* Hap thought. *But something was in the way. Something hard and cold. Cold as ice . . .*

Eldon went on. "He told Julian there were pretty circles in the ice. 'Circles within circles! It's beautiful! Go and see!' he said."

And when I searched that wall of ice, I saw something . . . a pattern, Hap recalled. *Circles inside circles, getting smaller. . . .* His chest heaved and his heart drummed.

"Julian ran onto the ice," Eldon said. "I went after him, told him to slow down. I was a few steps behind when I saw them—the circles. Julian laughed and called them pretty, but I knew why the rings were there. That was where the ice was melting from below. I screamed at Julian to stop."

Hap's teeth hurt—he was clenching his jaw. *I tried to break through the wall, because I thought my lost memories were on the other side. So I pushed against the circles. . . .*

Eldon's voice dropped to a whisper. "Julian tried, but before he could stop, he slid a little further. The ice broke under his feet."

And the wall shattered.

"He fell in, and he didn't come up. I turned to call for help, but the green-eyed man was gone."

But my memories weren't on the other side. Something else was on the other side.

"I didn't know what to do. I was just a boy myself. I finally crawled toward the hole on my hands and knees and reached in. The water was so, . . ."

Cold. And fear. And nothingness. That's what was on the other side.

". . . so cold. I tried to find him, anything to grab on to, but there was nothing. That was the end of him. Julian was gone."

It was death. My death. I died.

Eldon was breathing as if he'd run a mile. "And all the

good in my life perished with him. I ran home and could barely get the words out. My mother collapsed. My father ran out to find Julian, but he couldn't. The current under the ice must have taken him away. My father screamed at me, asking how I could let that happen. 'You were supposed to keep him safe,' he said. He was right, of course. I couldn't stand it, being the one to blame. Every night I wished it was me who had fallen through the ice, and Julian the one who'd run home."

Hap shot up from his chair, so fast that the others stared. "I—I don't feel well. Excuse me," he stammered, and he walked to the stairs, fighting the urge to sprint until he was out of sight.

There was a knock on Hap's door within the hour.

"Come in," he muttered. He sat in his chair with his back to the door, looking out the pair of windows.

"I don't blame you for leaving," Umber said behind him. Hap heard a chair scraping on the floor, and then Umber sat beside him and put his heels on the windowsill. "It's almost too much to take. I feel a little sick myself."

Hap closed his eyes. "It's true. I was the boy who fell through the ice."

He could hear Umber scratching his chin beside him.

"I still might have called the story a coincidence, except for the appearance of the green-eyed man."

"Do you think it's WN? The man who left me for you to find?"

"I asked Eldon if he ever learned the stranger's name. He didn't. But yes, I suppose it was him." The chair creaked as Umber slid it closer to Hap's. "Do you remember the cloak you were wearing when we first found you? It was still damp, as I recall."

Hap squeezed his eyelids tighter as the meaning sank in. *Still damp.* "The cloak I drowned in. But it was seven years later. . . . How can it be?"

"That's what Meddlers do," Umber said softly. "They can leap across time. And apparently bring somebody with them. It was part of WN's plan for you and me to come together. Why seven years later? I don't know. But these consequences . . . they are terrible."

Hap opened his eyes to glare at Umber. "I hate WN. I hate what he did."

"I would too."

"He killed me, and turned me into . . . something not even human."

"Hap, you're neither dead nor inhuman. You—"

Hap smacked the wall with his fist. "He stole my life, Lord

Umber. And my mother and father died because of what he did to me. I had a family. He destroyed it."

Umber nodded. "But you still have a brother, it seems."

Hap shook his head. "Did you see the way he looked at me?" He pointed with two fingers toward his eyes. "He didn't just see the brother he lost. He saw the eyes of the man who killed his brother."

Umber slumped in his chair. "Do you want Eldon to know the truth?"

Hap groaned. "I don't know. When I look at him, I remember nothing. He was my brother, but he's a stranger. He doesn't mean anything to me. And I'm not the person I was. Did you hear him? He said Julian was simple and didn't talk much. He smiled and laughed all the time. He was *happy*." Hap dropped his head into his hands. "No, don't tell him. I wish he'd never found me. All this time I wanted to know who I am, and now I wish I'd never learned."

"Poor Eldon," Umber said after a silence. "You missed the rest of his story. He felt so guilty over losing Julian that he ran away from home. This all happened in Meer, incidentally—it's a kingdom hundreds of miles south, beyond the great forest. Eldon barely survived a year on his own before he wandered home. He missed his parents by days. The loss of both of their sons had driven them nearly mad, and they'd sailed away in their little fishing boat, down the river and to the sea. Some neighbors took Eldon in, but he grew restless as time went by. A few years later he went to the nearest port and signed on with a merchant ship, hoping his travels would someday help him find his folks. Months ago he finally heard about the mysterious fisherman and his wife living in Kurahaven, and he got here as soon as he could. But once again he just missed them. Fate has been cruel to that young man."

"Fate wasn't cruel," Hap muttered thickly. "The Meddler was."

Umber tilted his head back and puffed air at the ceiling.

"Where is Eldon now?" Hap asked.

"Balfour took him to the inn he used to run in town. I'll pay for his lodging. We'll let him rest for a few days and eat like a king. Then, if it's all right with you, Hap, I'm going to send him down to my shipping company and have Hoyle find him a job. I have vast enterprises. There's a place for him somewhere."

Hap felt his eyes moisten. "I would like that."

"But I think we'll settle him somewhere besides Kurahaven. It might be hard for you, running into him now and then. We won't send him too far. But far enough. We'll keep an eye on him, see how he's doing. Fair enough?"

"Thank you," Hap said, but the words came out strangely

because of the way his lips stiffened and twisted. Umber excused himself, and Hap dove onto his bed, face down.

They were right here all along, Hap thought, thinking of the reclusive pair that he often saw out the window of the Aerie, catching fish, filling their water barrels, gathering wood for their fires. *My mother and father. And I didn't even know it.* He wished he could sleep, as others did when they wanted to forget their troubles for a time. But there was no sleep for beings like him.

No rest for Meddlers.

arrived in this place

if I had been somehow

flung back in time. (Let us leave

aside for now my occasional suspicion

that this is all an elaborate fantasy

concocted by my own brain to comfort

me as I lie unconscious on the

verge of death.) But soon I learned

that I was in a different existence

altogether. After all, my world

was never populated by trolls,

goblins, ogres, sorcerers, dragons,

thumb-sized folk, and other fanta

CHAPTER
5

"*This is just what you need to get* your mind off things, Happenstance!" Umber said. "Your first journey into the hills that surround our fair city. The terrain is magnificent."

Hap leaned out the window and stared at the crags that loomed ahead. The road below turned more rugged with every spin of the carriage wheels. They'd rolled from paving stones to hard-packed dirt to a pair of narrow scratches between grass and brush.

"Before we get there," Umber said, "I have something to show you." He dug into a pocket and held an object out to Hap, nearly concealed between thumb and forefinger. Hap opened his hand to accept it, and a flat copper coin fell into his palm. It was old and tarnished, and its engravings were half worn. Hap stared at the image of a wide, flat-roofed structure on a foundation of steps, with columns across its entire width. It looked like some of the grander buildings in Kurahaven, and much like Umber's own shipping company headquarters. Words curved along the coin's edge: ONE CENT at the bottom, UNITED STATES OF AMERICA across the top, and just above the building a phrase from another language, which Hap somehow knew and instantly translated with his mysterious intelligence: *One out of many*. He turned the coin over and saw the profile of a bearded man.

"It was in my pocket when I awoke in this world," Umber said. "The only thing that came with me, aside from the computer."

Hap winced as his mind made the instant connections. It was probably WN who'd brought Umber to this world, just as WN had ended Hap's former life as a simple, happy country boy. "Was it valuable?" mumbled Hap, brushing the coin with his finger.

"In fact it was our humblest coin. And it went by the same name as one of our coins here. We called it a penny."

Hap shook his head. *Penny,* he thought.

"Just a coincidence, but it did make me wonder," Umber said. "Do you want your old name back, Hap? It should be your choice. Would you rather be Julian Penny?"

Hap let his head sag back and closed his eyes. "No," he finally said. "There is no Julian anymore. I'm Happenstance now."

The carriage groaned to a stop at the foot of the rocky hills. A company of eight was gathered there, plus a pair of packhorses. Hap saw the two princes among the group. Argent raised a gloved hand in greeting. Hap was sure that a cold, dark look flashed on Loden's face when the youngest prince saw Umber.

Dodd had driven the carriage. He said quietly from his perch on the driver's seat, "Enjoy yourselves. And Hap: *Don't let Umber near the arrows and bows; he's liable to shoot himself in the nose.* Dodd grinned and snapped the reins, and the carriage rolled away.

Umber sniffed. "One of his lesser poems. Come, Hap." They hoisted their overstuffed packs onto their shoulders and joined the hunting party.

Loden had masked his moment of displeasure with a convincing smile. "Umber, my friend. I did not know you would be joining us."

"I invited him," Argent said, glancing sideways at his brother. "There are issues of some importance that I'd like to discuss."

"Really? I would like to hear those myself, if you don't mind."

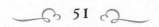

Argent shrugged. "If it suits you, brother."

Loden's eyes narrowed for a heartbeat. "If it involves the welfare of the kingdom, then I am naturally inclined to offer my point of view. But please, Argent, remember that this hunt is meant to be a pleasant diversion after so many weeks of toil rebuilding the city. Let's not occupy every moment with business. It wouldn't be fair to our esteemed guest!"

Loden clapped a hand on Umber's shoulder. Umber stiffened under the touch but forced a smile. "Discuss what you like. I am happy just to spend time in your company."

"Let us go," Argent said. He gave Hap a disapproving glance. "Umber, you and your . . . *ward* . . . don't need to carry your packs. The horses will bear them for you."

"I don't object to hunting in principle," Umber told Hap as they hiked upward. "It seems natural enough. The human species has forever been hunters. And I have no objection to the consumption of animal flesh. Heaven knows I've sent schools of fish down my throat, flocks of foul, and herds of cattle. It's just that I, personally, couldn't stand to bring suffering to a beast."

Umber looked forward and back to make sure the others were out of earshot. "And I'll never understand the impulse to kill a creature merely because it is fantastic, mysterious, or frightening. Like this death-boar the princes are after."

When Hap had first heard the word "death-boar," an image had popped into his mind. That was the way his mysterious brain worked: It contained a hidden reservoir of knowledge, and the introduction of a strange term would often summon forth its meaning. And so he knew what the thing was: a monster that was part boar and part man, armed with claws, teeth, and tusks, and surely dangerous to pursue.

"But this death-boar is probably not an animal at all, Hap," Umber said, lowering his voice even more. "I've learned a bit about them in my travels. There are no great populations of these creatures, only rare sightings hundreds of miles apart. And in this world, that generally means we're talking about the unnatural: a human being, cursed to live in beastly form. Which makes the idea of this hunt even more ghastly. No, with any luck this death-boar will escape unharmed." Umber gave Hap a playful punch on the shoulder. "After we've had a good look, of course!"

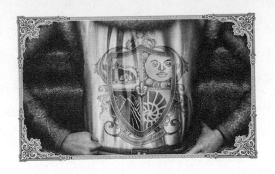

CHAPTER
6

Argent stood waiting for Umber and
Hap to catch up. He was the eldest of the princes, with a face
as cold, craggy, and foreboding as the mountainsides around
them. "Let us walk together, Umber."

The prince did not have idle chatter in mind. He asked for
Umber's opinion on the ongoing repairs to the harbor and the
city, and then moved on to a variety of proposals that Umber had
apparently made. They talked about a new system of roads and
bridges, improvements in public health and sanitation, and the
expansion of the kingdom's libraries and universities. It was all
frightfully boring, Hap decided, particularly because Argent had
a tendency to seize each topic and turn it in all directions until
every possible detail had been shaken loose and examined.

Hap's attention wandered, only to return when Argent's tone sharpened. "And what would be the point of *that?*" Argent was saying.

Umber bowed his head briefly before answering. "Your Highness, I merely suggest that it would benefit the kingdom to expand our efforts to educate the common folk. While the children of noblemen are certainly—"

"Really, Umber, you can be so eccentric at times," said a velvet voice close behind them. Hap turned. It was Loden. Hap hadn't heard the youngest prince approach them from behind.

"You always talk of the spread of knowledge as a wonderful thing," Loden said, with a cool smile and half-lidded eyes. "But have you considered that the common folk might be better off in a state of blissful ignorance, knowing that wise men such as us are making the right decisions for them?"

Umber's jaw tensed for a moment before he replied. "Forgive me for disagreeing, Prince Loden, but I believe that ignorance is rarely blissful. Why not illuminate every mind we can, down to the humblest farmer? Who knows what geniuses might be flushed out with a little prodding, like birds from the brush? And that would serve you well, my princes. After all, the greatness of a kingdom is measured by the accomplishments of its people."

Loden raised an eyebrow. "If you ask me, Umber, the greatness of a kingdom is best measured by the deeds of its kings."

"In part, Your Eminence," Umber countered. "Still, a king is only one man, yet thousands of brilliant artists, musicians, scholars, and engineers can thrive under his benevolent rule. Why, our Celador is entering a golden age as we speak, and this glory has been earned not through battles won by the king, but through a peaceful expansion of trade and the impressive accomplishments of its people."

"But most of those accomplishments flow from you, Lord Umber," Argent said. "And you are no common man."

"Not only from me, my prince! Others have built upon my humble contributions in ways that—"

"This is all very amusing, Umber, but the debate ends here," Loden said, raising a hand. "We are close to the Falls of the Mist, where I was told the creature has been seen."

Umber turned away so the princes would not see the color rising in his face. Something caught his attention, and he pointed over the tops of the trees that formed a dense barrier on the side of the trail. "What's that up there?"

Hap looked, along with the princes, at a wisp of smoke, visible only for a moment before a thin breeze swept it away. Umber's gaze leveled, and Hap saw what had caught his eye this time: a narrow path, easy to miss, sliced into the dense trees. Umber took a few steps down it and peered into the shadows.

Hap heard Loden's voice behind him, directed at Argent. "Just a deer path."

"Really, Loden? And have the deer built themselves a fire?" Argent replied. One of Argent's servants snorted as he suppressed a laugh.

"Perhaps we should see who's down there," Umber said.

"A waste of time. The Falls of the Mist are where we'll find our prey," Loden said. His tone was so emphatic that it drew a curious look from many.

"It won't take long," Argent said, looking sideways at Loden, who had taken a few more steps down the main trail. "If someone is down there, they might know about the habits of this death-boar. I will go with Umber. Wait for us here if you like."

Loden sighed. "Fine. I'll join you, if you insist on this pointless detour." He called to one of the men gathered nearby. "Larcombe, you're with me. The rest of you stay."

Umber waved for Hap to follow. "That Larcombe reminds me of a reptile," he whispered after Loden's servant walked by, and Hap agreed. Larcombe was lean and sinewy, with a cool, unexpressive face. He rarely spoke to anyone besides Loden, and then only in a whisper, and he had the unpleasant habit of licking his lips.

Umber and Hap were at the back of the group and so were the last to arrive at the end of the trail. There they found the source of the smoke: a tiny, crudely built house in a lonesome glade. Its small yard was tilled and planted, with neat rows of cabbage, turnips, and lettuce, and beanstalks twined around poles. A foursome of goats chewed and stared from behind wooden rails. Everything was silent, as if even the animals hesitated to make a sound.

"Hello?" called Prince Argent, breaking the calm like a clap of thunder. "Is anybody at home?"

There was no reply. Hap looked at Umber and saw that Umber's curiosity had by now been piqued: He was bobbing up and down on the balls of his feet, and his glance was darting back and forth, absorbing the scene.

"As I said, a waste of time," Loden muttered. "Let us resume our hunt."

"The door is ajar," Umber said, and he walked briskly toward the house. Argent followed, and Loden, after an angry look at the sky, hurried to catch up.

Hap went after them, anxious not to be left alone with Larcombe. Umber and the princes had already stepped inside, and he heard Umber's voice: "Oh! Pardon us, madam."

Hap saw her through the open door: a woman in a simple dress and apron, huddled in a chair in the corner, biting the knuckles of one hand.

Argent clasped his hands behind his back. "Woman, didn't you hear me call from outside?"

"I am sorry," she replied in a quaking voice. "My hearing isn't what it was. Are you . . . are you gentlemen of Kurahaven?"

"These are the princes Argent and Loden," Umber said.

The woman threw herself from the chair to press her palms and forehead on the floor. "Forgive me, Your Highnesses! I didn't know!"

Argent bent down and took her by the elbow, lifting her to her feet. "Not recognizing us when you've never seen us is not a crime, good woman. Take your seat again and be at ease."

Hap watched, fascinated and surprised by how kind the prince could be when kindness was needed. It was a side of the stern man he supposed many never got to see. Umber smiled at the sight—but his gaze was also lively, searching the small room up and down, left and right.

Argent took the woman's hand. "What is your name, my lady?"

She looked up at Argent with watery eyes. "Ludmilla."

"Ah, Ludmilla. We only wish to know if you have seen any sign of the death-boar."

The woman's glance darted from face to face. Her attention was held for a moment by Hap's unusual eyes, and then, as she looked over Hap's shoulder, her body stiffened. Hap turned to see what the matter was, and saw Larcombe a few strides outside the door, watching her with a cold stare and touching the handle of his sheathed knife.

"D-death b-boar?" she stuttered. "I have seen no death-boar here, Your Highness."

"As I expected," Loden huffed. "Enough of this. Let us get to the falls while there is still daylight."

Argent reached into a pocket and drew out a gold coin. He pressed it into the woman's quivering hand. "We are sorry for disturbing you, Ludmilla. Don't be afraid. If this monster is about, we will hunt it and slay it."

As Ludmilla bowed her head and thanked Argent, Umber leaned toward Hap and whispered, "Watch my left foot. But don't react."

Hap looked down. Umber swiveled his foot to the side and back again, revealing for a moment something that made Hap's heart flip inside his chest. There was a deep impression of a cloven hoof in the dirt floor. The print was so wide and long that Umber's foot could barely conceal it.

"Let's go," Umber said. They followed the princes toward the door. Umber put a hand on Hap's shoulder just before they crossed the threshold, stopping him there. He waited for both princes to take a few strides into the glade, and then turned back to the woman, who stared with wide watery eyes.

"Ludmilla," he said, "my name is Umber. I don't know if you've heard of me."

"Lord Umber of the Aerie," she whispered back. Her eyes grew even wider.

"That's right. I get the feeling that something's troubling you, Ludmilla," Umber said quietly, glancing out the door. "Is there anything you'd like to tell me? Don't be afraid. I'll do everything in my power to protect you."

Ludmilla's face trembled, and she pinched her bottom lip between her teeth. She seemed on the verge of speaking when Loden stepped into the doorway again.

"Are you coming, Umber?" he said, bumping the threshold with a fist.

"Of course," Umber replied with a bright smile. "You know me, Loden. I was asking dear Ludmilla if she'd seen any other magical creatures about. Sadly, she has not."

"I know you very well," Loden said. He mimicked Umber's smile. "Now let's get on with our hunt."

Loden stayed close to Umber the rest of the way, and so Hap could only imagine what questions were going through

Umber's mind. That enormous print—was it made by the death-boar? But Ludmilla had denied having seen the death-boar—was she protecting the creature? And why had Loden seemed determined to keep Umber from speaking to her?

The late afternoon air was still, but a sound like the wind rushing through the leaves could be heard ahead. It grew to a dull roar as they advanced. A thin fog drifted toward them.

"The Falls of the Mist," Loden said. "Brother, do you remember the last time we hunted here?"

Prince Argent, who was walking ahead of them, turned and nodded. "We brought home the great hart. Its head is still on the wall in Father's room."

"My fondest memory," Loden replied. "Do you remember how Galbus cried when he saw it?" Everyone laughed at the remark, apart from Hap and Umber. Loden grinned and gestured up the rising path. "Everyone—let us approach quietly now. The lair of this monster may be just ahead."

The party treaded softly through a dense stand of trees. They gathered at the edge of an open space filled with mist. The hiss of the falls had grown to a roar, and through the veil of fog Hap could dimly see water tumbling into a deep pool.

"Look!" whispered Larcombe. Hap was surprised to hear the fellow speak at all. Larcombe was pointing at the wide stream that snaked away from the falls, where large cloven hoof prints traced the muddy bank and disappeared into the fog. *The same kind we saw in that house,* Hap thought.

"The lair is here. It's true!" Loden said. He put a hand on his brother's shoulder. "Argent, when we slew the hart, we did it by climbing those rocks beside the falls. Do you remember? The mist is thinner there, and if the creature lurks behind the falls, we'll spot him."

Argent smiled at the memory. "Yes. There's something like a grotto behind the cascades."

Loden tapped his bow against Argent's. "What do you say? Perhaps it's a lucky spot for us."

Argent met Loden's gaze for a long while. "Why not?" he finally said.

The corner of Loden's mouth curved up. "The rest of you, spread out among the trees, out of sight. Keep your bows ready, in case we flush the creature out. And sound your horns if it runs. Come, brother!"

Umber watched the princes head into the mist. Their bodies blurred and finally vanished completely when they began their climb up the steep shoulder of rock beside the falls. The men fanned out among the line of trees that half encircled the falls. Umber and Hap were left with Grumman, the fellow who'd led the packhorse. Grumman tied the horse to a sturdy tree and strapped a quiver of arrows across his back. He held a second bow out to Umber.

"Will you join the hunt, Lord Umber?"

Umber raised his palms. "I've been advised not to handle weapons, Grumman. In the strongest terms."

Grumman smirked. "Very well, sir."

"Let's take a look around, Hap," Umber said. He led Hap away from the falls. They walked until they came to a deep cleft in the forest floor. Below them the stream rushed between steep banks of dirt where roots stuck out like grasping fingers.

Umber stopped and rubbed an earlobe between his fingers, frowning. "There's something odd going on here, don't you think?" he whispered.

Hap nodded, though he couldn't imagine what it was.

"Did you see those prints? If that's the lair, there would be lots of prints, going in and out. But there was just one set going *toward* the falls. That seems awfully convenient for a hunting party to find. And that woman in the house—why was she so—?"

Umber stopped himself abruptly and put a finger to his lips. With the other hand he pointed up the ravine. Hap heard something coming their way, from around a bend in the stream: footsteps. *Or hoofsteps,* Hap thought, because when they weren't squelching in the mud or splashing in the water, they clacked against hard stones.

CHAPTER
7

Hap saw a shadow first, and then an arm that looked only partially human—thick and coarsely haired. The rest of the death-boar appeared, dripping wet, around the bend in the ravine. Umber squeezed Hap's forearm. Hap glanced up and saw Umber's face filled with wonder and joy, like a child seeing his first rainbow.

The creature was tall as a man, but his head was grotesquely large. He had the face of a boar: a tapering jaw, flat snout, broad pointed ears, and a wild tuft of hair on top. Yellowed tusks curled up from the lower jaw. The feet were those of a swine, but the hands were a grotesque compromise between man and pig. He wore a pair of ragged trousers tied at the waist with a length of rope, while his thick torso was bare. The leathery skin was mottled pink and tan and bristled with spiny black hair.

Splash, squish, thunk: The death-boar picked his way across water, mud, and smooth stones as quietly as he could. *He's afraid,* Hap thought, as he saw the creature cast a worried glance over his shoulder.

Umber's hand tightened on Hap's arm as the boar passed directly underneath them, panting hoarsely. Hap held his breath and wasn't planning to release it until the creature was out of sight around the next curve of the stream.

But the death-boar stopped. He froze in place for a moment with his back to them. Hap heard a deep snuffling. The beast whirled about, and his yellow-brown eyes turned up to where they stood.

"Wait," Umber whispered, as Hap twisted to run. Umber's grip tightened a little more, holding Hap to the spot.

The death-boar looked to the left and right of Umber and Hap. *Wondering if there are more of us,* Hap thought. He expected the creature to climb the banks to attack. Hap figured his own legs could carry him to safety, leaping clear across the ravine if necessary. It was Umber who was in danger if the monster came after them.

But the death-boar only raised his strange hands—with a normal thumb beside cloven, jointed hooves. It was an

awkward motion that looked like begging or praying. He shook his head right and left, and a desperate whine escaped the brutish jaw. The sound pinched Hap's heart.

"You have nothing to fear from us," Umber told him.

The death-boar pressed one hand to his chest, where a man's heart would be. Umber opened his mouth to speak again, but a chilling sound came from the direction of the falls: a shriek of terror and surprise, cut off with a sudden *thump*. The shouts of other men came next. Umber and Hap both turned to look, but the thick forest and the mists beyond made it impossible to see what had happened. Behind him Hap heard feet pounding the mud and water. The death-boar charged wildly downstream, no longer caring how much noise he made.

Umber's face went pale. He took a final longing glance at the fleeing creature and raced toward the Falls of the Mist. "Come on!"

They weaved through the trees, hopping over roots and fallen limbs, and burst into the clearing. Someone was lying by the falls with his legs splayed in an awkward position. A bow was nearby, and arrows were scattered across the ground. Two of the party already knelt beside the wounded man, and more were running back from the positions they'd taken surrounding the falls.

Between the kneeling men Hap saw part of a short silver cape that the man wore. "It's Prince Argent," he said, feeling as if something thick and warm had gotten stuck halfway down his throat. The edge of the river, only a few inches deep, washed under Argent's back. When it emerged on the other side, it had taken on a pinkish hue.

Umber ran to the prince's side. "What happened?" he cried.

Grumman was there, his cheeks slick with tears. "He—he fell! I heard him scream, and saw him come out of the mist!"

"Careful!" Umber shouted to one of the other men, who tried to shift the prince's limbs into a more comfortable position. "Move him as little as you can!"

The other men gathered around the fallen prince. They covered their mouths and clutched their stomachs. *Someone's missing,* Hap thought. And then he heard Loden's cries.

"Argent! Brother! Are you all right? Answer me! Tell me you aren't hurt!" The prince's ghostly form was just visible as he hastened down the ledge, sliding recklessly across the stones. He leaped from the final ledge and ran to the group. When he saw Argent on the rocky ground, he choked back a scream and clutched his hair. "*No!* This cannot be!"

Umber had two fingers pressed on Argent's neck, under the corner of his jaw. "He's alive," he said quietly.

"What?" cried Loden. He dropped to his knees, shoving Grumman out of the way. He seized his brother's hand and kissed it. "Alive? Thank the stars!"

Argent's eyes were shut, but his lips quivered, attempting to form words. Loden leaned close, putting his mouth near Argent's ear. "Don't try to speak, brother! Save your strength. I will stay right beside you." Loden looked up at the others. "He was behind me—we'd almost reached the perch we were seeking. The stones were wet from the falls. I was about to tell him to be careful . . . and then I heard him scream. Oh, and it was my idea to go up there! I will never forgive myself!"

Loden bowed his head, and his shoulders shook. Around Argent's broken form, men bore the sort of expressions Hap thought he might see if arrows had pierced their bodies. Umber's eyes gleamed with tears, but his gaze was fixed upon Loden with an expression that Hap could not decipher.

The elder prince's eyes fluttered half open. They rolled left, then right, and widened when they settled on Umber. The fingers of Argent's free hand curled and uncurled in a weak but unmistakable gesture: *Come here.* The lips moved, soundlessly, but the name they formed was easy to read. Umber stepped closer and dropped to his knees.

"I'm here, my prince. What is it?"

Loden reached across his fallen brother and put an

open hand on Umber's chest, warding him away. "Not now, Umber! All of you, stand back and let my brother breathe!"

Umber seemed to bite back the words he really wanted to say. "I think he wants to tell me something."

Argent took a gasping breath, as if to gather whatever strength was left. His free hand rose, trembling, toward Loden's face. *Or his neck,* Hap thought. But the effort was too much for the gravely wounded man. The hand thumped on the ground. Argent looked at Loden, then again at Umber. He tried one last time to form a word, but it died on his lips.

They moved silently through the night. One man led the way with a lantern raised in one hand. The packhorse clopped behind; even its head was bowed. Two men came next, carrying a litter between them. One was Loden, who insisted on bearing the load and would let nobody take his place, even when the tired fellow at the other end of the litter called for relief. The covered figure on the litter never moved, even when one of the bearers stumbled.

Another man was chosen to run ahead of the others. Hap wondered if he should have volunteered. After all, he needed no torch or lantern to see, and his tireless legs could cover the ground with twice the speed. But he would never want to be the one to bring the terrible news to the kingdom: Prince Argent, the dour, sensible, capable man who was to inherit the throne from the ailing king, was dead.

CHAPTER
8

Gray clouds drew over the city like a funeral cloak. People walked softly through the streets, staring down at the paving stones or up at the great palace. A day before, craftsmen had swarmed over the dockyards and up the scaffolding on the walls of the storm-damaged buildings. But now the hammers and saws were silent.

There was a funeral procession the next afternoon, and the citizens of Kurahaven lined the streets, with hats removed from every head. A team of horses drew the bier with Prince Argent's body. The prince's personal guard came next, with their lips pressed into pale thin lines. Next came Loden, with his face arranged into the precise expression a grief-stricken brother ought to bear. After them came Galbus, wobbly in his saddle, gazing with bleary eyes at nothing.

Happenstance watched the procession pass, standing with Umber, Balfour, Sophie, Lady Truden, and Oates. Umber bowed his head as Argent went by, but lifted it to stare keenly at Loden. The youngest prince looked his way for only a moment, and acknowledged Umber's stare by subtly clamping his jaw.

Umber waited, then spoke quietly to Balfour. "I want to send one of the guards to talk to that woman who lives near the falls. She might speak openly if Loden is not around."

"A terrible thing," Umber said. He slumped at the table and ground his fingertips into the skin beside his eyes. Hap watched Umber carefully, afraid that the death of Argent might send Umber into one of his episodes of terrible sadness. Lady Truden clearly had the same fear, because she kept finding reasons to wander through the grand hall, peering sideways at Umber with every pass.

Balfour emerged from the kitchen of the Aerie with a steaming pot of coffee, a pitcher of milk, and a plate of small, flat, round cakes, steaming hot and studded with dark spots. Umber managed a weak but grateful smile at the sight.

"Hope I made these right. I followed your instructions to the letter," Balfour said.

"Ah. If anything can lift a fellow's spirits, then it is what Balfour brings us now," Umber said, taking the dish and holding it in front of Hap. "Happenstance, meet the peerless chocolate chip cookie. And shame on me for taking so long to invent it. Of course, we needed a source of chocolate first, which was only recently discovered."

Hap lifted a cookie from the dish. It was warm in his hands, and when he bent it, breaking it in two, steam escaped, and the dark substance—*chocolate,* Umber called it—oozed out in a melted string. Umber bit off half a cookie, closed his eyes, and hummed with pleasure. "Well done, Balfour," he sighed.

Hap took a cautious bite, and flavor exploded on his tongue—salty, sweet, and buttery at the same time, and easily the most delicious thing he'd ever tried. He crammed the rest into his mouth and had to force himself to chew slowly to extend the moment. When they finished, Umber searched the plate for crumbs, picking them up with a moistened fingertip. "Those were delicious, but it'll take more than sweets to lift my spirits," Umber said. "This city feels haunted now. We could use another journey; that would do the trick."

Balfour sat beside Umber and drew papers from his pocket. "Interesting that you should mention that. While you were on the hunt, an emissary from Sarnica came to the Aerie. You are invited to their annual festival of games, as a guest of their king."

Umber straightened in his chair. One side of his lip curled up. "*Sarnica*? A horrible place ruled by a horrible man. Ugh, Brugador."

Balfour nodded. "Normally, I wouldn't bother to pass the invitation on to you—for obvious reasons. But you might find the nature of this event interesting."

Umber leaned forward, waiting.

"It is not just their usual athletic competition. This year, they are calling it the Dragon Games," Balfour said. "Umber, Brugador has come into possession of living, breathing dragons."

Umber stared, blinking. Then he rocked back in his chair. "Impossible. Nobody *possesses* dragons. How could you catch them? How could you keep them?"

"I had the same questions. The emissary said they stole a cache of eggs."

Umber shook his head, as if the news were inconceivable. "But . . . how could one find the dragon's lair, and get into it? How could you get the eggs to hatch? These are mysteries that have never been answered!" He slapped the table. "Balfour, what makes you think we can even believe this emissary?"

Balfour answered quietly. "Hameron is behind this, Umber.

He brought the eggs to Sarnica. And learned how to hatch them, apparently."

Hameron, Hap thought, repeating the name inwardly. He'd never heard it before.

Umber groaned and raked his hair with his fingers. "That miserable, greedy, worthless, soulless glory hound. Oh, he must be proud of himself, discovering what I could never find. I would have been content to see the dragon's lair, but this villain stole the eggs! I don't know if I'm more impressed or outraged."

Balfour nodded. "Will we go, then?"

Hap's spirits reached a new depth, even before the inevitable answer. "Of course we will," Umber replied. "I can't resist the chance to finally see a living dragon. Hameron knows that, of course. We'll have to hold our noses against the stench of that awful country, but we'll go, all right. May I see the invitation?"

Balfour passed the folded parchment to Umber, who looked at it with his fingers flicking his chin. "Dragon Games. Hmm. What do you suppose they're doing with the dragons, anyway?"

"I asked, but the emissary was tight-lipped," Balfour said. "He said only that it would be a spectacle like no other."

"I don't like the sound of that," Umber said, squeezing one

eye nearly shut. "Well, we'll find out when we get there. But how shall we travel? Hoyle would chew off my ears if we used Boroon again, with so much shipping to be done. It'll be the *Bounder*, I suppose." A crafty grin appeared. "And something special, besides, if I can arrange it. But tell Captain Sandar that we'll leave on the *Bounder* in three days. I have business to take care of first, and a meeting at the palace. Then we'll see about these Dragon Games."

CHAPTER
9

A servant led Umber and Hap down
a wide curving stair and into the heart of the palace. He
stopped and pointed to their destination, through a marble
threshold. As they approached it, Hap felt a cool breeze wash
over his face. He followed Umber through the opening, and
his eyes widened when he saw what was inside.

The chamber had a round vaulted ceiling over a triangular
pool of clear water that bubbled high in the center. Three
channels were cut into the stone floor, where the water
flowed out from the corners of the pool and disappeared
through tunnels in the wall. Hap knew that this water fed
the fountains in the courtyard and gardens and filled the
crystalline moat outside the castle walls. It was a lovely sight,

and for a moment he was glad that Umber had insisted on bringing him to the palace for this meeting.

"Welcome to the Heartspring," said Prince Galbus. He was sitting on one of the benches that surrounded the pool. "I'm glad you came, Master Happenstance. I hoped Umber would bring you along." He stood and walked to them, without his usual wobbles and stumbles, across the tiny bridge that arched over the nearest channel. A headache seemed to plague him, as his fingers rubbed the bridge of his nose from time to time.

"The Heartspring is our endless source of fresh water. The palace was built over this spot so that no army could lay siege and make us die of thirst." Galbus had a cup in his hand. He dipped it into the spring and drank deep. "It's the sweetest water one could taste. But I never drank from it much myself. I imbibed other things."

There was a different look in the prince's eye, Hap thought. Not just the sadness of mourning—there was a clarity Hap hadn't noticed before. Galbus's gaze went past Hap's shoulder, to the open door through which they had just entered.

"Brother, is that you?" Galbus called. Hap saw Umber's posture stiffen as the youngest prince peered around the threshold.

"I didn't mean to disturb your conversation," Loden said.

Hap saw Umber's nostrils flare. He wondered if Umber was thinking the same thing he was: that Loden had been lurking around the corner, listening.

"Not at all, brother," Galbus said. "In fact, please join us. I have something to say to Umber, and I meant to tell you as well."

Loden glided into the room, handsome and graceful as always. He smiled at Umber, and Umber nodded back. Hap's collar seemed to be shrinking around his neck. There was a tension in the air that he could feel pressing against his lungs. Galbus embraced Loden, thumping his back. *Prince Galbus is blind to the danger that Umber sees,* Hap thought.

Galbus cleared his throat and let his gaze wander to the ceiling before looking directly at Umber again. "I know what people think of me," he said with a hollow laugh. "The prince of folly. An intoxicated fool who fritters away his days on wine and nonsense. And I earned that reputation, every scrap of it. I even cultivated it. This palace had no court jester—none was needed, with me about. But can you understand *why* I came to be the man I am?"

The middle prince looked from Umber to Loden. When neither offered an answer, he shrugged. "What else was there left for me to become? Argent was already everything a king had to be. Noble and stalwart. Not a man of vision, perhaps, but sensible and fair. He was the pillar we all leaned upon. I could not be like him, because two such princes could not dwell together." Galbus smiled at Loden. "And you, little brother. All the merits Argent did not inherit were left to you. The keen intelligence. The sparkling wit. The diplomat's charm."

Umber gaped as if he thought something remarkable was happening. Loden was doing his best to listen calmly, but one of his brown eyes twitched at the corner.

Galbus stood straighter. Now that he was out of his usual drunken slouch, he was taller than Hap had realized. "I know what everyone expects," Galbus said. "With Argent gone, and our father fading away, they all presume a worthless soul like me will step aside as the heir to the throne and let his more capable younger brother take his place."

Loden smiled and bowed. "My brother, it would be my honor to—"

"Hear me out," Galbus said, raising his hand. The smile vanished from Loden's face.

"It never occurred to me that this could happen," Galbus said. "Argent seemed as solid and eternal as the mountains. But now that he is gone, it seems a great whooshing gap has opened before me. A gap that I suddenly wonder if I might fill after all."

Umber glanced at Hap and raised his eyebrows.

Galbus tugged at the hem of his shirt. "I think it is time for me to leave folly behind. I have played the fool for too long. But I haven't been blind to the virtues of my brothers and the needs of the kingdom. You may not believe this, but I have paid some attention. My brother, my friends: I love our nation, our people, our glorious city. And I believe that, after all, I might like to be its king."

Hap could hardly believe the transformation that had taken place in the suddenly sober prince. Loden, meanwhile, had undergone a change of his own. He looked as if something rancid were caught in his mouth that he could neither swallow down nor spit out. Abruptly the youngest prince regained his composure. With a quick shake he affected a new expression: softened eyes, a slight tilt to the head, and a warm smile. It was the face of a man both impressed and moved.

"Lord Umber," Galbus said, "you are this kingdom's most valued citizen and trusted friend. I will count on your wisdom always. In return I think you will find me more open to your ideas than my father or poor Argent." Umber bowed his head. Galbus reached his hand out to Loden. "And you, my wise and clever brother: Of course I will need your counsel as well. You too will be my trusted advisor."

Loden smiled back and clasped the hand between his own. "Of course, dear brother. My heart and mind are yours."

Umber's expression didn't change as they left the palace and climbed into the carriage. But when they clattered through the passage in the walls and onto the streets of Kurahaven, he tilted his head back and laughed. "I think Loden got the shock of his life just now. Galbus grew up overnight! Who'd have guessed?"

"He's like a different person," said Hap.

"It boggles the brain," Umber said. "Now I just have to figure out a polite way to tell him to watch his back with that viper Loden slinking around."

Hap rubbed the front of his neck. "You think Prince Loden would hurt his brother—*both* his brothers?"

Umber sniffed. "He'd lop off his own right arm if that made him king. Loden does what suits Loden best. No matter what price someone has to pay." He leaned back on the bench and smiled with his eyes closed. "Imagine what I could accomplish with Galbus on the throne. It's almost too much to ask." Umber tugged his ear as he pondered that for a while. Then he leaned out the window, rapped on the side of the carriage, and shouted to the driver, "Dodd! Dodd, good fellow! Did I mention I need to stop by the shipping company?"

* * *

The Umber Shipping Company, one of countless enterprises that Umber owned, was in a stately marble building that loomed over the harbor. "I have some business to attend to, but the conversation will be so dull that I can't bring myself to make you sit in," Umber told Hap as they walked inside. "Why don't you take a look around? I'll find you when I'm done."

Hap wandered about. The building was crammed with crates of goods from distant ports, and desks and offices where clerks with feathered pens and furrowed brows scribbled notes and numbers. There were curiosities as well: models of merchant ships were lined up on shelves, and maps showed ports around the known world. Hap had just discovered the source of Umber's beloved coffee in some exotic destination when a shadow crossed his back.

"If *you're* here, Umber must be here," said Hoyle. Hap squeezed his teeth together.

"Um. Hello, Madam Hoyle," Hap said. She stared back with one eye half closed. The silence was torture. Hap tried to think of something to say to end it. "Er . . . it must be terrible with so many of your ships ruined by the storm."

"Terrible?" Hoyle cried. "It's the best thing that ever happened to us." She rolled her eyes when she saw Hap's confused look. "Silly boy. The storm did equal damage to our competitors' ships. The difference is, our coffers were already full of gold   thanks to my foresight and frugal nature, I might add. Now we're snatching up all the best materials to build new ships in our own shipyards, while our competitors lag behind. By the year's end, when the new fleet swims—and all with Umber's advanced design—nobody will be able to compete!" A wolfish smile spread across her face, and she rubbed her palms together, producing a rasping sound. The smile disappeared just as quickly when she saw a young man approaching. Hap recognized him. His name was Flugel, and he excelled at ferreting out whatever Umber needed from the markets and merchants of Kurahaven. Cradled under one arm Flugel had a glass sphere that was bigger than his head.

"What are you up to, Flugel?" snapped Hoyle.

"One of the captains found another one of these," Flugel said. He held up the hollow sphere. It was a milky color with writing scratched on its surface. "Umber is here, isn't he? I saw his carriage outside."

Hoyle looked over her shoulder and held out her hands. "Give it here. I'll see that he gets it."

Flugel nearly handed it over, but pulled it back. "Hold on. Did you show him the others I brought in?"

Hoyle's fingers curled like talons. "Just give it to me and be on your way!"

"Show me the other *whats*?" Umber said. He had emerged

from the room where he'd been engaged, and was giving Hoyle a sour glare.

"It's not important," Hoyle said. She tried to snatch the globe, but Flugel raised it over his head with both hands, where she couldn't reach it. Hap covered his mouth to smother a laugh, because the tiny, fuming Hoyle was leaping and trying to grab the sphere, like a child pursuing a toy.

"I think it has your name on it, Lord Umber," said Flugel. He passed the object to Umber.

Hoyle huffed and crossed her arms. "Splendid. I know *just* what's going to happen next. This will inspire you to run off one of your ridiculous journeys." Hap nodded. On that subject he completely agreed with Hoyle.

Umber held the sphere up to the sunlight streaming through the window. "You might be right, Flugel, about my name. How strange! The etching is a little worn—the rest is hard to read." He tapped his chin with his fingers. "Flugel, you said there were others?"

"This is the fourth one. Ships have found them floating in the open sea. And if they found four of them . . ."

Umber completed the thought. "How many more must be out there? Hundreds?" He turned to glare at Hoyle. "Get me the others, Hoyle. I am *not* pleased."

"I should have smashed them," muttered Hoyle as she

stomped into her office. "Don't even think about taking Boroon again for a month!" She slammed the door.

Umber handed the sphere to Hap. "You have better eyes than me, Hap. What do you think that says under my name?"

Hap stared at the thin scratches on the glass. "Umm . . . the next word might be HELP. And the third is . . . DESOLAS, I think. And under that it's just the letter C."

"Right," Umber said. "But do you see that curl on the bottom of the C? That writing looks familiar."

Hap looked up at Umber. "You know who wrote this?"

"I believe so. It's Caspar."

Hap had heard the name before. "Your old librarian? Smudge's brother?"

Umber wagged his head as if he could barely believe it. "That's the one. The traitor who stole a trunk full of my materials, went off in search of fortune and power, and left me with his nutty brother to run my archives."

But there was something else about Caspar, Hap knew. "And he's the one who knows about the Meddlers. Green-eyed people like me."

"That's our man," Umber said, and this time he smiled. "And now he wants my help? Oh, I'll give him a hand, all right. Assuming we can find the scoundrel."

with the sorceress Juriana?
I detest being her jailor,
but there is no other
option. I can't believe her
when she claims to have
renounced evil. And even
without the amulets,
rings, and other items
that amplify her powers,
she may be dangerous.
Who knows what secret
caches sh

CHAPTER
10

The four glass objects sat in a row on the desk in the archives. None of them was a perfect sphere, Hap could see; there was a slight irregularity to their shapes, and the milky color varied widely from one to the next. Smudge—the boorish and mildly crazed fellow who kept Umber's archives— bent his shaggy head to read the message scratched on each:

UMBER

HELP

DESOLAS

C

"Yes. Brother Caspar wrote this," Smudge whispered hoarsely. He looked at Umber with red-rimmed eyes. "Will you help him? Will you find him?"

"I'll find him, all right," Umber said, grinding a fist inside his other palm. "If we can figure out where he is. What is Desolas, Smudge? It must be a place, but none of the captains has heard of it."

Smudge tugged his beard with both hands, splitting it. "Desolas. Desolas . . . I've heard that name before. But when?"

"Your brother knew I'd ask you," Umber said. "He's counting on you to remember, Smudge. Look, maybe this will help." Umber spread a wide parchment across the desk. It was a map of the Rulian Sea. "This is where the spheres were found," Umber said, tracing the map with his finger. "Our captains say the prevailing currents would have brought the spheres from the west, over here. That doesn't narrow it down much. But does that tickle your memory at all? Think, Smudge!"

Smudge squeezed his eyes shut as he concentrated. He rocked in his seat, tugging his forked beard with one hand, then the other. "Desolas. In the Inferno." He opened his eyes. "That's the place! Brother Caspar is there."

"The Inferno," Umber said. He leaned back and patted his stomach, digesting the thought.

"Before Brother left, I saw him with scrolls and maps. One map showed the Inferno, and an island in the middle named Desolas. Brother was angry when he saw me looking. I asked what was on Desolas, but he told me there was nothing."

Hap didn't like the direction of the conversation. "What is the Inferno, Lord Umber?"

Umber smiled. "Never been there myself. It's on my to-do list, though! The Inferno is a ring of volcanoes in the Rulian Sea. Mariners don't like to get too close, with all the fire and smoke and molten rock." Hap's face must have lost all its color, because Umber quickly added, "But I'm sure it's not as bad as it sounds!"

Smudge leaned over and seized Umber's wrist. He choked out his words. "I know you are angry at Brother Caspar. But please. Bring him back. Please, Lord Umber."

Umber put his hand on top of Smudge's. "Oh, you know me, Smudge. If he needs rescuing, I'll do my best. Now if you don't mind, you're squeezing a bit too hard."

When Umber and Hap left the archives and stepped into the grand hall, they found Welkin and Barkin, two of Umber's trusted guards, waiting for them. They looked dusty and tired.

"Back already?" Umber said. He turned to Hap. "I sent these two to talk to that woman we met in the forest. So, boys, what did you learn?"

"Hard to say," Barkin said. There was a grim look on his face.

"We found the house, right where you said it would be. Except it wasn't there anymore," Welkin added.

"Burned to the ground, Lord Umber. The embers were still hot when we got there."

Umber's jaw went slack.

"There were people inside, as far as we could tell," Barkin said. "Two of them."

"Ah, Ludmilla," Umber mumbled. "And the death-boar, I'm sure. Was the beast her poor cursed husband? Brother? Son?" He thumped his fist against his mouth.

"Something else you should know, Lord Umber," Welkin said. He exchanged an uneasy glance with Barkin. "On the way there we ran into a party coming back to Kurahaven. We hid, so they didn't see us."

"Let me guess," Umber said quietly. "Larcombe was among them. They wore no uniforms, but you recognized some of Loden's guard."

Welkin's eyebrows shot up. "How'd you know?"

Umber waved his hand. "Never mind. Thank you, boys. You did well to avoid being seen, and to rush back with the news. Don't speak of it to anyone. You can go now."

When the two were gone, Umber slumped into a chair. Hap stood beside him. "I don't understand, Lord Umber. What do you think happened?"

Umber rested his head, temple on fist. "I have a pretty good idea, and I don't think it's just my imagination. In a nutshell: The man cursed to live as the death-boar lived deep in the woods with Ludmilla, just trying to live a secret, peaceful life. Somehow Loden learned about them. He threatened to kill or capture the death-boar unless the poor creature did one simple favor: Lure a hunting party to the Falls of the Mist. There Loden shoved Argent off the rocks. Then he sent Larcombe to silence the two who might speak of the treachery."

Hap put a hand on the table to steady himself. "That's horrible."

Umber nodded. "That's Loden. The stench of it all disgusts me. I'm sending word to Galbus to warn him. And then I'm glad we're getting away from Kurahaven for a while. I don't think I could be civil to dear Prince Loden if we met."

Sophie was hunched over a table with a brush in one hand and the tip of her tongue sticking out from the corner of her mouth. Her damaged arm, which ended at a scarred stump at her wrist, was holding the parchment down at the corner. Hap rarely got more than a glimpse of the wound, because she was painfully conscious of it and kept it out of sight. But she did not know that he was there for the moment. His heart ached for her, but he was also glad that the injury had not subdued her talents. Sophie was a splendid artist, and with the aid of a false hand that Umber had devised to help her hold a bow, she was also a superb archer.

Hap waited until she paused to dip the brush in a jar of ink. "Hello, Sophie."

"Oh—hello, Hap," she answered. She slid her damaged arm under the table's edge.

"Don't let me interrupt you," Hap said.

"It's fine. I was working on a study of the sea-giants." She frowned at the parchment. "But I don't think I got them right. They were scarier than this."

"I'm sure you drew them wonderfully," Hap said. "But soon you'll have something else to sketch and paint. Dragons, maybe."

Sophie turned her face away from Hap and looked out the narrow window high in the wall. "I'm not going on this journey, Hap."

Hap stared. "I thought you always went."

"Not this time."

"But why?"

"I . . . um, I just have too many things to do."

Hap scrunched his brow. This didn't make any sense. "But—you have to come!"

She spun in her seat and leaned over her sketch again. "I don't want to talk about it, really. I'm sorry, Hap."

"But—"

"Do you mind, Hap? I need to finish this now, and I have to concentrate."

Hap winced. "Very well," he said, and left the room.

The *Bounder* was about to sail with the morning tide when a royal messenger rode into the harbor, leaped off his horse, and ran to the dock, shouting and waving. "A letter for Umber!" he cried.

"Who's it from?" Umber called.

"His Highness Prince Galbus," said the messenger, running up the gangplank. Umber tucked the letter into his vest. Minutes later the last mooring line was untied, and the *Bounder* eased away from the dock.

Once the ship cleared the harbor, Captain Sandar turned her west, and she pelted over the waves. Hap felt the warm sun on his back, but it didn't cure the chill that swept his bones every time he ventured onto the water. But at least he understood why he was afraid. *I drowned,* he thought. *When I was Julian Penny, I fell through the ice and drowned.*

"Wonderful to be off on a new adventure, isn't it?" Umber said, holding on to one of the ropes that angled down from the ship's mast.

"Of course, Lord Umber," Hap lied.

"First we'll look for Caspar. Then it's on to Sarnica and the Dragon Games. The *Bounder* will take us on the first part of our journey, but I have arranged a rendezvous with some special transportation later on. But don't ask me what it is, and don't go asking Oates, either. I want to surprise you!"

Hap gripped the railing a little tighter. Coming from Umber, *special* was not a promising word, and a surprise was not a welcome development. Another thing troubled Hap: Captain Sandar, who always brimmed with confidence, was pacing back and forth with a troubled look in his eye. The sailors who manned the ship looked just as ill at ease, and they whispered quietly among themselves.

"Why does everyone look so worried?" asked Hap.

"Oh, sailors get that way. I'm sure they're wondering how we're going to get this ship inside the Inferno. They've probably heard that nobody who sails in gets out alive." Umber saw the stricken look on Hap's face and added, "But Caspar got in, didn't he?"

Hap fought the temptation to say, *Right, and now he needs help getting out.*

Several times that day Hap came upon Umber hunched over the prince's letter, grinning widely, and once even pressing the paper to his chest. But whenever someone approached, Umber tucked it out of sight, so Hap decided not to ask him what it said.

After two days at sea a wide column of smoke appeared on the horizon. As the *Bounder* sailed closer, the smoke's extraordinary size became apparent. It was at least two miles across. *Or is it steam?* Hap wondered, because it came straight out of the sea, where jagged projections of living rock, craggy black or oozing molten orange, boiled the water. There were fissures and short cones amid the rock, shooting fountains of lava high above the *Bounder's* masts. Flakes of ash came down like snow.

Sailors lined the rail and stared. "This is a demon's nest," one said.

"Enough of that talk!" shouted Sandar. "That's close enough for now, Mister Greenway," he called to the man at the helm. Hap saw sweat beading the captain's brow. Sandar looked to Umber.

Umber cleared his throat, aware that the sailors were keeping a wary eye on him, clearly hoping he wouldn't ask them to do something reckless. "Can we get inside the ring?"

Sandar puffed out a deep breath. He called up to a sailor perched in the lookout atop the mast. "Hannigan! Is there a way in?"

Hannigan shaded his eyes. "Not that I can see," he shouted down. "But just now the smoke cleared for a moment—I thought I saw something inside. Like a tower, very tall!"

Sandar looked at Umber, who smiled and shrugged. The captain tugged at his chin, and more color drained from his face. "Circle it, Mister Greenway," Sandar called. "But keep our distance, you hear?"

"Don't have to say that twice," Greenway muttered, turning the wheel.

One sailor tossed a bucket on a rope over the side and hauled it up full of water. He dipped a cautious hand inside. "Feel that," he said to a shipmate. The other fellow put a finger in, and his eyes widened. A dozen other sailors lined up for a try, and Umber joined them.

"Oh!" Umber said when he plunged his hand in. "That would make for a nice warm bath! Anybody want to take a dip? Ha, ha!" He looked around, and was disappointed when none of the crew laughed with him.

There was only a gentle breeze to propel them around the Inferno, and so the *Bounder* ambled past the smoking, spewing fissures. Hap felt a tap on his shoulder. It was Umber, pointing at an object bobbing in the waves: another of the milky globes.

Umber leaned against the rail and watched carefully, looking for a wider gap between the volcanic fissures. Once he called to Sandar: "That might be it! Mark this spot please, Captain!" Most of the crew shot Umber a disbelieving look before staring dolefully at one another.

Hap could not imagine how the *Bounder* would get inside the Inferno. It seemed designed to keep intruders out. He kept an eye on one of the more spectacular fissures as they glided by, and saw that the eruption rose and fell in rhythm, pausing as if to rest every minute or so.

The *Bounder* returned at last to where she had begun to circle. "Captain, I think the place I pointed out is the best way through," Umber said. Sandar nodded grimly, and the *Bounder* returned to the spot.

The ship dropped anchor outside the gap. Sandar shook his head as he stared at the treacherous passage. He stepped close to Umber and spoke quietly, so his crew could not hear. "Lord Umber, please. This would be suicide."

Umber frowned and stared at the gap.

Hap offered an observation. "I think the eruptions get bigger and smaller. But not all at the same time." As soon as the words left his mouth and he understood what they implied, he instantly regretted uttering them.

Umber blinked quickly, leaned over the side, and kept time by tapping the rail. "Yes! Brilliant, Happenstance!" he shouted a minute later. "If the cycles are predictable, we

can time it just right! Captain, would you bring me an hourglass?"

Within a half an hour it was obvious that Hap and Umber were right. Every so often the eruptions on both sides of the gap lost their intensity at the same time.

"I still can't risk the *Bounder* in that passage," Sandar said. "I'm sorry, Umber, but with this weak breeze, I don't think she's nimble enough to shoot through in time. Look at that flaming stuff in the air—her sails would catch fire. But I think the jolly boat, with some good oarsmen—and your man Oates among them—could make it. Would that be all right with you?"

Umber rubbed his hands together and grinned. "That'll do just fine!"

Sandar turned to the crew. "I need six men to man the oars for Lord Umber. Would anyone like to go?"

The men stared at the boiling fissures. Not a foot stepped forward or hand rose skyward.

"What if there were five gold pieces for every oarsman?" Umber asked, and there were suddenly more volunteers than seats on the boat.

The smaller boat edged closer to the gap. On either side there was an ugly heap of jagged black stone, steaming

where it touched the water and vomiting dark smoke and glowing magma. The colossal wall of vapor blotted out the sky ahead of them. Chunks of gray stuff bobbed in the water, thumping against the boat. Umber, who sat at the bow, reached over and plucked one up. He held it high for Hap to see. "Pumice!" he cried. "Volcanic rock. The only stone that floats!"

Hap was at the stern with a bucket of water between his feet. If any molten rock or flaming ash landed in the boat, it was his job to douse it. Balfour, who sat beside Umber, had another bucket. Most of the oarsmen, Oates among them, had dunked cloths in the ocean and draped them over their heads and shoulders. Hap dipped his hand into the water—it was nearly painful to touch. *How nice,* he thought. *If I drown this time, I can get boiled, too.*

"Hold us here for now, my friends," Umber said, and they stopped rowing with the Inferno just a hundred feet away. Hap felt the heat on his face. Men wiped their sleeves across their eyes to keep the perspiration from stinging.

Umber wore his usual giddy grin as he looked from the small hourglass in his hand to the pair of fissures. First on the left side, and then on the right, the eruptions lost their intensity. The jets of lava that shot as high as the mast of the *Bounder* simmered down to half that height.

"Now! Go!" Umber cried, pointing forward. "We have less than a minute!"

The men pulled on their oars, and the jolly boat shot forward. The oars circled and plunged into the water, and the oarsmen grunted with the effort. Hap lifted the bucket, ready to hurl water. They slid through the wall of steam, which thinned to a white haze near the sea.

"For five measly pieces of gold," an oarsman muttered. "My mother birthed a fool!"

"Shut up and pull!" cried the man beside him.

Red heat washed over them as they entered the gap, with the eruptions nearer than ever. Bits of molten rock rained down on either side, trailing smoke and sizzling as they hit the sea.

"We're going to make it!" cried an oarsman, half grunting and half shouting. His eyes looked ready to spring from their sockets. On their left, the fountain of flame roared and grew, rising and spreading. Hap held his breath.

They were through. The air cooled, and the boat emerged from the curtain of steam into the interior of the Inferno. The oarsmen were facing the stern, so Umber, Balfour, and Hap got the first look at what lay inside. Hap's muscles went weak at the sight. He didn't realize he'd dropped the bucket until he felt the pain of it landing on his foot.

One by one the oarsmen turned to look over their shoulders. Their oars slipped from their hands. Some stood up, a reflex inspired by awe. They tugged the wet cloths off their heads as if doffing hats.

"Desolas," Umber said.

CHAPTER
II

The wall of steam rose a mile high, surrounding them and blocking the world from sight. The sun dazzled above, inside a circle of blue that blurred at the edges.

Amid the inner sea, a half mile from where they floated, there was an island. It was only a few hundred strides from one end to the other, white and sandy at its edges, with strange trees lining the shore—tall with ribbed trunks and broad plumes of fronds at the tops. Stranger still were the three structures in the center, which prompted everyone in the boat to gape in silence.

The tallest was a castle of gleaming black rock. The word for that mineral sprang into Hap's mind: *obsidian.* The castle had a narrow tower at one corner that looked needle-thin from this distance. It shot higher into the air than Hap imagined a tower could ever stand, at least twice as high as the tallest spire of the palace at Kurahaven.

Beside the castle, even more remarkable, was a glittering pyramid made of glass. Hap's keen eyes showed him what the others could not yet see: The structure was made of the same spheres that had led them to this spot—thousands upon thousands, stacked in diminishing rows.

Finally, being carved from an enormous block of stone, there was the titanic figure of a man. It stood a hundred feet high and was covered to the shoulders in scaffolding. The body was still emerging from rock, while the head and shoulders were finished. There were hordes of pale figures scrambling over the scaffolding, and the *chip, chip* of hammer on stone could be heard across the water. Flecks of rock fell from the colossus like rain. Hap leaned forward, narrowing his eyes to sharpen their focus.

"Hap," Umber said. "You see better than the rest of us. Those people on the scaffolding . . . those aren't really . . ."

Hap shook his head. "No. They aren't people."

"What are they, then?" said Oates.

Hap shrugged. "They're smaller, I think. . . . I have no idea."

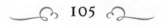

"Let's get closer and find out!" Umber said brightly. "Hap, do you know what my old archivist, Caspar, looked like?"

"No, Lord Umber."

"You do now. That's the man, right there." Umber gestured toward the enormous statue with his thumb. He chuckled and crossed his arms. "Well, he always wanted fame and glory. He looks like the king of the world here. So why call for help?"

The boat drew closer to the island, giving them a better look at the countless tiny figures. They weren't just on the scaffolding; they were polishing the glass at the foot of the pyramid, walking the parapets of the castle, and marching in and out of dark holes in the island.

"How many are there?" asked Balfour.

"Thousands," said Umber. "They don't seem hostile. They haven't even noticed us. Oh—except for that little fellow." A large arrowhead of stone jutted from the near side of the island, and one of the creatures had ventured out to stare at them. It had short bowed legs and long arms with high knobby shoulders, all sinew and muscle. Its face was wider than long, with a curled slit for a nose and a wide mouth that curved dolefully down. The back of its skull tapered to a pointed crest. It was naked, with no hint of gender and hairless skin as pale and smooth as marble. Hap peered at the other creatures in the distance. Most were waist-high, while a few, like the nearest, stood only as tall as a man's knee.

"Are they gnomes? Elves? Hobgoblins?" Balfour asked.

"I don't think so," Umber said. He groped at his chin. "You don't suppose . . ." He leaned over the bow, gripping the sides. "Balfour! I think those are the *bidmis*."

This remark caused the oarsmen to look at each other and shrug. "What's a bidmi?" asked Oates.

"Creatures of legend—or so I thought," Umber said. Every man in the boat leaned closer to hear the words. "They will do the bidding of any person who awakens them. Nobody knew where to find them. Apparently the answer was in my archives, and Caspar discovered it."

As if responding to the name, a lanky man appeared on the terrace of the castle. He leaned on the balcony, grabbed the top of his head, and shouted with joy. "Umber! Lord Umber! Oh, thank the heavens above, you are here!"

"And there is the weasel himself," Umber said from the side of his mouth while raising his hand in greeting.

Caspar raced down a staircase that descended the castle wall and dashed onto the jutting rock where the single bidmi stood watching.

"Look at him, Umber," Balfour murmured. Hap could see there was something wrong with the fellow rushing toward

them. His teeth were clenched, the tendons in his neck popped, and his bleary eyes were underscored by black crescents. His voice cracked and quavered when he spoke to them with his palms raised up. "Don't touch the shore, whatever you do! And don't show any weapons or make a hostile gesture, or they'll destroy you!"

Oars splashed in the water as the sailors reversed their paddles while staring at the hordes of creatures on the island. Hap heard one of the men whimper, "Knew this was a mistake!"

"We'll be fine. Keep us here, boys," Umber told them, before turning back to Caspar. "We got your—" Umber began, but Caspar cut him off with a desperate wave of his hands.

Caspar put a trembling finger to his lips. The bidmi looked up at him and cocked its head. It narrowed its tiny dark eyes. "Master," it said, flashing pure white teeth with sharp, even points like the blade of a saw. "What do you bid me?" The voice was a thin screech, as unpleasant as a rake dragged over slate.

Caspar groaned and pressed a hand against his forehead. "I bid you to climb to the top of the pyramid. The globe on the top doesn't please me—it's the same color as the rest of them! Take it down and replace it with a new globe, of a different color."

The creature bent an arm across its narrow, waspish waist

and bowed. "As you bid me." It turned and loped toward the gleaming glass structure.

Caspar watched with his shoulders twitching until the bidmi was some distance away, and then fell on his knees and held his clasped hands toward Umber. Tears rolled down his face. "Umber! Lord Umber! My friend, can you please forgive me?"

Umber sniffed out a laugh. "Of course you're sorry, now that you need my help. Should your brother forgive you too?"

Caspar winced as the words stung. Hap saw the resemblance to Smudge in the wide-set eyes and the shape of the mouth. This man was a taller, less unkempt version of his brother, with long hair that hung straight past his shoulders.

"How is Smudge?" Caspar muttered.

"About the same, aside from the wound in his heart," Umber said.

Caspar stared at the rock under his feet. Every part of him seemed to twitch: shoulders, hands, eyes, and mouth. "I was going to come back for him, when I made my fortune."

"I doubt that," said Oates.

Caspar glared back at the big man, and then softened his expression for Umber. "I'm desperate, Umber. I've gotten myself into a fix, and I don't know to escape."

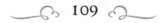

"You look like you're going mad, to be honest," Umber said. "Well, get in the boat. We know how to get through the—"

"I can't! I can't leave the shore!" cried Caspar. He dug his fingers into his scalp. "They won't let me. These are the bidmis, Umber. I found the bidmis, and I woke them."

Umber nodded. "And is it true? They'll do anything you ask?"

Caspar tugged at his hair and cackled. "Ha! It is true—but there are *laws*, you see! Of course I didn't know them until the foul creatures were unleashed, and there's the problem!"

"Here come your little friends," Oates said.

Caspar turned and snarled at the trio of bidmis that loped toward them. "You see, Umber? They come again! 'What do you bid me,' they will say, and I must give them something to do! There is no peace, no sleep—what have I done to deserve this curse?"

The bidmis arrived. "What do you bid me?" screeched the smallest of the three. The sound crawled up Hap's spine like a spider.

Caspar fell on his knees. "Why can't you help with the statue?" he croaked.

"There are enough to do that bidding," said the creature. "What do you bid me?"

Caspar pressed his palms against his eyes. "I don't know. I can't think. . . ."

The bidmi clacked its white teeth together. The others joined in, and soon it seemed that every creature on the island stopped what it was doing to make the same terrifying sound: *clack-click-clack-clack-click* . . .

"Master, what do you bid me?" repeated the nearest creature, stepping closer. "Or has the master run out of bidding?" It rejoined the clacking of the others and brought its snapping jaws near Caspar's knee.

Caspar crawled backward, pushing with his hands. "Please . . . give me time. . . . Wait, wait . . . I know!" He pointed toward the pyramid of glass. "Tear it down! It doesn't please me! Smash it to pieces; turn it back into sand!"

The bidmi bowed. "As you bid me." The clacking of teeth ceased at once, the myriad bidmis went back to their tasks, and the three creatures ran toward the pyramid.

"Do you see, Umber?" Caspar wailed. "Of course I'm going mad. They will do whatever I ask—but only what is possible on this tiny island. And they finish it all so quickly, and then they ask me again and again, 'Master, what do you bid me?'"

The sound of shattering glass reached Hap's ears. He looked toward the towering pyramid. Even as the first bidmi climbed up its side with a new ball of glass, obeying Caspar's earlier command, hundreds of its brethren attacked the spheres at the base. The walls shifted, and globes began to roll off the sides. As they tumbled down, the bidmis stomped, grinding them into bits. Hap's stomach lurched. The pyramid had an awesome beauty, and the destruction was terrible to witness.

"Why don't you just tell the bidmis to drown themselves, or bury themselves in a hole?" Oates said. The sailors looked at Oates, jutting their bottom lips and nodding at what sounded like a sensible idea.

"You think I haven't thought of that, you great oaf?" Caspar cried. "It's one of their bloody laws: *The master must not order his bidmis to destroy themselves, for who will serve the master?* Oh, it sounds wonderful—an army of invincible creatures to do anything you command. Infinite obedience, ultimate power! But the blasted *laws* spoil everything. *The master must never leave the island. . . . The master must not ask the impossible. . . . No other may walk upon the island, for we serve only the master. . . . The master must not ask for the same task more than—*" Caspar interrupted his own words. "Umber! Who is that boy with you?"

Hap had been staring at the pyramid's slow disintegration. He turned to see Caspar gaping at him.

"This is Happenstance," said Umber. "My ward."

Caspar's fingers fluttered at his lips. "Happenstance? But. . . those eyes . . . he looks like a . . . *Umber, do you realize what he is?*"

"I'm well aware," Umber replied evenly.

"A Meddler! How did you find him? Where did he come from?" Caspar rose awkwardly to his feet and groped at the air in Hap's direction. "Boy—Happenstance! You can help me! Can you see my fate? Can you see how I can be saved?"

Hap looked at Umber, who sighed and glanced at the sailors in the boat. Umber had always intended for Hap's origin and abilities to remain a secret, but now the sailors stared with lifted brows. Hap walked down the center of the craft, joining Umber at the prow where he could more easily speak to Caspar.

"I know what you're talking about," Hap told Caspar. "The filaments. But I don't see them all the time. I don't see them now."

Caspar moaned. "A Meddler . . . the thing I most wanted to find, and it turned up after I left." He laughed, but it was a mad, unnerving sound without a shred of humor.

"You were the expert on Meddlers, Caspar," Umber said. "But you took the knowledge with you when you deserted us. So I have some questions, if you're sane enough to answer."

Caspar looked up with his wild eyes barely visible through

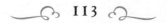

the long hair that had fallen across his face. "Questions? What questions?"

Umber glanced at Hap and gave him a reassuring nod. "Do the initials WN mean anything to you? They were on a note that told me where to find Happenstance. I believe that person was another Meddler."

Caspar's head lifted at the mention of WN. "What other questions do you have?"

Umber narrowed his eyes. "Several. What are the Meddlers? Where do they come from? How did Happenstance become one? And how can the boy understand those filaments better, and how to use them?"

A wild grin distorted Caspar's face. He used both hands to push his hair away from his eyes. "Oh, I know where to find the answers to those questions—and many you have not asked. But first, Umber, you must rescue me from this torment."

Umber put his fists on his hips. "Come on, Caspar. You have my word; I will search for an answer, but—"

Caspar waved his arms and screamed, "You're not leaving until you do what I've asked! I can order the bidmis to devour you—they'll be on you before you can paddle twice!"

Behind them the sailors gasped, and the knuckles they had wrapped around the oars turned white. The boat rocked as

Oates leaped to his feet, glaring at Caspar. Umber patted the air with one hand to calm them.

"Save me, Umber," Caspar whined. He trembled and wrapped his arms around his stomach. "You can have it back. All of it."

"All of what, Caspar?"

"The stuff I took from your archives. The things I learned about the Meddlers."

"Where is it, Caspar? Here, with you?"

Caspar shook his head. "In a safe place. Not here. I'll show you, if you get me out of this mess!"

Umber sat on the side of the boat and crossed his legs. "Very well, Caspar. Tell me about this place and what you've been through. Perhaps when I hear your story, I will find an answer."

the biggest problem

faced has been the

matter of transcribing. How

do I get the information

from the Reboot computer

onto paper, into a form

that I can share? I could

spend every hour committing

to paper the fundamentals

of medicine, architectural

drawings, schematics for

inventions, musical compositions,

and the like. The solution

CHAPTER
12

Ringing, clinking, splintering, and smashing: The sounds were both musical and harsh. Hundreds of spheres at a time rolled down the pyramid's shifting walls and were crushed under the feet of the bidmis. Already a quarter of the magnificent construction was gone. At the same time thousands more of the tiny creatures still chipped away at the enormous statue of Caspar.

"I was clever to get the message to you!" Caspar said, with the mirthless grin of a skull. "The bidmis won't allow me to call for help, but I found a way. I saw currents in the water—the heat of the molten rock makes it flow, and one stream led right out of the Inferno. So I ordered the bidmis to make the glass spheres. I stole all I could and scratched out my message, and I dropped them in the current, and it worked. Wasn't I clever, Umber? Almost as clever as you!"

"Ingenious," Umber said.

"But how do they make the glass?" Balfour asked.

"From sand," Caspar said. He pointed toward the dark holes in the island. "Somewhere beneath us there are volcanic fires. They melt the sand into glass down there. That is all I know—I am not allowed so far below."

"Don't distract him, my friend," Umber said quietly to Balfour. "Caspar, what led you here? Something in my archives, I presume."

"A scroll—ancient and partial. Took forever to translate. Showed the location. Said a vast army of invincible creatures waits for a master to awaken them so they may do his bidding . . . but that's all it said! That's all the legend of the bidmis has ever said, anywhere! Nothing about the rules!" Caspar couldn't seem to decide whether to whisper or shout his story, and his voice had finally risen to a scream.

"Cling to your wits, Caspar," Umber pleaded. "You're right—I've heard of the bidmis, but never these conditions you mention. You said it was a partial scroll. Perhaps the missing part was your downfall. But tell me what happened when you got here."

Caspar nodded quickly. "Yes, yes, I will tell! We finally got

here—how long ago, I can't remember. Months, I guess—it seems like a thousand years! It was a Meddler I really wanted to find, you know, but this seemed just as grand. And besides, if they would follow any command, couldn't I make them bring me one of those green-eyed folk?" Caspar's desperate, hungry stare fell on Hap again for a moment before he continued. "It took so long to find a ship that would take me into the Inferno—three turned back without even trying, and I had to start all over! But finally I met a braver soul. It was Captain Blacktree, and his ship, the . . . I forget the name. . . . The *Audacious*."

"I used to know Blacktree," said one of the oarsmen. "The *Audacious* was a little ship. A dozen crew, maybe. Blacktree was a bit of a smuggler," he added with a shrug when Umber looked back.

"Yes, a tiny ship," Caspar said. "Small and quick enough to get through the gap in The Inferno. But . . . then . . . what . . . what was I saying?" Caspar slurred his last few words. His eyes rolled up, flashing blood-streaked whites, and his head sagged to one side.

Umber leaned forward, staring. "He's exhausted," he said quietly. "We may be able to—"

Caspar gasped and jolted awake. "What? What! Umber!" He stared in panic until his bleary eyes found their boat again. Then he exhaled deeply and dug his fingers into his cheeks. "Was afraid I only dreamed that you were here. So tired ...," he muttered. It seemed to take a mighty effort for him to string his thoughts together. "Where was I? Yes, we got here. Desolas was ... barren. Empty. Just sand and rock and these strange trees. We looked around and found a hole that led to winding stairs. And at the bottom of the stairs ... a chamber with an iron door, and the door had an iron ring on it that you could use to knock. We tugged at the door ... wouldn't budge. There were words carved in the door, and I recognized the old language from the scroll. It said, "Knock thrice and master you shall be."

"I thought of you at that moment, Umber," Caspar said. "How jealous you'd be if you could see me there, on the threshold of ... a greater discovery than you ever made. I thought I would order my new servants to ... build me a great palace ... fetch me a Meddler ... fetch you as well, so you could see what I had done—me, your poor humble archivist, eclipsing your fame!"

Umber interlaced his fingers and tapped his thumbs together. "You were never poor, Caspar. But go on. You knocked."

Caspar's mouth twisted into a grimace. "I knocked ... three times. For a while nothing happened. Blacktree laughed and called me a fool. And then ... *we heard them.*" Caspar shivered.

"On the other side of the door. Countless thumping footsteps, louder and louder. Some of the men ran, but Blacktree stayed. The door screeched and opened, and we saw eyes, as many as the stars, shining in the light of our torches. One of the bidmis, the smallest of all . . . stepped out and asked, 'Who has knocked?' But it was looking at *me* all the while; they all were, because they knew it was *me*. And I told them, 'I did.' And then they poured out of the darkness with their teeth snapping. They flowed past me like water around a stone, and they fell on Blacktree and the fools who had stayed in the chamber, and went up the stairs after the rest of the men." Caspar lowered his face into his palms.

It was one of the sailors who spoke next, while clutching his throat. "But . . . what happened to those men? The crew of the *Audacious*?"

Caspar lifted his head. He gnashed his teeth up and down and pointed down his throat. "All gone!" he howled. "The men on the *Audacious* would have been all right, because they were offshore, but they fired arrows at the bidmis, and the little monsters got them. . . . Umber, *they even ate the boat, for heaven's sake!*"

The faces of the sailors, and Balfour and Oates as well, turned as white as the sand. From the inner island came the loudest crash of all as the bulk of the unsteady pyramid shifted and collapsed, with the globes flowing and rolling across the ground like an ocean wave crashing on the shore. In a frenzy thousands of bidmis leaped onto the fallen spheres and shattered them under their bare feet, somehow without drawing a drop of blood.

Despite the noise Caspar's head bobbed again. He bit his knuckle to keep himself awake.

"What else can you tell me, Caspar?" Umber said.

Caspar shook his head. "Nothing . . . Ever since that moment, these devils haunt me, asking again and again. . . . I spend every moment dreaming of new tasks for them . . . never sleeping more than minutes, eating nothing but the vile leaves they pull from the sea and those . . . *things* from those trees."

"Coconuts," Umber said, pointing at the clusters of enormous nuts in the tops of the trees. "They shouldn't grow around here, but the volcanoes must keep it warm enough."

"Who cares," Caspar muttered into his hand.

Balfour cleared his throat. "Visitors."

A flock of bidmis, the few not busy with the smashing of the pyramid or the sculpting of the statue, trotted up to Caspar. The smallest of them spoke. "What do you bid—"

"Pick up every stone on the beach!" screamed Caspar, with spittle flying. "Put them in piles of a thousand stones, no more and no less!" He lurched to his feet and slapped the side of his

head with his hands. His wild, drifting gaze took a moment to find the boat again. "Well, Umber? Well? You who know so much about the strange and terrible—tell me how to escape!"

Umber spread a hand over his own heart. "Caspar, I'm at a loss. You need to let us go. I'll search my archives again, and send messages to every learned man I know, and—"

"No!" bellowed Caspar, shaking his fists over his head. "You'll stay right there and figure it out! Clever, sneaky Umber! You probably know the answer already, and you don't want to say! And *you*," he cried, pointing at Hap. "You can change my fate! That's what you Meddlers do. So change it! Change it, or the bidmis will destroy you all!"

"Caspar!" snapped Umber. Caspar stopped his rant and wiped a hand across his spittle-covered mouth. "Give me some time. Let me think in silence," Umber said.

"But you must—"

"Shhh!" Umber hissed. "All of you! I'm thinking." He rested his chin on his hand and narrowed his eyes in concentration.

On the jutting rock Caspar sat again and hugged his knees to his chest. Before long his eyelids fluttered and finally closed entirely. His head lolled from side to side before settling awkwardly to the left.

Umber leaned forward and studied him. Then he turned

and pointed to the oars, made a rowing motion, and asked for stealth with a finger against his lips. The sailors, gulping and shivering, dipped their oars quietly and turned the boat about. To Hap, every drop that fell off the oars sounded like a boulder splashing, even though the smashing of glass continued from the island. The pyramid, Hap saw, was nearly gone.

Every muscle in his body was as taut as a bowstring as they slid away from the island. *Don't wake up,* he silently called to Caspar. Hap felt sorry for the man, but feared him more. In his desperation to escape he was ready to send others to their deaths.

When they were a stone's throw from Desolas, Umber motioned for them to row faster. "We need to get farther away," he whispered.

How far? wondered Hap. The boat picked up speed. When they were a third of the distance to the wall of steam and smoke, a strange silence fell inside The Inferno.

"No more smashing glass," Oates said, grunting with effort as he pulled on the oars.

"Hap, what do you see?" asked Umber.

Hap narrowed his eyes to sharpen his vision. He saw hundreds of bidmis heading for where Caspar sat, still dozing. Hap bit his lip as a tiny bidmi stepped in front of Caspar. A moment later Caspar's head sprang up, and he scrambled to his feet. Hap heard his scream carry across the waves as Caspar spotted their boat in the distance. Caspar leaped up and down, shouting an order and pointing their way. The hundreds of bidmis plunged into the water, churning it into a white froth that moved swiftly toward their boat. Countless more dropped whatever they were doing and followed. They leaped off the scaffolding of the statue without regard for height, they streamed out from the castle, and they charged by the thousands out of holes in the ground.

"Row, men, row!" shouted Umber, pointing to the passage through the Inferno.

The oarsmen pulled, hissing through their teeth, and the boat picked up speed. Hap stared back at the froth that pursued them. It was shaped like a wedge, with one swift swimmer ahead of the others. Hap saw thousands of little hands rising and slashing, and heads bobbing in the foam, and heard the *clack-click-clack* of their teeth.

Balfour pushed a water barrel overboard to lighten the boat's load. It bobbed in their wake. Soon the bidmis overtook it, and it was chewed and torn to pieces in an instant. Facing backward as they rowed, the crew had all too good a look at the spectacle.

"They're catching up!" cried an oarsman.

"We just have to make it past the fissures! That's where

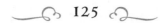

their domain ends!" shouted Umber. "I hope," he added in a whisper that only Hap could hear.

The men strained and grunted. Sweat rolled past their eyes, and their chests heaved. Only Oates was unaffected by the effort, and he rowed so fiercely that the boat lurched every time his oar stabbed the sea. Still, the distance between them and the relentless horde quickly shrank. Soon barely a hundred feet separated them, and the splashing and clacking were deafening.

Hap turned to look at the raging plumes of lava and smoke just ahead. Both fissures were furiously erupting, raining molten death into the channel. "Lord Umber," he said, pulling Umber's sleeve.

"I know! Fill the buckets," Umber said. Hap was startled to see an exuberant grin on Umber's face. Umber raised his voice for all to hear. "Aim a little starboard now—yes, perfect! I think a lull is due there any moment."

The eruption to their right began to ebb just as they entered the wall of steam. Hap looked back. He could see every tooth in the nearest bidmi's mouth, and the ferocious glint in its eyes. Behind it was a vast mob of snapping jaws and flailing arms. Then the creatures were obscured by the mist, and oppressive heat struck the boat from either side.

Hap and Umber held buckets poised. A flaming chunk

dropped into the boat, landing on the floor, where it smoldered and ate into the planks until Hap doused it. The sailors stared up as they rowed, and one leaped from his seat to avoid an orange blob of molten rock. Umber caught another in his bucket, where it hissed like a snake. And then they were through the gap, into the clear, with the *Bounder* dead ahead.

With red faces, open mouths, and lolling tongues the sailors stared at the wall of steam and smoke, dreading the sight of those countless swimming creatures. Hap held his breath.

"They stopped," Balfour said. Another beat passed, and then a wild celebration erupted. The sailors wept, shouted, and embraced. Hap got his hair tousled more than once, until the hurrahs settled into sighs of relief.

"Twenty-six," snarled Oates, glaring at Umber.

"Twenty-six?" asked Umber.

"That's how many times you've nearly ended my life, by my count."

Umber flashed a broad smile. "That's nearly three cats' worth!"

Hours later the Inferno was a dwindling mushroom on the horizon, and the *Bounder* coursed over rolling waves with a crisp wind urging her along.

Dinner was spread for Umber's party. They dined under a

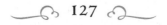

bittersweet cloud, glad to have escaped but sorry for Caspar's plight. Captain Sandar joined them, and so Umber had a new audience for their story. "We had to sneak away," Umber finally said. "For our own sakes, and because it was the only way to help him. He was too desperate to understand that."

"Caspar was a wreck," Balfour said. "How much longer can he stand it?"

"Why doesn't he just jump off that tower of his? That'll end his troubles," said Oates.

Umber shot Oates a poisonous look. "Because he's hanging on to hope, and I admire him for it. You live with a curse yourself, Oates. You ought to have more sympathy." Oates sniffed and stuffed half a biscuit into his mouth.

Hap leaned forward. "You'll try to help him, then, Lord Umber?"

"Of course," Umber said. "If I can. Aside from being the humane thing to do, it's also a way to learn more about you and your green-eyed brethren, Hap. We need to get our hands on the archives he stole. As for his current plight, maybe Smudge can find something in my library that Caspar didn't think to steal. It's worth asking Turiana, too, as unpleasant as that may be. And we can inquire with some other parties."

"So shall I turn us about and head for Kurahaven?" Sandar asked.

"Not yet. I can't miss these Dragon Games," said Umber. "Balfour, dear friend, I'll have you stay on the *Bounder* when we make our rendezvous. Hap, Oates, and I will press on. You'll return to Kurahaven to look into Caspar's quandary."

"Fair enough," Balfour said, rubbing the side of his neck. "I'm getting too rickety for these adventures, anyhow."

Captain Sandar drummed the table with his fingers. "What's this mysterious rendezvous, Lord Umber? Who are we meeting? I should tell my lookout what he's looking out for."

Umber tilted his chair back, put his hands behind his head, and grinned. "You'll find out soon enough. As soon as tomorrow morning, I think. You know the place?"

"Your rendezvous point? A barren rock in the middle of the sea, as far as I can tell," Sandar said.

"That's the spot! It's time to hoist my pennant from the top of the mast, so the other party can identify us. And by the way, Captain, do you think your cook can whip me up some coffee?"

Hap saw Balfour at the prow of the ship, watching the moon rise. "I'm sorry you won't come with us to Sarnica," Hap said.

Balfour rocked his head from side to side, producing a

symphony of bony crackles. "Just as well. I've been feeling a little worn out lately, to tell you the truth. No bed seems as comfortable as my own."

"I feel the same way," Hap said. "I wish we were all going back."

Balfour laughed. "Honestly, Happenstance. You look like you're barely twelve, but on the inside I think you're an old man like me. Boys are supposed to crave adventure, didn't you know?" He smiled, while rubbing the place where his neck met his shoulder.

Hap noticed the wince of pain. "Does it hurt, getting older?"

Balfour raised an eyebrow. "That's a funny question. Parts of me ache, that's for sure. But my brain feels the same as ever. It's a queer thing, growing up. The years pile up, Hap, but at the same time I'm still every age I ever was. When we stood before those sea-giants, I felt five years old, awed and scared. When I see a pretty young lady, I'm eighteen again! And when my bones remind me, I feel all of my sixty years. All those ages are still inside me, all at once. The years stack up like sediment, and the layers remain. You'll see one day." Balfour yawned, bunching his fists over his shoulders. "I just wanted to see the moon rise. But you ought to stay here for a while, Hap, and get used to the sight of water. I know how it strikes fear in your heart."

Hap nodded and folded his arms tight against his chest.

"And here's another reason to keep watch, Hap: Umber tells me the leviathans swim these waters."

"Leviathans . . . like Boroon?" Hap asked, turning to watch the sea.

"Yes. And it's said that when the moon rises high, they leap from the water to catch it in their mouths." Balfour fell silent to watch the silver orb, nearly full, clear the horizon. Its reflection was a river of glittering shards. "What do you suppose the moon is, Hap?"

Hap puckered his mouth on one side. "I don't know. I've never thought about it."

"Umber said it's a dusty ball of cold rock, with a side we never see. And those dark marks on it? He says those are from other bits of rock slamming into it." Balfour chuffed out a laugh. "He has the oddest ideas, doesn't he?"

"He does," Hap said. Balfour didn't know what Hap knew— that Umber was certainly right, about the moon and many other things. Umber was from a world apart from this one. It was an existence where technology and the scope of human knowledge were far advanced; where men had walked on the surface of that moon. Hap knew this because Umber had showed him on the remarkable machine he had brought with him from his other world. "A lot of strange ideas," he murmured.

Balfour nodded. "Good night, Hap. Keep an eye out for those leviathans."

Hap watched Balfour walk gingerly down the stairs to the lower deck, feeling a touch of guilt. The more he grew to like the man, the more uneasy he felt about keeping secrets from him. But he knew he must never tell what he'd learned about Umber.

He sighed and looked at the sea. Instinct told him to sit, but he fought the urge. *Nothing is going to happen,* he told himself. *The sea is calm. There's no danger. Stay here and watch for the leviathans—that's something I'd like to see. And maybe if I can stay through the night, I'll conquer this silly fear.* And so he remained there as most of the crew, except the helmsman and a watchman, slept in their quarters below.

All night a friendly breeze drove the *Bounder* forward. Hap spent hours wondering if he could have helped Caspar escape from his plight. *Perhaps if I'd seen the filaments,* he said inwardly, thinking about the strange threads he'd seen before. One had emanated from his own body, as if it belonged to him. Another seemed to belong to an enemy of his who'd met a brutal fate. *Does everyone have a filament?* he wondered. He thought about the sound that he'd detected when he touched the threads— an otherworldly music that hummed with elusive meaning.

Umber wanted him to explore and master those visions. The

thought made Hap's stomach twist because of the terrifying responsibility that Umber had given him. In Umber's former world, civilization had collapsed, a catastrophe fueled by fanatic hatred and technology of awesome destructive power. Somehow, probably with the help of the mysterious WN, Umber had barely escaped a violent death in that existence. Now Umber had a plan. He wanted Hap to leap across to that other world and use his untapped abilities to undo the terrible fate that awaited humanity there. Was it truly possible? Hap had no idea.

Perhaps it was coincidence, or perhaps it was because he was thinking about the filaments, but Hap felt the disturbing sensation that always heralded their appearance. A sudden chill coursed through his limbs, as if his blood were turning to ice. The cold was swept away by a burst of heat that brought beads of perspiration to his forehead and left a lingering warmth in his eyes. It all happened quickly—much faster than before—but he knew what he'd see when it passed.

A filament. It emerged from his chest and floated across the deck, rippling with a motion unaffected by the sea breeze.

Lights of infinite color pulsed and flowed inside the thread. Hap stared and finally reached out and passed his hand through the apparition. There was no weight, no resistance. It wasn't warm or cold. He didn't feel it at all as he watched it travel through his palm and emerge on the other side. But he *sensed* it. And he heard strange music, like chimes, bells, and wind blowing through reeds.

"What are you saying?" he whispered. And the slightest, vaguest suggestion of meaning whispered back. It didn't come as words. He had to guess at what it meant. And he thought it said: *Follow. Important.*

The thread led toward the stern of the *Bounder*. Hap traced its path with his hand before him, palm out, to let the filament pass through. The threads he'd seen before hadn't lasted long, and he wanted this one to linger so he could learn from it. He had a feeling it would. *It's stronger,* he thought. *Or maybe I'm just seeing it better.*

A surprising thing happened when he'd taken a few steps. The thread divided before him, showing two paths. One led the way he'd expected to go, down the center of the deck and past the ship's wheel, where the helmsman kept the ship on course. The other path hugged the rail of the ship.

"Which way?" Hap whispered. Then he decided to see what the thread told him. He stood where it forked, with a palm on each of the split threads. Again no words came to him, but he could sense a difference. Instinct tugged him toward the ship's rail.

He moved slowly, making as little noise he could. The

helmsman's head was turned the other way, and Hap wondered if he wasn't meant to be seen. He heard gentle snoring ahead, and was amused to see the watchman sitting on a barrel, dozing with his head resting on a furled canvas. *Not watching much,* Hap thought.

The stern was just ahead, and the thread ended there, flickering gently back and forth at the tip like a serpent's tongue. Hap stared at it, wondering what to do next.

He heard a gasp from the middle of the deck. It was the helmsman. The man was staring out toward the horizon, and Hap nearly cried out himself when he followed the helmsman's gaze. Far away, out in the ocean, still rising from the water, was a leviathan. It was not as large as the great Boroon, but it was awesome still. Its head pointed up, and its enormous fins were spread like the wings of a bird. Nearly the entire beast had emerged from the water, showing a pale belly lined with deep grooves. The cavernous mouth opened wide, and it looked indeed like it was leaping up to swallow the moon. It seemed to suspend itself in the air forever, until it finally came down, cleaving the sea and creating a billowing, surging wave that crested and crashed.

Hap's awe turned to frustration when he looked down and saw that the filament had vanished. "Come back," he whispered, hoping he could summon it again.

The deck lifted under his feet and sank again. He stared down at the planks, wondering what had caused the feeling, and it dawned on him that the whole ship must have risen for a moment, lifted by a surge from the depths. "What?" he asked, just as something titanic burst out of the water beside the ship, blotting out the night sky with a mountain of barnacle-speckled flesh.

When the first leviathan had leaped, he'd wished it were closer. But not this close. It was twice the size of the *Bounder*, dwarfing the ship as it flew skyward. Hap could see the fluked tail just under the surface, and the leviathan poised as if standing for a moment on solid ground. It was amazing enough to stand on Boroon's back and marvel at the immense size of the creature, but this spectacle, with nearly the entire leviathan out of the water and reaching for the moon, was beyond imagination.

The beast could have broken the ship into splinters, but Hap saw with relief that it was falling beside them instead. Down it came, carving a valley in the ocean and hurling up giant waves. The sight was so amazing that Hap opened his mouth to shriek with joy. As he gathered his shout, he wondered if the thread had delivered him to this spot just so he could witness the leap of the leviathan. But the thrill turned to panic when he saw the wave coming fast at him, rising and cresting as it approached.

The wave missed all of the ship except for the stern. It spilled onto the deck, scooped Hap off his feet, and lifted him high. He tried to scream, but water filled his mouth. He reached for the railing but only brushed it with groping fingers. Then he fell, and he knew he'd dropped below the level of the deck. He plunged into the sea, with bubbles and foam all around, and the crashing wave made him tumble, so that for a moment he didn't know which way was up. Panic paralyzed him until he sensed his body rising. He clawed at the water, throwing it behind him, and finally broke the surface. There he saw the *Bounder*, fast departing. As he opened his mouth again to shout, another wave struck his face. He choked and sputtered, paddling furiously with his hands and kicking to stay afloat. By the time he caught his breath enough to make a sound the ship was far away, and the same whistling wind that drove her swiftly across the waves brushed his voice aside as he howled for help.

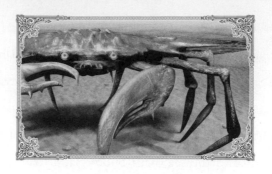

CHAPTER
13

Hap shouted until his voice was a feeble rasp and the *Bounder* was a speck on the horizon. He felt his heart pounding in his temples. A blinding white light filled his mind as he rose and fell with the waves. Some instinct told him how to keep afloat by moving his open hands in circles and kicking gently. The ocean lapped at his mouth, and he had to spit salty water out again and again. *My boots,* he realized amid his panicked thoughts. They had filled with water, and the weight tugged him down. He kicked them off, and that made it easier to keep his head high.

A barrel from the deck of the *Bounder* bobbed in the water nearby. He didn't know how to swim, so it took a great deal of awkward thrashing before he was able to throw his arms across it.

"Turn around," he croaked at the ship. He was sure that they would realize he was missing and come looking for him. Didn't the helmsman see him go overboard? Didn't the watchman wake up in time to notice? He beat his fist on the barrel, cursing the filament that had brought him to this fate.

Hap looked at the eastern sky. There was no hint of sunlight there. Dawn was hours away. But there was something else to the south, coming out of the sea. He wondered if it was another leviathan, at rest on the surface. But it was solid and fixed, with a low jagged peak at its center. *An island,* he realized.

He turned the barrel in that direction and began to kick his feet, heading for the scrap of land. There was a flare of pain where his chest touched the barrel: The locket that Nima had given him was pressing into his flesh. He thought of the amazing pearl inside, an object of great value. What had she said when she gave it to him? *It may be useful in a difficult spot someday. Or it might help a friend in need. Your heart will tell you when to use it.* Well, this was a difficult spot, but the pearl was worthless. Only his kicking legs could save him from a watery death. Then, he hoped, when somebody on the *Bounder* finally realized that he must have fallen overboard, the ship would retrace its journey. Surely they would spot the same island and find him there.

Hours later he finally drew close, still pushing the barrel before him. His thighs ached, and the muscles in one calf had knotted up for a while. Umber had always wondered if there were limits to Hap's endurance. *Now he'll know,* Hap thought. *If they ever find me.*

The place was an islet, he decided, too small to be called an island. There were signs of shipwrecks in the surrounding shallows. A rotting mast angled out of the water to his right. To his left, waves rolled over the barely exposed flank of a sunken vessel.

His toes scraped the bottom as he kicked downward. He let go of the barrel and stood up in waist-high water. Despite everything, he smiled—few things had ever felt as welcome as the feeling of land under his feet, even if it was just soggy muck that filled the spaces between his bare toes. He waded to the shore.

The first blush of the rising sun could be seen over the islet. The broken fragments of ships, some weathered from age and some fresher, were scattered on the shore. *Ships get wrecked here because the island sticks up in the middle of nowhere,* Hap reasoned. *They strike it in fog, or in the middle of the night—the* Bounder *might have, if they'd steered a little farther to the south.*

The islet was mostly rock, with dark craggy holes in the ocean-battered shore. The only feature of note was the small, steep hill. Terns and gulls dotted the sand and rock, turning their heads sideways to stare with one eye.

Hap thought he might see the ship if he climbed to the peak. But before he took a step, his instinct told him that something was behind him. He couldn't have said how he knew—a hint of a shadow, or a sound softer than a breath. But it was enough to make him whirl around, and when he did, he saw a stranger.

The man was dressed in a glistening silver tunic and leggings. He had a satchel at his side, with the strap over the opposite shoulder. His long hair was the most curious color: white, with flecks of color inside the strands. *Just like Eldon told us,* Hap thought, and his shoulders jerked as his attention was seized by the stranger's glittering green eyes.

"And there you are," the man said. "The bird afraid to fly. The bud afraid to bloom."

Hap stepped back, caught his heel on a stone, and landed on his rump. That mocking musical voice was familiar. He'd heard it on the first day of his existence, in the buried city of Alzumar. "You're *him,*" he croaked.

WN bowed deeply, then spread his arms wide and shook them. "Why do you *hesitate?* Why don't you *dare?* Here's a fine adventure, and you probably wish you were cowering back in your little nest in the Aerie right now. How maddening!"

Hap's mouth flapped without a word coming out. A white-hot rage built up inside him that practically steamed out of his pores. When he finally managed to speak, it was through teeth clamped tight. "You're a *murderer*. You made Julian Penny drown."

WN rolled his eyes and gave an exaggerated sigh. "Oh, fuss and drama! History will never miss Julian. And who'd rather be a simple-minded peasant than a fabulous being like you or me?"

Hap felt something he'd never experienced before—a furious urge to do physical harm. He scooped sand and rock in one hand and flung it at WN, who grinned and hid his face behind his elbow. Hap's chest heaved, and his breath hissed out his nose. "You had no *right*. And it wasn't just Julian's life you took—now my parents are dead as well! And my brother's life was ruined!"

WN chuckled as he flicked the sand off his clothes. "Yes, your silly brother showed up and spilled those beans. I didn't see that twist ahead! Well, our gift is not a perfect one. You'll learn that for yourself one day."

Hap wished Oates were there to give this monster the throttling he deserved. His anger was so complete that it overwhelmed his wits, and he couldn't think of a thing to say. But WN could. He cupped his hand against the side of his mouth—another theatrical gesture that made Hap loathe him even more. "I won't dillydally, because a terrible someone is on my trail, and getting closer."

"Whatever it is, I hope it catches you," Hap said.

"Don't say that!" WN replied, in his maddening singsong way. "You'd better hope I stay a leap ahead of his clutches. Because as soon as he catches me, the hunt begins for you!"

"For me?" cried Hap. "What have I ever done?"

"You *exist*, my boy," WN said. "I broke the rules when I made you, you see."

Hap's voice rose to a shriek. "What rules? How did you make me? What did you do to Julian?"

WN waved off the questions. "Never mind that. Get on with it! You were made for a purpose, Happenstance. Your powers elude you because you resist them."

"I know about the *purpose*," Hap said. "I'm supposed to save Umber's old world. I promised Umber I would try."

WN smirked. "Is that what you think the whole point is?"

"Isn't it?"

The green-eyed man raised his hands, palms up. "Maybe yes, maybe no . . . or maybe it's all just willy-nilly!"

Hap pushed himself to his feet and raised his fists. "What do you want from me? Why don't you just say it?"

WN ignored him. He wasn't looking at Hap anymore—he

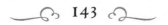

was staring at the space between them. He waved his long fingers in the air and rocked his hands back and forth. *He's seeing a filament,* Hap realized. *Mine!*

"More trials ahead," WN whispered, as if sharing a delightful secret. "Violence and pain. Dangers galore. You will be tested, infant Meddler. Will you survive? And all your friends? Hard to say."

"What dangers?" cried Hap. "Should we turn away?"

WN laughed. "And how would you know which way to turn? I tell you this, though: Never look for me to save your timid hide. It's sink or swim, perish or flourish, derring-do or duly die! You won't see me again—not until you've become what you must." He looked over his shoulder, suddenly nervous. "But I mustn't linger—here we have a fateful place, and meeting you is like lighting a signal fire for our executioner."

"You're just going to leave me here?" Hap cried.

"Why, I think your ship is coming," WN said, pointing over Hap's shoulder. Even as Hap turned, he guessed that it was a diversion, and his senses sharpened. There was a quiet *whoosh* like a twig being whipped through the air. And for a fraction of a second there was a strange phenomenon that he could only describe as a burst of darkness.

When he turned back, it didn't surprise him at all to see that WN had vanished. He looked at the beach where the green-eyed man had stood. There was a cluster of footprints, with no marks leading in or away in the smooth surrounding sand.

The sky abruptly brightened as the sun pierced the horizon. As if that were a signal, the birds spread their wings and left the islet, hundreds in all. Hap watched them fly. He wondered if he was the only living creature left on the tiny speck of rock in the middle of the sea.

A hollow scraping sound came from his left. There was a crevice in the rock there, where seawater washed in and formed a pool. It was shadowy, but that didn't keep him from seeing the tip of a claw rise up, and then another beside it. The rest of the creature emerged. It was a crab of remarkable size, with a wide body as big as a shield, and eyes on short stalks. The shell was covered in horned projections. Its foremost legs ended in fat pincers.

The crab perched on the edge of the crevice, cleaning its pincers with its mouth—a strange, wide mouth with mandibles at its corners. It made a gargling, rattling noise as it cleaned, and its wiry antennae quivered in the air. The eyes turned on the ends of their stalks, scanning the surroundings. The gaze seemed to pass right over Hap, but then the stalks twisted back, and the eyes looked directly at him.

"Somebody's here," a voice said.

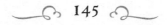

Hap was still dizzy from his encounter with WN, and it took him a moment to realize that the crab itself had spoken. "Um . . . excuse me?" he replied.

"Who is king nowadays?" another voice said.

Hap stared. The crab's mouth had moved each time he heard a voice. He was sure it was the creature that had spoken. But the second voice was different—it was a woman's voice, while the first had been a man's.

"Are—are you talking to me?" Hap asked.

"Do you have any candy?" the crab said. This was the voice of a child.

"Who cares," replied a voice that sounded like the first one he'd heard. "We don't eat candy."

"Quiet, all of you," said the woman's voice. "You'll wake the others."

Hap stared, without a clue of what to say or do. *What is happening here?* he asked himself.

The crab scuttled sideways toward him and stopped a few paces away. Hap took a wary step back.

"How many survivors? How many dead?" said yet another voice. This new voice spoke in a different language from the common tongue. Hap understood the words, nevertheless—for reasons nobody knew, he could interpret any language, written or spoken, current or ancient, that he had encountered.

"Survivors? D-d-dead?" Hap stammered. "Er . . . nobody's dead. I'm the only one here."

"What ship?" This time it was an old woman's voice.

"Huh?" Hap said, feeling bewildered and foolish. "No ship—I mean, there *was* a ship, but I fell off and swam here. . . ."

There was a chorus of whispered replies, and questions he could not answer, in voices young and old, in tongues familiar and strange. "The lad says no ship." "Boy, who rules Londria?" "No more survivors?" "What year is this?" "Quiet, dost thou want the others to hear?" The crab scuttled forward some more. Hap edged back, eyeing the dangerous-looking pincers.

A new voice spoke up behind him. "Someone's here!" Hap turned to see a second crab climbing out of another hole in the rock, dripping seawater off its shell. Beyond, another pair of claws trembled over the lip of a crevice. Each of those crabs began to chatter like the first, in voice after voice. "Is there news from Andobar?" "Is the war still going?" "How many survivors?" "Who is it, a pirate?" "Are there lots of dead?"

Hap turned to speak to the first crab. "Wh-what are you? *Who* are you? How can you speak like that, in so many voices?"

"We are like you," an old man said. "Washed up on shore."

"I was first mate on the *Fury*," said a deep voice.

"I was on the *Sapphire,* a merchant ship bound for Gordania," said another voice in another tongue.

"We were lost in a fog," said an old woman.

Hap's head swiveled left and right. The crabs were creeping toward him, and he saw the pincers flexing. Farther down the shore, out of a bigger hole in the coastline, a dozen more emerged and scuttled in his direction.

"Do you mean . . . you're *people?*" Hap said.

"We were." The voice changed every time. "Until our ships wrecked upon this rock."

A scraping, tapping sound made Hap turn around. Behind his back the pair of crabs had raced across the rocky shore. When he looked at them, they paused. Antennae quivered, and froth bubbled from their wide mouths. Next he heard scrabbling in the other direction. When he whipped his head around again, the first crab froze, but alarmingly near.

"Please don't come closer," he said, swiveling his head. He bent his knees, ready to spring. In the distance dozens more of the creatures swarmed at him, wide thorny disks propped up on crusty legs.

"Don't run. Everybody runs, except the ones that already drowned," the first voice said. From the corner of his eye Hap saw another crab rush at him with claws extended. The creature was faster than he expected. As Hap leaped, its pincer caught the cuff of his trousers. Hap tumbled across the stony ground, bruising his bare foot.

"There's no point to running," a girl's voice said. "Just lie down and shut your eyes."

"If you were people once, what happened to you?" Hap cried, and then he clapped a hand across his mouth because he saw the answer. He'd landed next to a hole where the ground had collapsed long ago into the sea-carved space below. There was water down there, sloshing with the force of the waves, that barely covered a pile of bones and grinning skulls.

"The crabs got me," a voice said. Other voices answered, from the other crabs. "And me." "Same for me." "And me as well."

The full horror of what had happened to the poor folk who'd washed up on the islet struck Hap. He felt a wave of pain. It was from biting his palm. "Get away from me!" he shouted.

"But we're hungry." "There's no place to run." "Forget it, child—nobody ever gets away." "Hurry, before everyone else gets here!"

The horde came for him with pincers snapping. Hap snatched up a piece of driftwood that would make a decent club and ran inland, leaving them far behind. The crabs were quick, but he could leap and move faster than anyone they'd met before. The rugged rock scraped his soles and nicked his toes as he ran. When he looked behind, he saw that every crab along the shore was in pursuit.

The rising sun had bleached away the night, and the stars sputtered and disappeared. Hap trotted up the hill, which rose no higher than the mast of the *Bounder*. It grew so steep that he needed his hands to climb. He prayed that when he reached the small, flat peak, he would see the ship cutting through the waves, close enough to notice him desperately waving his arms.

"No," he groaned as he surveyed an endless, empty sea. When he looked down at the other side of the tiny islet, he cried aloud.

More crabs, dozens upon dozens, were coming up from the opposite coast. They spread out, pincer to pincer, and approached slowly as the terrain angled higher. Hap grabbed a handful of his own hair, realizing what a foolish mistake he'd made. By climbing the hill, he'd cut himself off from escape. He was surrounded.

The voices rose up from below. "They always go up the hill," said one that was far ahead of the others. It came up the steepest part of the slope, digging the tips of its sharp claws into cracks in the rock. With its broad shell tipped sideways, it looked unbalanced. Hap ran closer, put the end of his stick under its belly and pried it away. The crab teetered, snapped a pincer in his direction, and fell away, making a hollow sound as it clattered on the rock, fell onto its mates, and finally landed on its back with its claws frantically waving.

A shadow crossed the sun. Hap looked up, fully expecting to see some other monstrosity swooping down on him, but the bright rays burned his eyes and he looked away. To his left, a fat claw appeared at the crest of the hill. He raced over and used the stick to send another crab tumbling. That crab latched onto another, and both rolled down together.

The voices rose to a shout that made it hard to think. He thought he heard his own name somehow amid the riot. "How do you know my name?" he screamed back at them. *There are too many; they're coming too fast,* he thought as he pried two more off the edge. He tried not to think about the horrible, imminent fate: his bones picked clean by the crabs, and his voice joining their chorus, waiting for the next poor castaways on this fiendish rock.

He heard his name again, above the other voices. "Happenstance!" It even sounded like Umber. How could that be? But he couldn't risk a look around, because there was no time. Another crab came to the crest. Hap ran to the spot, nearly too late, and rammed the driftwood under its mouth, shoving the thing back. A pincer reached out and closed on the wood, splintering it. Hap imagined his bones crunching just as easily. The crab pulled the driftwood from Hap's hand and tilted backward, almost tipping over. But somehow it found its balance and reached the summit. Hap stepped away. He couldn't turn his back on the nearest creature, even though he heard more claws scraping at the edge behind him.

I'll have to jump, Hap thought, though he knew it was senseless. The crabs below were spread too wide and deep. They seemed to know that he would jump, because they waited with pincers raised high.

Claws snapped at his knees, forcing him back. Hap shrieked when something touched his shoulder and stuck there. When he whirled, he saw a strange cord dangling before his eyes. He slapped at it, meaning to swipe it away, but it stuck to his hand. And then he heard the voice that sounded like Umber's again. "Hold on, Hap!"

His gaze followed the cord up from his hands and into the sky. It dangled from the strangest thing he'd yet seen. Floating above him was what looked like an enormous elongated egg with a long basket suspended from its bottom. Umber was leaning over the side of the basket, with a blood-stained cloth wrapped around his head. Oates was there too, with both hands on the cord. Hap gripped it tight, and his feet left the ground as Oates hauled him high, and the horrible crabs wailed and cursed below in a hundred tongues.

...ruggle with ... question:
...hat innovations are safe to
introduce? After all, it was the
dizzying rush of technological
progress that also enabled the
destruction of the world I left
behind. Take my razors, for example.
Here I shave with a dull,
brutish thing. I could find ways
to produce better, sharper blades—
but then the swords and axes would
grow sharper and deadlier as well.
Does every advance I bring to this
civilization, therefore, no matter
how beneficial, also hasten its

CHAPTER
14

Hap tumbled into the basket. Now that he was safe from a gruesome death and even more horrible fate, he curled up in a ball, clenched his teeth, and buried his face in the crook of his arm. His heart thumped so loudly in his ears that he could barely hear Umber's giddy shouts.

"Did you see them, Oates? I think those were the soul crabs! It's a mariner's legend, and now we've found them. Ha, what a jaunt this turned out to be! Pilot, be a good fellow and mark this spot on the maps; I may want to come back."

Hap moaned at the thought of ever returning. Umber dropped to his knees and spoke gently by Hap's ear. "We are so glad to see you. I am so sorry, my friend. That wave swept you overboard, didn't it? I fell out of bed when it hit, and cracked my head on the floor."

"I hope it knocked some sense into you," said Oates.

"Far from amusing, Oates," Umber said. "Hap, everyone was so worried about me—I was unconscious for hours and bleeding like a spigot—that they forgot to check on anybody else. Poor Sandar was beside himself when we realized you were gone. The watchman had fallen asleep, and Sandar would've had him flogged if I hadn't intervened. He'll be so glad we found you!" Hap felt Umber's hand squeeze his shoulder. "Are you all right, Hap?"

Hap couldn't stop shaking. "Th-th-those things . . . those crabs . . ."

"Soul crabs," Umber said. "Had to be! They feast on shipwreck victims, and the memories of the victims live on in the crabs. Let us hope it is only some dim copy of their memories, and not really their souls."

The thought made Hap shiver more. He kept his arm across his face. "We're flying, aren't we?"

Umber chuckled. "We certainly are. You're aboard the *Silkship* now. You should pick your head up and look around; it's really something. No? Well, when you're ready. Anyway, by the time we realized you were missing from the *Bounder*, this craft had found us, so we took up the search.

Good thing, too. The *Bounder* wouldn't have made it here fast enough."

Hap curled himself into a tighter ball, with his knees in his chest. He knew he had to tell Umber about the appearance of WN, but he couldn't bear to yet. "I can't take any more," he moaned.

Umber patted his shoulder. "Now, Happenstance . . ."

"Please, Lord Umber. First it was those bidmis that almost killed us. Then those awful crabs . . . I want to go back to the Aerie. No more horrible little monsters!"

Oates spoke up. "If that's how you feel, you'd better keep your face covered."

Hap froze, and his breath caught in his throat. He took his arm from his face slowly, revealing his surroundings like a curtain unveiling a stage. The basket was a small space, shaped like a boat but made of sheets of silk stretched between narrow tubes of wood. He saw Umber, smiling down with the bloody bandage around his head. He saw Oates, looking on with his arms folded and then nodding to one side. Hap followed the gesture and saw another man. *That must be Pilot,* he thought. Pilot's skin was dark, almost the color of Umber's beloved coffee. His hair was black and finely curled, and his close-cropped beard was in the shape of an anchor. He had chiseled features and a fierce demeanor. But it was the thing on Pilot's shoulder that made Hap sit up and crawl backward.

The creature was stranger than the bidmis, more grotesque than the soul crabs. It had the legs and body of a spider, but a head like a human infant's. The creature mewled at him, and Hap saw a pair of wriggling fangs inside the mouth. "Urp," was all he could say, as he clapped his hand over his mouth and tried not to be ill.

He averted his gaze and saw another one of the things perched upside down on the ceiling of the basket. And then, from a hole in the ceiling that led to an enormous, hollow space above, a third spidery creature crawled into view.

"They won't hurt you, Hap," Umber said cheerfully.

Hap tried to nod, but his head wanted to shake no, and so he ended up swirling his head in an awkward circle. "What are they?" he finally croaked into his palm.

"Spider-folk, we call them," Umber replied. "Lovely creatures, once you get used to their looks. But Hap, you really need to meet Pilot. The *Silkship* is his craft. Do you think you can stand up?"

Hap felt like a fawn wobbling to its feet for the first time, but he managed to stand. "Hello," he said to Pilot.

"These are my rules," Pilot snapped. "Don't bother my crew. Don't touch what does not belong to you, especially the helmstones. And don't ask questions about my secrets."

"What are helmstones?" Hap asked, before he thought better of it.

Pilot glared back. "Shall I go over the rules again?"

"You're being rude to the boy," Oates said.

"Am I. And perhaps you'd prefer other transportation?"

"I certainly would," Oates said. He was sitting on the floor of the basket with his legs stretched before him. "It was Umber's idea to fly around in this puffed-up bladder of yours."

"Gentlemen, please," Umber said with a nervous chuckle. "No need to bicker. Pilot, I think Hap understands the rules. He merely wondered where the helmstones were, so he knew not to touch them. The answer is right there, Hap." Umber pointed toward the front of the basket, where a tapering space could be closed off with a gray curtain that was pushed to one side. Hap saw a large ship's wheel mounted flat on a pedestal. It had four sky-blue, apple-size crystals embedded around its perimeter. Hap wondered what they were for, but he held the question within, along with all the others that sprang to mind.

Pilot stared with his lip twitching on one side. Finally, he turned away and spoke to the spidery creatures. "Quellen and Gossilen: Inspect the outer skin, my dears. We have more weight than I'd like aboard." He looked with narrowed eyes at the pile of boxes and packs in one corner. Hap recognized their stuff from the *Bounder.*

The creature on Pilot's shoulder climbed down his body and scuttled across the floor with its head raised high. Its speed and agility made Hap shiver. The spidery thing that was hanging on the ceiling dropped by a thread that emerged from the tip of its abdomen; it then pinched off the thread and followed its sibling. The two creatures raced up the side of the basket, climbed one of the cords that attached it to the cocoon above, and disappeared over the curving outer edge.

Hap looked at the third monstrosity. It was smiling and eyeing him with its head angled nearly sideways.

Pilot gave Hap a wary look, then spoke to the creature. "Rest if you'd like, Arabell. I will be at the helm for a while." He strode to the front of the *Silkship* and closed the curtain behind him.

Hap turned to stare blankly at Umber, whose wide grin faded only a little when he saw Hap's expression. "But Happenstance," he said, "aren't you amazed to be here?"

"Not everyone is crazy like you, Umber," Oates said, stuffing a pack behind his head for a pillow. "Look at us, floating around like a soap bubble. This thing could pop any minute now."

Umber clapped a hand on Hap's shoulder. "Ignore him and try to enjoy this, Hap. We're flying!" He steered Hap to the side

of the basket. Hap peered over the edge. *Flying,* he thought. He wrapped his arm around one of the cords that suspended the basket. The sea stretched to infinity ahead, forming a gentle curve at the horizon. He could see the island of the soul crabs shrinking away behind them, and he thought about his strange meeting on that shore.

"When I was on that island, I saw him," he said quietly.

"Excuse me?" Umber replied, and his jaw dropped when he saw the look in Hap's eye. "You can't mean WN! You do? I can't believe it—tell me everything, Hap, every detail you can remember!"

Umber had listened with his eyes on the ceiling of clouds overhead, but he turned to Hap once the story was done. "Is that all? Did he say anything else? Even if it didn't seem important, I want to know."

Hap shook his head. His memory was sharp, and he'd managed to convey nearly the entire exchange, word for word. "I think that was everything."

"He's mischievous, this green-eyed man," Umber said. "This is like a game for him."

"I hate him so much," Hap muttered.

"No doubt." Umber tugged at his chin. "I guess this means we don't have all the time in the world to develop your skills.

Whoever is after WN will eventually come for you." The skin on Hap's arms turned to gooseflesh as he remembered Occo, the last horrible creature that had come hunting for him. Umber put a hand on his shoulder. "Don't fear, Hap. Your powers will emerge. And when the time is right to leave this world, you can take me with you if you like. After all, it's my civilization you're saving."

Hap nodded and sniffed, and he stared at the watery horizon.

"By the way," Umber said, "I might be jumping to a silly conclusion, but we may finally know WN's name."

"What? How?"

Umber smiled. "Consider what he told us to call you: *Happenstance*. That's a witty name for a boy who might someday steer destiny. And now think back to your conversation, because I believe he let his name slip. He teased you with it." Umber grinned and folded his arms.

Hap's mind turned back to what the green-eyed man had said. A phrase leaped out in his memory, and he gasped. "Oh! I see. Do you really think that's his name?" Hap asked.

Umber tilted his head and bobbed his shoulders. "It'll do for now."

The spidercraft rose into the clouds, and mist obscured everything from view. It was eerie and beautiful, but all Hap could think about was the vast distance between them and the sea below. "But how?" he asked. "How can we fly?"

Umber peered around to see if Pilot was near, then leaned toward Hap so his whisper could be heard. "The *Silkship* is the only craft of its kind in the world, as far as I know," he said. "We are in its gondola now. Above us is the envelope—what Pilot calls the cocoon. Come on—I don't think he'll mind if we take a peek up there." Umber led Hap to the center of the gondola, where a narrow ladder made of knotty cord rose into the open space above. "You first. I'll follow."

As Hap climbed, Umber educated. "It takes three remarkable elements to make this ship work. One is the spider-folk. You know how spiders spin webs? Well, the silk those creatures produce is astonishing in its versatility. The ladder you're climbing was made by them, and the rope that saved you from the soul crabs. The craft itself is made almost entirely from bamboo and spider-silk, and that's why it's all so light. But though the silk weighs almost nothing, it is stronger than you can imagine. Like iron!"

Hap emerged in a large hollow space. *The cocoon,* he thought. He stepped onto a narrow platform of webbing that ringed the opening. All around, on the lower third of the cocoon, there grew a forest of puffy pale-blue mushrooms that rose almost knee-high.

"And now you see the second element," Umber said brightly, climbing up behind him. "Those are *puffers*, Hap. Pilot won't tell anyone where he finds them, but this odd species of mushroom releases a gas that is lighter than air. That gas fills the cocoon, and up we go! Listen carefully, now."

Hap heard the wind ruffling over the skin of the craft. There was also a scratching sound overhead, and there he saw the sunlit silhouettes of two spider-folk on the outside of the cocoon. Then he detected a softer sound, the one Umber wanted him to notice: little puffs of air, like breathing. He looked down and saw the mushrooms slowly swelling and then thinning as they exhaled, most likely through the vents under their caps. "And those are the second element. Isn't it wonderful?" Umber said reverently beside him.

It was, Hap admitted with a nod. "What is the third element?"

"The helmstones," Umber said. "Those crystals are among the most powerful magical objects I've seen. They're like magnets, each drawn to a different point of the compass, and that attraction is strong enough to move the ship in all but the strongest winds. Watch Pilot steer sometime. You'll see how it works."

Hap was startled by a tug at his leg. He looked down, and his entire body twitched when he saw one of the spider-folk staring up at him. His bare feet felt terribly vulnerable. He mashed his lips together to contain a shout.

"Hello, Arabell," Umber said. The creature kept its gaze fixed on Hap. She even raised herself on her rearmost legs, putting another on Hap's knee. Hap stared back. The thing horrified him, with her child's face and stringy black hair threaded with beads of silver and gold. The human head was attached to a small arachnid body that tapered to a point. The limbs were thin and knobby-kneed. Hap's stomach lurched when he looked at the tip of the leg on his knee: It ended in a dreadful, random mix of tiny fingers and hairy claws.

"You can tell Arabell from the others by the number of legs," Umber said. "She has six. Gossilen has five, and Quellen seven. Also, Arabell is our raven-haired beauty."

Arabell's mouth spread into a crooked smile with only two fangs for teeth. She mewled up at Hap and made sounds that were almost words, like an infant learning to talk. Then she turned her head and rubbed her cheek against his shin.

"Look at that," Umber cried, sounding a little offended. "She didn't warm up to me until my third trip on this craft! Arabell, you've broken my heart!"

Arabell turned her head to inspect Hap's other leg, where his pants had been torn by one of the soul crabs. She made a chirping sound and with two of her legs reached for the tapered end of her body, where a stream of fine silky thread appeared.

"What is she doing?" Hap asked uneasily.

Umber's eyes gleamed with curiosity. He squatted to see better. "Don't move, Hap. See the spinnerets—those fingerlike things at the tip of her abdomen? She's making thread with them. Those spinnerets are covered with tiny spigots that can produce all manner of silk—thick, thin, sticky and nonsticky, sheets of silk, you name it."

Arabell's legs moved swiftly, pulling thread from the wriggling spinnerets and passing it forward. With the tip of one claw, she pierced the ragged edges of Hap's torn trousers. She threaded the holes with the silk and pulled the tear shut. Before a minute passed, the repair was done, and it was hard to see that the trousers had ever been damaged. Arabell brought her legs to her mouth to nibble off the bits of silk that remained, then looked at him and grinned. Hap stared down, dry-mouthed.

"Er, Hap . . . what do you say to Arabell?" Umber prompted.

"Oh. Um. Thank you, Arabell. And it's nice to meet you," Hap said. Against his better instincts he extended a hand. Arabell chirped again and gripped his hand with surprising strength. The fingers were soft against his, while the claws pinched without breaking his skin. Another of her arms went to his knee, another to his waist, another to his elbow, and suddenly she was crawling up his body, until they were nose to nose. Hap shifted his feet to keep the weight from toppling him over. Her breath brushed his face. She angled her head from side to side, gazing at Hap.

"Steady, Hap. I think it's your eyes that amaze her."

Hap waited, trying not to shiver. A moment later Arabell's face reddened. *She's blushing,* Hap thought. Something akin to a giggle escaped her fanged mouth, and she hopped down and scrambled out of sight down the ladder.

Umber chattered as they climbed down from the cocoon. "Their bite isn't poisonous, Hap. It just numbs you, and enough will knock you out. The perfect anesthetic, actually, if we could bottle it. And they can—oh, look! We're over the clouds."

For a moment Hap forgot the ordeals he'd faced. Below them was a landscape of billowing, towering, foamy white, and ahead the sun was rising for a second time, this time above the sea of clouds. Even Oates leaned over the wall of the gondola to gape.

"There's a sight that can lift any spirit," Umber said.

Hap nodded. But before long a frown settled back on his face. Umber put a hand on his shoulder.

"I know the last day has been a nightmare," Umber said. "Aside from nearly drowning and being devoured by giant crabs, is anything troubling you?"

Hap chewed his lip for a while before answering. "When I got swept overboard . . . It was because I saw a filament, and I followed it. I could have been killed, Lord Umber. I thought I could trust the filaments. But now they scare me."

Umber drummed on the side of the gondola and stared at the clouds. "You know how important it is to understand them."

Hap shrugged. Of course he knew. The fate of a billion lives in another world depended on his mastery of the filaments. That was the power that he was supposed to embrace. It was the reason he existed.

"Keep in mind," Umber said, doling his words carefully, "that the filaments represent destiny, which can be either good or bad—or somewhere in the middle. The trick will be to figure out which is which. And who knows? Perhaps falling overboard and meeting Willy Nilly—if that is WN's real name—was the best thing that could have happened to you."

At the nose of the gondola the curtain was swept aside, and Pilot strode out. He reached up and pulled a ring that dangled from the cocoon above. Hap heard a hissing sound, and at once the craft began to descend.

"What now, Pilot?" Umber asked.

"Time to feed the crew," Pilot said as the *Silkship* fell into the clouds, toward the sea.

The three creatures perched on the edge of the gondola wall. Pilot handed Arabell a barbed harpoon with a ring at one end. Quellen, the seven-legged creature with yellow hair tied back in a yellow ribbon, spun a long line of thread, which she tied to the ring; auburn-haired Gossilen chirped and mewled while watching the water below.

"You don't understand what they're saying, by any chance?" Umber asked Hap.

Hap shook his head. The noises these creatures made meant nothing to him. He had the feeling they had invented the language on their own.

The *Silkship* leveled off thirty feet over the waves. Pilot scanned the ocean from the helm. A few minutes later Gossilen screeched and pointed. Hap saw what she had spotted. A dark shape moved just under the waves—quite large, as far as Hap could tell. Pilot turned the wheel, and the craft responded. Soon they were cruising right behind the dark shape.

"That's a shark," Umber said, squinting down.

Arabell pressed the tip of her abdomen to the side of the gondola and anchored a line of silk to a gluey mass. She crawled down the outside and then let herself drop, weaving a dragline of thread behind her. Hap saw her spinnerets wriggling.

Pilot had left the curtain open, and Hap could see him at the helm as he turned the wheel to adjust their course. Besides the four blue helmstones embedded in the edge of the wheel, there was a larger white crystal mounted at the nose of the ship. To steer the ship, Hap realized, Pilot would rotate the wheel and align the proper stone with the white crystal. He could also slide the entire wheel forward on its pedestal, pushing it closer to the crystal, which made the *Silkship* accelerate. Pulling the wheel back had the opposite effect.

Hap leaned over the gondola's wall and watched Arabell drifting over the water, hanging from the gray strand. Pilot's skill brought her directly over the dark swimming shape. She raised the harpoon and hurled it down. There was a tiny splash as it pierced the surface, and then the sea erupted as the shark's body contorted.

The craft began to rise again, and the shark was hauled, thrashing, out of the water. Quellen held the end of the line that was attached to the harpoon, and she stuck it to the side of the gondola. Gossilen leaped off the wall, trailing her own silk dragline, to join Arabell below.

"Amazing," Umber said in a hush.

"Sickening," Oates muttered.

Hap thought they were both right. There was a savage beauty to the attack. Fearless Arabell spewed silk onto the shark's fins and tails. The shark writhed and snapped, but Arabell was too agile. Gossilen arrived and covered the shark's head with silk. She bound the jaws shut and then sank her fangs into the gills. Arabell nipped the shark on its pale belly. Soon the shark's writhing weakened, until it barely moved at all. By then Quellen had joined the others. The ship cruised on, slowly rising, trailing the spider-folk and their prey. When Hap heard the awful slurping sounds that drifted up to the gondola, he pushed away from the wall and sat on the floor, feeling vaguely ill.

CHAPTER
15

When the spider-folk were done feeding, they let the shriveled carcass of the shark splash into the ocean and climbed back to the gondola. They pulled their draglines after them and devoured the silk. "That way they don't waste the protein," Umber explained. "Makes it easier for them to spin more."

Hap's stomach heaved again when he looked at the creatures' swollen bellies, which had doubled in size. He wrinkled his nose as Umber produced dinner from his pack: cheese, fruit, bread, salted meat, and a jug of cider. *I'm supposed to eat after that?* Hap mused, shaking his head. But Oates dove in with his usual gusto, and it was soon obvious that the food would be gone altogether if Hap didn't seize his share.

While they dined sitting on the floor with their meal spread on a cloth, Pilot came back from the nose of the craft and stared down at his passengers. "It will be dark soon. You'll want hammocks, I suppose."

"If you don't mind," Umber said. "They're quite comfortable, Hap. Try one, even if you won't sleep in it."

Pilot raised an eyebrow at the comment but said nothing. He turned to the trio of creatures resting at the rear of the gondola. "Three hammocks, my dears." He looked sideways at Oates's considerable bulk. "Better use thicker cord for one of them." Oates frowned up at him.

The spider-folk sprang up, eager as puppies, to the hammocks. They climbed one wall of the gondola, and each anchored a thread there and then dropped to the floor, spinning a line as she ran to the opposite wall to fasten the other end. They went back and forth in that fashion until seven lines for the length of each hammock had been strung, and then each wove more lines across the breadth. Hap watched, astonished by their speedy work. Barely a minute had passed before the hammocks were finished. The creatures stood before them, smiling broadly. They bent their front legs and lowered their heads, in a gesture that reminded Hap of a bow.

Umber bowed in reply. "Wonderful work, girls. Thank you

kindly." The creatures giggled and scuttled forward to rub their cheeks against Pilot's leg.

Oates stood up, brushed crumbs off his lap, and walked to the sturdiest hammock. Without hesitating, he spread the webbing wide and lowered himself into it. He shut his eyes, locked his hands behind his head, and yawned like a bear.

Umber chuckled. "One of you never sleeps; the other would sleep all day if he could."

The sea glowed orange as the sun touched the horizon. Pilot stayed at the helm, studying a map by lamplight. Umber frowned as he sketched in one of the little notebooks he kept in his vest. The furrows in his brow deepened, and he finally snapped the notebook shut and crammed it into his pocket. "Curse it all. I'm trying to draw those soul crabs, but I'm nowhere near the artist that Sophie is."

"I wish she was here. Why didn't you bring her, Lord Umber?" Hap asked.

Umber pursed his lips and winced, as if he regretted letting the name slip. "Oh. I suppose I ought to tell you. But you have to promise me something."

"Promise you what, Lord Umber?"

"You're going to be angry when you hear the reason. But you cannot act on that anger, no matter how tempted you'll

be in the days ahead. Do you agree?" Umber stared at Hap with his eyebrows raised. "If you're not sure, it might be better if you don't know."

Hap stared back. In his mind he saw Sophie's pretty, fragile face. He saw, too, the arm without a hand that she took care to hide from sight. "I would like to know. I promise."

Umber rubbed his hands on his knees and took a deep breath. "Do you know where Sophie is from?"

"I always thought she was from Kurahaven," Hap replied.

Umber shook his head. "In fact, she's from Sarnica."

"Sarnica?" Hap sat up a little straighter. "Isn't that where—"

"Exactly," Umber said. "Sophie's only family was her father, Albin. Albin was a fletcher—an arrow maker, you know—and he was the one who taught her archery. He was a master archer himself, but by the time Sophie was twelve, her skill had surpassed his. Sophie became a bit of a legend in her town— the little girl who could stick an arrow in a bull's-eye from a hundred paces. In fact hardly anyone noticed what a splendid artist she also was, in charcoal or ink or paint or any other medium she tried.

"Albin was so proud that he entered her in a contest with the finest marksmen in Sarnica. Unfortunately, a cruel prince of Sarnica was in the same contest. That was Magador, son of Brugador, the king of Sarnica. Magador fancied himself the best bowman in his kingdom, and when this little girl defeated him with her last shot, he burned with rage. The vile man ordered that another contest be held the next day. And that night his men made sure that Sophie would never hold a bow again. They beat Sophie's father terribly, and dragged her—"

"Stop!" Hap cried, holding up his hand. Everything in his stomach had suddenly soured. "Please, Lord Umber. I don't want to hear it."

Umber's face had reddened as he told the tale. He wiped his palm across the corner of one eye. "Come to think it, I don't want to tell it."

Hap shuddered. He was learning more about the world every day. There was beauty and kindness in it, but also depths of evil that he could not fathom. Sophie was as gentle and harmless as the morning dew. What sort of man would maim her, simply to avenge his wounded pride?

"Let me tell you this, though," Umber said. "While Sophie was healing, her father got word that the prince was still furious about losing to her, since the folk kept talking about his defeat. Sophie and her father had to flee. They took passage on a ship bound for Kurahaven. But the poor man fell ill on the journey, and he died soon after they arrived. A week later Balfour and I met Sophie on the streets of Kurahaven. Only a month before, she had been the beloved child of a prosperous craftsman. When we found her, she was a street urchin. Her only possession was a stick of charcoal, but she was creating the most remarkable picture on the stone walls of the harbor—a beautiful drawing of the Aerie. It occurred to me that I could use an artist to illustrate my books, and that was that—Sophie joined our household."

Hap became aware of a sharp whistling noise. It was the sound of his own breath, he realized, hissing from his nose as if he were a bull about to charge. He glanced at Umber, who was appraising him with one eye narrowed.

"I said you'd be angry," Umber said.

Hap's fists felt hot, and the urge to strike something nearly overwhelmed him. He closed his eyes to calm himself.

"As I said, you need to keep a lid on that anger," Umber said. "We might run into this Magador during the Dragon Games." He yawned and scratched his chest. "And now I think it's time to get some sleep. We'll reach Sarnica before sunrise and disembark while it's still dark outside. Good night, Hap. Wake me up if anything really interesting happens."

Umber climbed into his hammock. Before he dozed off, Hap saw him read the note from Prince Galbus again, three times or more, smiling all the while. And then Hap was the only human awake on the *Silkship*. Pilot seemed confident in the course he'd set, because he sat in a woven chair that hung from the ceiling and slept with his head slumped to one side. Gossilen, who seemed to be Pilot's favorite of the spider-folk, clung to the roof of the gondola, peering forward into the night.

Hap leaned on the gondola wall and watched the stars for a while before deciding to give the hammock a try. He spread it wide and climbed in, nearly losing his balance before getting the knack and settling down. *It is comfortable,* he thought, but it troubled him to feel so much like a fly trapped in a giant web. His unease grew a hundredfold as the hammock tilted from an added weight on one side and tiny claws and fingers tugged at his arm. He stared, saucer-eyed, as Quellen and Arabell climbed into the hammock with him. They moved to either side, burrowed into his armpits, folded their many legs, and closed their eyes. Hap gulped. He lay motionless for hours. After seeing what they'd done to the shark, he was afraid to startle the sleeping creatures.

As he listened to the deep, easy breathing of the others, and even the spider-folk nestled against him, he wondered again what sleep was like. He closed his eyes and let his chest gently rise and fall. But it was only an imitation, not the soft glide into unconscious peace that others had described.

He could not sleep. It was his nightly reminder that he was different and strange.

"Quellen! Arabell!" boomed Pilot. His jaw slid back and forth as he stared at the spider-folk at Hap's side. Their eyes blinked open, and they wriggled their fangs and gazed up at their master. The gondola was still lit only by the single lamp at the helm. "Weave the mooring lines," Pilot snapped.

Hap didn't like the angry look Pilot was shooting at him—after all, he hadn't invited the little monsters to join him. But he was relieved to be able to move again. He hopped down and dug his other pair of boots from his pack.

Umber sat up in his hammock and rubbed the sleep from his eyes. "Are we there yet?"

"Within the hour," Pilot replied. "I will anchor the craft on the cliffs a mile north of the city, as we agreed."

"Splendid," Umber said, tipping himself out of the hammock and onto his feet. He dabbed with his fingertips at the bandage around his head and struck a few ridiculous poses as he stretched his muscles. Then he put his heel to Oates's hammock and rocked it. "Come on, big fella. Rise and shine."

Oates's eyes sprung wide and he sat up too quickly. The hammock turned sideways and dumped him onto the floor.

The spider-folk giggled as Oates sat up, rubbing the side of his face. "Forgot where I was," Oates said, glaring sideways at the creatures.

Hap went to the wall of the gondola and peered out into the dark. "That must be Sarnica," he said, pointing.

"What? You can see it?" Pilot looked over his shoulder from the helm. Hap dropped his arm. Umber preferred that he keep his special abilities a secret, but he'd momentarily forgotten.

"Hap's eyes can pierce the darkness, Pilot," Umber explained. "I should have told you, I suppose—you might find it handy while he's on board."

Pilot gave Hap a cold, appraising look. "What sort of child is this, Umber?"

"A perfectly nice one," Umber replied stiffly.

Pilot snorted. "Where do you see land?" he asked Hap.

"That way, sir."

"And is there a point that rises above the rest?"

Hap pointed again. "Yes. To the left. I mean port. I mean south . . . you know."

Pilot shook his head and rolled his eyes. But he also spun the wheel to align the stones, which turned them toward the elevated point on the extreme end of Sarnica.

If that's an island, it's a big one, Hap observed. He saw a city

in the distance, on the tip of the island, guarded by a rugged stone wall and dominated by a primitive castle.

"I see it now," Pilot said, as they neared the coast. He brought the ship close to the waves and aimed for a vast, imposing cliff that spread wide across the near side of the island.

"Big cliffs," said Oates.

Umber nodded. "Five hundred feet, at least."

Hap saw Pilot leaning out to stare at the sheer wall of rock that loomed ahead. "Are you looking for something?" Hap asked.

Pilot gave him a stern look, and then shrugged. "A cavity where this ship can be concealed. Close to the top, if possible."

Hap looked at the cliff. It was craggy enough to offer many such possibilities, but one place looked especially inviting. "About two hundred yards that way," he said, extending his arm. "It's deep and wide, and there's a ledge sticking out on top like an awning."

Pilot raised his eyebrows and even smiled a little. He slid the wheel back, away from the large white crystal, and the *Silkship* slowed to a crawl. From far below came a noise like thunder: waves hammering at the foot of the cliff.

"Perfect," said Pilot, as a yawning hole loomed before them. The crevice plunged deep into the face of the cliff.

Hap supposed nobody had ever set foot in this inaccessible place before. The *Silkship* glided in, and the three spider-folk dropped from the gondola, spinning draglines behind them and gripping the freshly spun mooring lines with their forelegs. They spread out and pulled the mooring lines taut until the gondola hovered a foot off the floor of the crevice, and then they produced a gluey thread that cemented the lines in place.

"They'll need a ladder," Pilot called. Quellen squeaked in reply. Gossilen joined her, and they crawled together up the back of the crevice, upside down on its roof, and straight up the cliff wall. They dropped down again moments later, holding hands—*Claws? Feet?* wondered Hap—and leaving a parallel pair of silk threads behind them. When they reached the bottom, Quellen climbed the same threads, this time weaving rungs between them. Hap shook his head, amazed. They'd made a perfect ladder, and it had taken only minutes.

After some quiet words with Umber, Pilot unlatched a door in the side of the gondola and swung it inward. The floor of the crevice was just a foot below, and Umber bounded out with a wide grin on his face and a pack slung over his shoulder. Oates stepped out next with the rest of their baggage gathered in his arms. Hap followed, relieved to feel solid rock beneath his feet once more. Whenever he'd walked on the paper-thin floor of the gondola, he'd felt certain he'd plunge through at any moment.

"Now what?" said Oates.

"Wait for dawn and climb the ladder," Umber said. "The road we need runs near the top of this cliff, and then it's maybe an hour by foot to Faldran."

"Faldran?" asked Hap.

"The chief city of Sarnica. Where the Dragon Games are. Where King Brugador lives. He calls himself king, but warlord is more like it, since he murdered his way to the throne and rules by brute force, and smells like bad meat."

Pilot hadn't left his ship. Hap saw him back at the helm, fiddling with the wheel and running his fingers across a map.

"What will Pilot do while we're gone?" asked Hap.

"We'll either leave Sarnica in three days or arrange other transportation home," Umber said. "It's up to Pilot whether he wanders off or stays here. But this is a perfect little hiding place you spotted, Hap. I think he's quite pleased with it."

Hap sat on a chunk of fallen stone to wait. All three of the spider-folk scuttled over and sat at his feet.

"They've really taken to you, Hap," Umber said. "I wonder what it is about you?"

Hap grimaced down at the creatures, not sure if he should be disgusted or flattered. They rocked their heads from side to

side, meeting his gaze. *It's my eyes,* he thought. He glanced at the gondola. He was sure Pilot had been glaring at him, but he turned away as soon as Hap looked in his direction. *It's not my fault they like me.*

When daylight broke, Oates lashed their packs together and hoisted them on his back, along with a pair of small wooden crates that Umber had brought. He bore the weight as if it all held nothing but feathers.

"You first, Oates," Umber said, shaking the ladder. "That way we can be sure it's safe, ha ha!"

Oates grumbled at the joke and began his climb. The silk looked so thin to Hap that he held his breath, certain it would snap. But Oates vanished safely over the ledge above.

"I'll be right behind you, Hap," Umber said. Hap went up the rungs, still wary, though he could feel the strength in the cords. On the wall of the cliff he saw Arabell climbing along with him, smiling his way.

"She's not coming with us, is she?" he said to Umber, just a few rungs below.

"I think she just wants to see you off," Umber said.

They arrived at the top to find Oates hunched down behind a shrub, tapping a finger against his lips. There were sounds ahead: the clattering of many hooves, and the cry of someone in terrible pain.

CHAPTER
16

Their shadows led them forward,
through heavy underbrush. The thump of hooves had faded
into the distance, but voices and sobs were just ahead. Umber
peered between branches and then straightened from his
crouch and walked into a clearing. Beside him Hap heard
Arabell squeak. She turned and scrabbled back toward the
cliff.

The road was beyond the thicket. Three people—a family,
it seemed to Hap—had camped beside it. They had a cart, and
a donkey tethered to a tree. Next to a smoldering campfire a
father and mother sat beside a teenage boy who was lying on
the ground. His teeth were bared, and his eyes were squeezed
shut, wringing tears from the corners.

rdon us, friends," Umber said. "Do you need help?" He

his hands palms out, to show that he meant no harm.

e heads of the man and woman snapped toward his voice.

ar widened their eyes, and despair stretched their mouths.

"He cut our boy with his sword, and for no good cause," wailed the woman. "The monster!" Her words alarmed her husband—he reached over and grasped her shoulder.

Hap looked at the young man on the ground. The mother clasped the son's hand between hers. His shirt was torn, and the father was using a cloth to press against a wound on his chest. The fabric was dark with blood. Hap's throat convulsed at the sight, and he covered his mouth with his hand.

"Oates, my medicine kit," Umber said. Oates shrugged the burden off his back and dug into one of the packs, finally extracting a tin box that he handed to Umber.

"Who did this?" Umber asked, as he kneeled beside the son and unlatched the box.

"It doesn't matter," the father said, looking nervously at the three of them. His gaze lingered a bit longer on Hap's eyes.

Umber pulled out a clear bottle stopped with cork and wax. "You have nothing to fear from us, my friend."

It was the wounded son who answered the question. "The bloody king's bloody son, that's who!" he said, wincing with the effort.

Hap felt a jolt pass through his chest. *Magador,* he th

snarling the name inside his head. *Right here, just a minute*

The image of Sophie's wounded arm flashed through his mi

Umber looked back at him and shook his head in a gestu

of disbelief.

"May I see the wound?" Umber asked the son gently. Then

he sucked in a breath and turned his head a little as the father

removed the cloth. "Ouch," Umber said. Before Hap could

look away, he saw the wound. It was a slice in the flesh, longer

than a hand. The mother cried out again at the sight and

gripped her son's arm.

"What's your name, friend?" Umber asked the son as he

uncorked the bottle.

"Steffan," the son replied, opening his eyes to look up at

Umber.

"It could have been worse, Steffan. The wound isn't deep—

it was a slash and not a thrust, I assume? Yes, I thought so. This

will sting, but not as bad as that sword." Umber poured some

of the bottle's clear contents on the wound. There were two

hisses: one from the potion as it bubbled in the wound, and

another through Steffan's gritted teeth.

Umber handed the bottle to the parents. "That will help

fight infection, but we need to close this wound. Do you have

any—?"

"Umber," interrupted Oates.

"Hold on, Oates," Umber said, waving him off. "I was saying, my friends, do you have needle and—?"

"Umber," Oates said again, louder.

Umber glared over his shoulder. "What is it, Oates? Can't you see that—"

Oates jabbed with his thumb. Behind him, barely visible through the undergrowth, stood a tall, familiar figure. When Umber looked his way, the figure nodded.

The anger dissolved from Umber's expression. One of his eyebrows went up, and he mumbled to himself. "Oh. Yes. Really? I suppose . . ." He turned back toward Steffan's mother and father and worked his jaw back and forth as he composed his thoughts. "Er. My friends. I believe we can help your son. But you might find the nature of the help . . ." Umber's fingers waggled in the air. ". . . a little . . ."

"Disgusting?" offered Oates.

Umber frowned at the big man and corrected him. *"Unusual."*

Steffan's parents looked at each other. "If you can help him, do it. We don't care how."

"Please," Steffan said.

Umber smiled and nodded. He called to the figure. "Do what you can, Pilot."

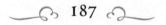

The mother and father's eyes expanded as the imposing figure strode out of the underbrush, tall and grim and dark of skin. And when Arabell and Gossilen crawled up from behind Pilot's back to perch on his shoulders, the father's eyes rolled up white and he toppled over.

Pilot frowned at the unconscious fellow. "Go on, girls," he said to the spider-folk, and they climbed down to the ground and scuttled to Steffan.

"No," moaned Steffan.

"They won't hurt you," Pilot snapped, a little cruelly. "How bad is the pain?"

"What do you think?" Steffan said, wincing and clenching his jaw.

"Arabell, just a nip," Pilot said.

Umber walked on his knees to the mother's side and put an arm around her shoulder. She trembled as Arabell approached the wound. "Courage, madam," he said. "Steffan, don't move an inch. And perhaps you should close your eyes."

Steffan looked ready to leap to his feet despite his terrible wound, but he took Umber's advice and turned his head away.

Arabell licked her lips at the sight of the bloody wound. She put her forelegs onto Steffan, who whined with fear. With a sudden, darting motion Arabell sank her fangs into Steffan's belly, and scuttled backward to avoid the arm that swatted at her by reflex.

Pilot glowered and stomped his foot. Umber called to him. "The boy couldn't help it, Pilot. Besides, Arabell's too clever to get hurt."

Steffan opened his eyes and stared down at his chest. His face shone with sweat. "Something . . . happening . . ."

"You're getting numb," Pilot said, still simmering.

"No more pain . . . no feeling at all . . ."

"If you strike at my creatures again, I'll triple your agony," Pilot said.

"Steady, Pilot," Umber said. "Hap, come here and hold Steffan's legs. Oates, you get the arms. Just to be sure."

Hap felt sick and dizzy, but he did as Umber asked, grabbing Steffan's ankles and gently pinning them down. As far as he could tell, the legs were limp and senseless. Arabell and Gossilen crept forward and went to work. Hap watched as much as he could bear. It was as fascinating as it was horrifying. The spider-folk sewed the boy's wound shut as neatly as Arabell had mended Hap's trousers. Gossilen turned her spinnerets toward the wound, and the little finger-shaped things spun out the finest thread Hap had seen yet. Arabell pierced the edges of the wound with her fangs and stitched the flesh, pulling it gently together. As they worked, Umber spoke to the mother—either to distract her from what was happening or to satisfy his own curiosity.

"Madam, how did you happen to be at this spot?"

"We were coming to watch the Dragon Games, sir, if we could. Steffan begged us to see the dragons. When it got too dark to go on, we stopped for the night."

"Why was Magador here just now?"

"I think he rode out from the city at dawn to go hunting. There were six of them riding together."

"And why did he hurt your son?"

"Magador never needs a reason. He invents one on the spot. We were sleeping when he rode up, and he said we should have bowed as he passed. Then he didn't like the way Steffan looked at him."

The father finally picked up his head again. "Quiet, woman. You want to get us killed?"

"We'll keep her words a secret," Umber assured him, "If you'll keep *this* a secret." He waved his hand toward the spider-folk and Pilot. "Don't tell anyone what has happened, or where it happened. In fact, I suggest you head back home—moving your son as gently as possible for a while."

"Who are you people?" whispered Steffan. His eyes were closed, and his voice was groggy.

"Regular folk like yourselves," Umber replied.

"I'm Oates; that's Umber, lord of the Aerie and the richest man in Kurahaven; this is an odd little boy named Happenstance; and that's Pilot, who owns a flying ship and these disgusting spiders," said Oates.

Umber groaned and clutched his forehead. "Oates, please tell me you packed your muzzle."

As they followed the dirt road, walking three across, Umber spoke of Pilot.

"I know very little about him or his ship. Those helmstones—I can't imagine how valuable they are. And those mushrooms of his. Remarkable."

"Where did those spider-folk come from?" asked Hap.

Umber laughed. "I'd give half my fortune to answer that question! Someplace only Pilot knows of. In fact I think everything—the helmstones, the mushrooms, and the spider-folk—comes from the same place. Because the *Silkship* couldn't exist without all three. I have a theory about—ah! That's a sight, isn't it?"

The road had climbed a small hill, and as they reached its peak, they saw a vast gray wall that began at the cliff's edge and reached out of sight to their right. Peaks of buildings were visible above the wall, and a hundred thin streams of smoke slithered high.

"The Wall of Sarnica," Umber said.

"It looks like it goes all the way across the island," observed Hap.

"It does," Umber said. "The city of Faldran occupies the tip of the island, and the whole end is walled off. It's quite a stronghold. An easy place to strike out from, and then retreat to and defend. Which helps if you're a petty tyrant like Brugador, with a thirst for violence. Happenstance, you've spent your days in Kurahaven, a land of prosperity and mercy. This is a grim, oppressive place. We'll all have to watch our tongues."

"And how am I supposed to do that?" said Oates. Hap was wondering the same thing.

Umber shrugged. "Just do the best you can. Shall we enter?"

There was a gate in the wall ahead of them. A group of sullen soldiers lounged at the base of the wall. One stepped in their path as they approached. His long face and drooping eyes reminded Hap of a hound. "What business do you have in Faldran?" the soldier asked.

Umber grinned. "And good morning to you, friend! I have been invited to the Dragon Games by Brugador himself." He produced a folded parchment from his vest and handed it to the soldier.

The soldier returned a suspicious glare. "Where are you from?"

"Kurahaven," Umber replied.

The eyes narrowed further. "Then why didn't you enter from the harbor side, if you had to take a ship?"

"We got dropped off up the coast. I wanted to see a little of your lovely countryside before the games," Umber said. His smile never faltered.

The soldier handed Umber the note but didn't move. Then his sour expression turned toward Oates, who was frowning back with his lip curled up on one side.

"What are *you* looking at?" the soldier said to Oates.

"A nasty man with a face like a dog," Oates replied, honest as always.

The soldier's face flushed scarlet. "Who are you calling dog-faced?"

"I don't know; we haven't been introduced," Oates said.

The other men overheard the exchange and got to their feet. Swords slid from their scabbards. Hap felt his legs begin to shake.

The tension was broken by the sound of hooves behind them. A party of horsemen crested the hill and rumbled toward the gate. The soldier smiled. "You can deal with *him* now."

The first rider clattered to a halt. He had black hair cropped

close, and gray eyes that were nearly hidden under half-closed lids. Something about his manner, and the feeling of coiled menace he radiated despite his sleepy-eyed stare, made every muscle in Hap's body go tense. "Is there a problem?" the rider asked.

"Strangers, sire," said the soldier, lowering his head.

Umber held up the parchment. "We are invited to the Dragon Games, at the request of your regent."

The black-haired man yanked the note away and examined it. His thick eyebrows rose. "You are Lord Umber?"

Umber bowed with his arms wide and one leg extended, heel to ground. "I am. And this is my ward, Happenstance, and my friend and servant, Oates."

The rider's sleepy eyes widened, and he turned a cold glare upon the soldier, who audibly gulped. "Was this sentry rude to you?" the rider asked.

Umber pondered the question too long, which sadly allowed Oates to reply first. "Very rude," Oates said.

The rider smashed the soldier across the face with the back of his hand. The soldier thumped to the ground and pinched his nose, which had turned into a fountain of blood. Hap watched with his jaw hanging slack. For an instant, as the blow was being delivered, he saw an expression of intense pleasure flash across the rider's face, as the teeth were bared in a savage grin. It disappeared a moment later.

"Mind how you treat the king's guests," the rider said with chilling calm as he rubbed his hand. His eyelids lowered again, giving him a sleepy, contented expression, as if the act of sudden violence had delivered the same effect as a flagon of wine. He turned back to Umber and smiled. *A wolf's grin,* thought Hap.

"I am Magador, son of Brugador. My father is keen to meet you, Umber. And there is another guest who waits eagerly for your arrival. Follow me into Faldran."

They walked on a cobblestone street through a dense city. There were handsome, older stone buildings with flimsier wooden structures crammed between, leaving only the narrowest alleys. They looked as if they'd been constructed a millennium apart. An ill smell hung in the air, trapped in the suffocating streets, safe from the ocean breeze that whistled over the rooftops.

The residents of Faldran were just waking. Windows creaked open, and faces peered out. None looked content, Hap thought, and most ducked out of sight when they spotted Magador. A door opened, and an elderly man stepped out, ready to dash a bucket of dirty water into the gutter, but he froze and held his breath until they went by.

Hap thought that if he'd had any manners, Magador would

have dismounted and walked beside them. But the prince of Sarnica looked down at Umber from his saddle. "Tell me, Lord Umber. I have never seen your Kurahaven. Can it compare to our grand city?"

"Oh, there's no comparison at all," Umber said. He winked at Hap when Magador turned away.

They turned onto another street that looked the same as the first, like a narrow canyon between walls of wood, brick and stone. *It's a maze in here,* Hap thought. He peered into the alleys, where glum figures slumped in doorways or slept on piles of rags. One man dozed with his head on his arms. When Hap saw that one of the arms ended at the wrist, his heart drummed angrily. *Magador,* he thought. *The man who hurt Sophie. Of all the people to run into.* He couldn't believe they were walking cordially behind the man. And he couldn't understand how Umber could smile and take in the sights like any curious visitor.

The road turned, and the castle loomed before them. It looked more like a fortress to Hap: imposing and blunt, without the architectural flourishes that adorned the jewel of Kurahaven.

A wide door stood open, guarded by a half-dozen men. They lowered their heads as Magador rode up. The prince dismounted and handed the reins to one of the guards. "This way," Magador told Umber.

A short, sooty corridor led them to a hall inside the castle. Only a fraction of daylight came through narrow windows. Candles provided the rest of the meager illumination. The furniture was rough-hewn. There were no tapestries on the walls, but plenty of mounted animal heads. Hap heard the faint buzz of flies.

Umber seemed about to speak, but a voice from the other end of the room rang out first. "I knew you'd be here. You couldn't resist, could you, Umber?"

Hap turned. The man who spoke was sitting in a chair with his feet propped on a stool. *Narrow* was the word that sprang to Hap's mind as he looked at the man. He had a narrow nose on a narrow face atop a narrow, bony frame. His hair was blond, almost white, with a dark streak on one side, and it hung limply to his shoulders.

Umber stared back with an artificial smile. "Hello, Hameron."

... Aerie with
in her arms. The child was desp...
ill and would clearly not survive.
She begged me to save the girl. S...
said she'd heard that I could work
miracles, was capable of anything.
I have never felt so hopeless, Balfour
I had her brought to the physician
that I have trained as well as I can.
But now I fear I've wasted much
time on frivolous things. Shouldn't all
my hours be spent relieving the suffering
of our people? Worse still, Balfour,
this event has triggered another of my
episodes. I can feel it coming—the
bottomless despair opening under my
feet and preparing to swallow me
whole. I pray...

CHAPTER
17

Hameron ambled over with his hands clasped behind his back and his shoulders bobbing. A long gray cape hung from his shoulders and nearly brushed the floor. The grin on his face was tainted by a sneer. "This time, Umber, I think you've been outdone."

"Have I?" Umber said.

"I remember you," Hameron said, looking distastefully at Oates. "Umber's bodyguard, I believe? Really, Umber, you have nothing to worry about here."

Oates glared down at the unpleasant man. Hameron chuckled and turned to Umber again. "Are you injured?"

"Had a spill along the way," Umber said, touching his bandage. "Nothing to be . . ." He stopped talking, because he had lost Hameron's attention. Like so many before, Hameron's eyes widened and his jaw dropped when he saw Hap's eyes.

"And what is *this?*" Hameron said. "One of your discoveries?"

"That is my ward, Happenstance," Umber said.

"Your *ward?*" Hameron glanced sideways at Umber with his lips pursed. "But such peculiar eyes. Surely this is another of your magical acquaintances? Like that stunning sea-creature of yours. What is her name, that fishy woman who rides the leviathan?"

Hap's temper had been rising, and the words came out before he could contain them. "Her name is Nima. And you shouldn't speak of her like that." He was sure his face was turning purple.

Hameron grinned. "Feisty! But Umber, you should teach your ward some manners."

"I haven't noticed a flaw in them," Umber replied.

Footsteps approached from another corridor, and four servants appeared. They bustled in and stopped nearby, keeping their faces turned to the floor and stealing glances at Magador. Hap pitied them for their dilemma: If they were caught looking, the prince would probably accuse them of insolence; if they didn't guess his wishes, he might punish them for incompetence. "Took you long enough," Magador said. Those words—and the way his eyes wakened from their sleepy, half-lidded expression—were enough to make the servants tremble. "Show the newcomers to their room. That one is Lord Umber, the man my father has been waiting for." Without a farewell Magador strode away, with the heels of his boots striking hard against the marble floor.

The servants rushed forward, bowed, and took the packs from Umber and Hap. There was a brief, awkward tug-of-war before Oates finally let his packs be taken. "This way, my lord," whispered one servant, and they all bustled toward the archway at the far end of the hall.

"Don't you want to know how I did it?" Hameron called after them.

Umber paused and turned, but did not speak.

"How I got the dragon eggs," Hameron added.

"Stole them, you mean," Umber replied.

"Come on, Umber. Do you call the eggs stolen that you eat for breakfast?"

"A dragon is not a chicken. It is a magnificent and intelligent creature."

Hameron chuckled and shook his head. "You can't stand it, can you? That I was the one who discovered the nesting caves and got away with the eggs. But now your curiosity is overwhelming your wounded pride—I know that look in your eye! Don't fear—you don't have to wait much longer. Go unpack your things. Then meet me here in an hour."

"It makes me sick to admit it," Umber said as he opened a small crate to see if the bottles he'd brought were still intact. "But I am itching to see a dragon. Curse that Hameron."

"I want to punch him," said Oates. He was stretched out on one of the beds in the dreary room where the servants had led them. "After I pummel Magador, of course."

Hap thought he'd like to see both of those things happen. "Who is Hameron, Lord Umber?"

Umber flipped the lid of the crate shut and sat wearily upon it. "Hameron fancies himself my rival when it comes to investigating the supernormal. He came to Kurahaven years back, proposing that we work together. I told him I didn't like his methods. Observing and chronicling is enough for me. I've got a couple of keepsakes, of course, but all Hameron wants to do is capture and kill, and show off his trophies.

"Hameron was furious when I scorned him, and he has tried to outshine me ever since. I heard a while ago that he'd attached himself to Brugador, the king of this land. Brugador was his patron, and in return Hameron brought back specimens, dead or alive, for Brugador's amusement. And now he's gone and done it, hasn't he? Stolen a cache of dragon eggs. That's no easy feat; I'll grant him that. Dragons don't like people messing with their broods. But to rob the eggs! Not in a million years would I do such a thing."

"And the eggs have hatched?" asked Hap.

"Apparently," Umber replied.

"I hope the dragons eat him," Oates said.

"He's so greasy it would probably make them ill," Umber replied. He slapped his knees and stood. "Hold your noses, everyone. It's time to allow an odious man his moment of triumph."

Hameron strutted down the corridor with his cape rippling behind him. He turned back now and then to grin at Umber. On their left a balcony faced the open air at the rear of the castle, revealing a well-protected harbor a hundred feet below. A steep road switched back and forth along the face of a sheer slope, linking the castle to the crowded docks.

"As you can see, there are many important visitors here for the games," Hameron said, waving at the harbor. Hap saw a variety of ships moored in the water, flying foreign pennants and flags.

"Yes, at least from the nations that Brugador hasn't plundered," Umber said. "But what are those big red ships?" The same two craft had caught Hap's eye. They were painted the same dark red but differed in form, like a spade and spear. The thick, blunt ship had three tall masts, while the sleek, narrow craft had no mast at all and narrow holes along its length. Each had an ominous, predatory look.

"Come now, Umber, you must have heard of Brugador's warships: the *Shark* and the *Eel*. Those are the most feared craft on the sea. The *Shark* is for sailing, and raiding afar. The *Eel* prowls the shipping lanes near Sarnica. That one is rowed by Brugador's slaves. You knew Brugador kept slaves, didn't you?"

Slaves? thought Hap. He felt the hair on the back of his neck stand up. Umber's expression didn't change, but when Hap looked at Oates, the big man's jaw was grinding.

When Umber didn't respond, Hameron prattled on. "Well, I can't imagine that pleases you, Umber, the famous freedom-lover. But there's not much to be done about it, is there? I'm afraid Sarnica is destined to be a formidable sea power. More ships are being built as we speak, in the shipyard on the other side of the island. But I don't think your good king has anything to worry about, Umber." Hameron smirked. "Yet."

"Celador is a peaceful kingdom with no taste for war," Umber said.

"A peaceful kingdom. Of course," Hameron said, sighing.

"That reminds me—there's an ambassador of sorts here. A friend of yours, I assume? He asked to be alerted when you arrived."

Umber smiled. "Bertram Charmaigne? Yes, I knew he was here."

Hameron rolled his eyes. "You might as well tell him he's wasting his time in this place. Brugador won't change his ways."

"Bertram is quite convincing," Umber said.

"Quite tiresome, if you ask me. He's your friend—you ought to tell him that there are some minds that are immune to his persuasion," Hameron said. He shoved a pair of heavy doors that swung inward. "Now here's something you'll appreciate, Umber: the Hall of Curiosities!"

They stepped into a long, high-ceilinged room. Hap's breath froze in his lungs for a moment. The place was crowded with strange creatures, all dead and preserved in part or in whole. He'd read about many of them in Umber's books and seen illustrations depicting them. Umber covered his mouth and breathed into his palm for a moment. "You've been busy, Hameron."

"Take a moment to peruse the collection, Umber. The dragons can wait," Hameron said. He leaned against a pillar and folded his arms.

Oates wandered ahead by himself, and Hap followed a stride behind Umber. Umber's eyes darted about in their sockets, taking it all in. But his lip was curled on one side, as if he'd eaten something distasteful.

There was a barrel-sized skull on a table. A sign beside it read GIANT'S SKULL. UNEARTHED IN LONDRIA.

After that was a stuffed head on a plaque—a frightening mix that was half human and half wolf.

Next was a coffin with a lid made of muddy glass. A skeleton was inside—perhaps only four feet long, but with the stout bones of a powerful being. A broad ax was laid across the ribs. A sign on the coffin said UNKNOWN DWERGH. Umber lingered there a bit longer. Hap saw Umber's hands bunched into fists, squeezing so hard that the knuckles turned white.

Hap looked over Umber's shoulder as they approached the next exhibit. It was a stone box with no lid. Inside was a shriveled form the size of a child. It had once been wrapped entirely in bands of cloth, but the wrappings were unwound to the shoulders, revealing a skull with a small forehead and a wide mouth lined with triangular teeth. Umber glared down at it. "This is a goblin mummy," he said.

"Quite a find," Hameron replied. He had crept up behind them.

"If they mummified it, it was one of their royalty. There was treasure with it, I assume?"

Hameron grinned. "Oh, yes. We took what we could, and then abandoned most of it on the way out, since a horde of goblins was on our heels."

Umber narrowed his eyes. "Rightfully so. This would be a sacred relic to the goblins. It should not have been removed."

"Seriously, Umber," Hameron sighed, crossing his arms. "Your ethics are so curious. What's the point of finding a thing if you don't bring it back? That's how I earn my living, you know."

"This should be returned to the place you found it," Umber said. "And that Dwergh as well. It's ghoulish."

Hameron clucked his tongue. "Your jealousy is getting the best of you, Umber. But I forgive you. And I'll still show you what you really want to see. Come on!" He brushed past them and disappeared around a corner into an adjacent hall.

"Do you want me to snap his bones?" Oates whispered as Umber walked by.

"Don't tempt me," Umber said.

They came to a guarded door. When the guards saw Hameron, they stepped aside, and Hameron pushed the door open. Beyond was a dark staircase, descending past curving walls of stone. As they followed Hameron down, he boasted all the while. "The first challenge was finding the nesting place in the sea cliffs of Chastor. That land is usually shrouded in mist, for one thing. And of course the dragons don't welcome human visitors. The first four scouts I sent did not return. But the fifth did the trick!"

Hap didn't hear a hint of regret in Hameron's voice when he spoke of the men he'd lost. Beside him Oates scrunched his brow.

"Once we had the spot, I made a wonderful discovery: The cliffs were full of crevices and cracks that I could use to approach unseen. I waited until the wind would carry my scent away, and made my approach."

The stairs landed in the middle of a corridor. From the left came a reddish glow and a rhythmic hissing. Hameron paused to look Umber in the eye. "I saw it all, Umber! Almost as close as I am to you right now. There's a great chamber deep in the cliff, with hundreds of eggs inside. Who knows how old they are? Thousands of years, perhaps. Maybe those are all the eggs there will ever be, and one day the dragons will be no more!"

Hap saw a familiar wide-eyed expression on Umber's face as he learned something new about the magical world. And he saw the pleasure that Hameron was taking in Umber's reaction. It all made Hap sick to his stomach.

"And you saw them hatch?" Umber asked, bouncing off his heels.

"Only one," Hameron replied. "I don't think they do it often. But they use *dragon fire*, Umber. Three dragons gathered around and bathed it in flame. I nearly passed out from the heat! It took all day, but finally the egg cracked open. A dragon born, before my eyes!"

"I wish I could have seen that," Umber said quietly.

"I can make that happen, old friend," Hameron said. "Come on." He led them down the left side of the corridor. Before he followed, Hap glanced the other way. It was unlit, but his nocturnal vision revealed what was there: rows of barred cells, filled with prisoners staring blindly at an endless night. *A dungeon,* Hap thought. The sight reminded him of how cruel Sarnica and its rulers were.

"Those are the Midnight Dungeons," Hameron called. "The king keeps the enemies he really detests in there. But that is not our destination, young ward of Umber. Come with me, and do not linger."

Hap followed, with the ghostly faces of the prisoners haunting his thoughts. The corridor soon opened into a larger space. Hameron paused there to make a dramatic, sweeping gesture. "This is the Dragon Incubator. This chamber once was built for another purpose, as you can see. But I insisted on using it to hatch the eggs."

Hap winced at the sight of the terrible machinery that had

been pushed to one side of the space. There were manacles on the walls, cages suspended from the floor, boards covered with spikes, and other instruments for the infliction of pain. When he turned away from those awful devices, he saw the source of the red glow and the hissing sound.

"It takes fire to make a dragon," Hameron said. "Here I can make all the flame we need." He pointed to three hearths in the far wall. The middle hearth had been filled with a conical pile of red-hot coals. And at the top of the pile there was an egg. At least, it was *shaped* like an egg. Its shell was unlike anything Hap had ever seen, and it shimmered as the intense heat washed over it.

"Will you look at that," Umber whispered.

"It looks like it's made of glass, doesn't it?" Hameron said. "Look, you can see the infant moving inside."

When Hap looked closer, he saw the tiny dragon through the murky crystal of the eggshell. Its head twitched, and the stub of the tail uncurled and curled again. Umber leaned so close Hap was afraid his hair would catch fire as he stared, awestruck, at the dragon egg.

Hap felt perspiration blossoming on his forehead. The room was oppressively hot. It would have been hotter still if it weren't for the opening in the hearth above the coals, which led to a chimney that must have vented somewhere high above.

"Look here, Umber," Hameron said, walking to a small, heavy crate on the other side of the room. There was a padlock, which Hameron opened with another key. Then he swung the lid open. It was full of more crystal-shelled dragon eggs.

Umber gasped. He reached out and brushed the shells with his fingertips. "They glow!" he said.

"Yes. Beautiful, aren't they?"

Umber sighed deeply. "May I hold one?"

"Certainly. They're not fragile at all, despite the glassy look."

Hap bit his lip. This was all wrong. He wanted Umber to be furious and disgusted. Instead he was behaving exactly as the loathsome Hameron wanted: giddy with wonder.

Umber held the egg with two hands. He sniffed it, put it to his ear, and gazed into the semitransparent shell before gently placing it down again. "When will that one hatch?" he asked, gesturing toward the egg in the fire.

"A day or two," Hameron replied. "It's hard to know for sure. Then it's a simple matter of feeding the baby. Fish and goat do just fine—that's what the dragons bring their young in the caves."

"How interesting. I'd love to see a living specimen," Umber said.

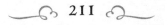

"You will have to wait until tomorrow for that."

"Why tomorrow?"

Hameron smiled and lifted an eyebrow. "The games, of course."

CHAPTER
18

"Where are we going now?" asked Oates.

"Looking for someone. In a tavern, not far from here."

They bustled through the winding streets of Faldran. It was nearly noon, and the city had grown crowded, as locals flooded in and visiting ships arrived in the harbor. Soldiers crowded the streets as well, looking for trouble and often causing it. They bullied commoners, picked fights, and seized what they wanted from the merchants who sold food from stalls.

"Who are we looking for?" Hap asked.

"Bertram Charmaigne. Bertram is an ambassador from Pernica, and a peacemaker of some renown. He's also a friend. Now where is that tavern . . . ?" Umber raised his face to examine the signs on the buildings in the square. "There it is: the Hare and Hedgehog. And just in time for lunch!"

They shared the tavern with dozens of foreign visitors. The people seemed to relax inside this haven with no soldiers strutting about, so it was a cheery oasis in an oppressed and gloomy city.

The table and chairs were rough-hewn, and dried grass was spread on the wide floorboards under their feet. At least five cats prowled under the tables. Umber ordered a vast quantity of food while they waited for his friend. Soon the table was covered with roasted lamb and fish, bowls of thick steaming soup with bobbing vegetables, and mugs of ale for Umber and Oates and cider for Hap.

Umber talked between bites. "Bertram is a remarkable fellow. In his youth he underwent a strange ordeal that left him a wounded but wizened soul."

"What happened?" Hap asked.

"I don't know if he would like details getting out, so I won't say more than that," Umber replied. "But this is a man who deserves your respect and admiration. Since his ordeal he has devoted his life to bringing understanding between different peoples, and peace between warring countries. He has spent many months in Sarnica, trying to persuade its king to give up his barbaric ways. But I don't think—" Umber glanced up as an open door brightened the room. "Bertram! Here!" he called, standing up raising his hand.

A man nodded from across the room and threaded his way through the tables toward them, pausing to shake hands and clasp the shoulders of some of the foreigners along the way. Hap had time to study him as he approached. Bertram was thin, and neither short nor tall. He had blue eyes under black brows and an uncommonly pale complexion, almost as white as snow. Between the smiles of greeting, his face settled into a saddened, tired expression. He was not an old man—younger than Umber, in fact, not yet thirty—but there was something ancient in his demeanor. The gray strands in his coal-black hair seemed years before their time.

"How nice to see you, Umber," he said, and they thumped each other on the back. The newcomer remarked on Umber's wound, and Umber assured him it was nothing. Bertram turned to Oates and extended a hand. "This must be the famous Mister Oates. A pleasure, sir. I know how greatly Umber appreciates your service."

"He does?" Oates asked, shaking the hand.

"Absolutely. And here we must have young Master Happenstance. Umber has told me about you in his letters," Bertram said.

"Hello, sir," Hap said. It pleased him to see that when their eyes met, Bertram did not show surprise or amazement.

"Sit and eat, Bert," said Umber.

Bertram reached for a chair, but stopped when he noticed his reflection in a dusty mirror on the wall behind their table. He clenched his jaw before taking a deep breath, and then chose a chair on the other side, with the mirror at his back. "Excuse me. I have disliked mirrors since I was a boy," he said. Hap found it a curious thing to say; he assumed it had something to do with the strange ordeal that Umber would not discuss.

Umber and Bertram traded news from their kingdoms as they dined. The fact of Prince Argent's death had already reached these shores, and Bertram expressed his sorrow and admiration for the fallen prince. He was delighted, though, to hear of the sudden change of character in Galbus. "One can't be both king and court jester," Bertram said. "Galbus understands this. Now, as necessity beckons, he attempts to answer the call. You may not believe this, Umber, but I always thought he had it in him."

"You're the best judge of character I know," Umber said. "I do believe you. And speaking of character, what is your opinion of King Brugador?"

Bertram looked left and right, and forced a weak smile.

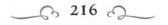

"I suppose I can tell you. A noisy room is better than a quiet corner for this kind of talk, if you ask me. Brugador is a criminal with a crown. A torturer, cutthroat, and pirate. He's built a pair of fearsome warships and uses them to plunder his neighboring islands. And I suppose you know that he's been enslaving captives to row his galley. *Slaves,* Umber. It sickens the soul to think of it. He's a nightmare, pure and simple, who dreams of expanding his navy and his tyranny. I could talk to him for a millennium without moving him an inch toward a better path. And the only thing worse is his son, Magador."

"We've met his son," Umber said.

"How unfortunate for you," Bertram said. "It seems the prince is either on the brink of violence, or in the act of violence." He sipped his ale and used a cloth to wipe foam from the corner of his mouth. Leaning toward Umber, he lowered his voice. "There are other things I need to tell you, another time."

Umber nodded.

"Do you know what we ought to do now?" Bertram asked. "Wander over to the athletic fields. The archery contest is happening as we speak. And the Running of the Harbor ends the day. Naturally, Prince Magador is expected to win both."

Another walk through winding streets led to an ancient athletic field. It was an oasis of green, wide and sunken below the level of the city, and surrounded by tiers of marble benches. In a line on the grass stood two dozen archery targets backed with haystacks. The contest must have just ended, because the archers were packing their gear, and people were filing out. Hap noticed that many were exchanging whispers and secret grins. He looked down at the field and saw Magador furiously prying arrows from a target. The prince turned to a group of soldiers nearby, shouted about something, and dashed the arrows to the ground. Hap hoped this meant that the prince had lost the competition.

Bertram led them down the stairs between the rows of seats. He met someone he seemed to know: an older man who limped up the stairs. "Parley! There you are. Who won the contest? What happened?"

Parley wasn't handsome—one eye was missing, in fact, and one of his arms was withered from an old injury—but he was instantly likable. "A farce is what happened," he said, chuckling. "Too bad you missed it! The early rounds were impressive. There are plenty of talented bowmen on this island. Magador is one of them, of course. But a funny thing happened once the final round started. Suddenly, nobody but Magador could come within a hand's breadth of the bull's-eye! Half of them missed the target altogether. I could have done better, and I'm half blind. And you know why they missed, of course."

Hap knew why. Magador's reputation was well known. Anybody who dared defeat him might win the contest but lose a hand, like Sophie. So nobody dared.

Bertram shook his head and smiled ruefully. "This fine fellow is Parley, my friend and courier," he said, but the introductions ended as a loud and angry voice rose toward them. Hap's jaw clenched as he saw Magador storm up the aisle, directly at them, grousing to the three sour-faced soldiers who followed him.

"Ridiculous," Magador growled. There was nothing sleepy about his expression at the moment. "What's the point of winning when the opponents don't even try to compete? As if I couldn't beat them in a fair contest!"

The prince was so preoccupied with his rant that he didn't notice Umber and the others until he was right on top of them. His face flushed a deeper, angrier shade of purple— *because we didn't leap out of his way,* Hap figured.

"Your Highness," Bertram said with a formal bow.

"Charmaigne," Magador muttered. He jabbed his head to acknowledge Umber, and ignored the others. Hap was glad for it. Parley winked at him, as well as a one-eyed man could.

"Congratulations on your victory," Bertram said.

Magador spat on the stairs. "Disgusting. A field of cowards. And the Running of the Harbor will be the same, you can wager."

Umber leaned forward. "Your Highness, what is the Running of the Harbor?"

Magador sneered at him, as if Umber were a fool for asking. "A race, of course. From the docks to the castle." Hap remembered the place: The castle sat high over the harbor, above a road that switched back and forth up the steep hill, with turns as tight as clothespins.

The prince glared at the crowd. "I can't be beaten in that race. But nobody will even try. We ought to just cancel it and declare me the winner." His gaze suddenly fell on Oates. "You look strong. Perhaps you'd like to enter?"

"I hate running," replied Oates.

Always honest, thought Hap, but he didn't like the way Magador glared at Oates. And then his head went numb when he heard the next thing that came out of Oates's mouth.

"Happenstance could beat you, though."

"Oates!" Umber cried. Happenstance felt dizzy, and he edged behind Umber, hoping to disappear. Bertram gave him a curious look, and Parley put a hand to his mouth and coughed, perhaps to hide a grin.

"Who? This green-eyed whelp?" Magador snorted as he brushed past Umber and loomed over Hap. He smelled like an animal.

"Yes, him," said Oates, despite Umber's stern glare and

shaking head. "He can run like the wind and leap like a flea."

"Is that so?" Magador flexed a fist as he looked Hap over from head to toe. "Fancy yourself a runner, boy?"

"Not really?" squeaked Hap. It came out like a question.

Umber spoke up. "Your Highness, we are merely visitors here. I'm sure young Happenstance would prefer—"

"Let him run," Magador said. "What harm could it do?"

"Good prince," Bertram began, "letting the boy run would violate your own rules. The entrants must submit their names before—"

Magador cut him off with a raised hand. "I can change the rules as I see fit. He will run."

Two hours later they made their way down the steep road to the harbor's edge. Parley explained the race as he hobbled beside them. "As I understand it, the first one to reach the top and ring the bell that stands before the castle is the winner. That is the one and only rule. A runner may take any path he wants. He can stay on the road as it zigzags, or scale the slopes between the switchbacks." Hap looked at the course. The question was, could one climb fast enough to make the shortcuts worth it?

"One other thing you should know, young man," Parley said. "Not everyone in this race is here to win. Some have entered to help their champion to victory, by sabotaging the other runners. You can be sure Magador has plenty of allies to guarantee his victory. And there are no rules forbidding contact between runners. The race can get violent."

"Violent?" cried Hap.

"Pushing, punching, tripping, scratching, gouging . . . anything goes," Parley said.

"Sorry about this," mumbled Oates.

"That settles it," Umber said. "Happenstance, just fall behind when the race begins, and stay out of harm's way. Pretend your leg is injured if that helps. There's nothing to gain by winning. And we know how Magador can't stand losing to children. Agreed?"

Hap nodded. *Even better, how about I turn around and run the other way?* he thought.

"Could you really win this, Happenstance?" asked Bertram.

"Don't doubt it for a minute, Bert," Umber said.

They reached the bottom of the road, with the harbor before them. From there Hap got an eyeful of Brugador's warships. They were even larger and more forbidding than he'd thought. From where he stood, he could see a ram that jutted from the prow of the narrow ship, the *Eel*, at the water line. It was obviously designed to punch a hole in any ship that it attacked and send it to the bottom of the sea. He saw the rows of dark slits in the side, where the oars would come out, and he wondered if the slaves who rowed the ship were inside right now.

Hap shaded his eyes and peered up at the castle looming at the crest of the hill. He could see the bell mounted at the top of the road. People hurried down the steep road, coming to watch. A few youngsters tried climbing the steep walls. Hap saw one lose his grip and slide down, landing on his rump in a cloud of dust while his friends laughed.

All work in the harbor had ceased, and crowds gathered on the docks and the roads while sailors clung to the rails of the vessels and climbed the masts. Runners prepared for the race, rubbing oil into their thighs and calves and stretching their legs. They were dressed in short leggings, and many were shirtless. Magador wore only a pair of light knee-length trousers. His body seemed chiseled from stone, and he prowled the ground with the power of a bear and the grace of a cat. His eyes had settled into their half-lidded stare, full of smug malice.

Hap wished the race were already over. His heart was beating faster by the minute, and the inside of his mouth had gone sticky and dry. Umber pulled Bertram aside, and they withdrew to a quiet spot and talked, quickly and seriously. Parley joined them, and he listened intently and nodded while Umber spoke.

"I really am sorry about this," Oates said to Hap.

"I know," Hap replied.

Oates sighed. "I'm causing trouble. I should just wear my muzzle the rest of the time we're here, so nothing else goes wrong."

Hap shrugged. He certainly wished Oates had been wearing it earlier that afternoon. "I'll be all right," Hap said. "I'll just stay out of the way."

"Still, I'd love to see his face if you beat him," muttered Oates.

There was a blare of trumpets, and the runners headed for the place where the race would start, on a dock that extended into the harbor. Umber hurried back to where Hap stood. "Go on, join the rest of them, Hap. Bertram has gone to the finish in case you need him up there. Good luck, and don't make it too obvious that you're not trying!" He grinned and gave Hap a playful punch on the shoulder.

Hap made his way into the crowd of runners. There were a hundred or more, and they all jostled for position—all except Magador, who stood undisturbed at the front of the line, where a ragged line of chalk marked the starting point. *He gets every advantage,* Hap thought bitterly. He let himself be pushed toward the back of the mob, where he could hear whispers among the other runners.

"What's the prize for second place?"

"Ten pieces of gold."

"That's better than the prize for first place: twenty pieces plus Magador's revenge!"

Hap found an open space near the back of the pack. Within a few seconds a brute of a man pushed through the crowd and stood beside him. He didn't look much like a runner. With his twisted nose and battered ears he looked more like a brawler. The man peered sideways at him. "You're that green-eyed boy."

Hap had no idea how to respond to such an obvious statement. "Yes," he finally said.

The man cracked his knuckles. "I hear you're quite the runner."

Hap shrugged. "I don't think I'll win."

The man pushed a thumb into one nostril and cleared out the other with a violent expulsion of air and snot. "You're right. You won't."

When Hap saw the wicked mischief in the fellow's eyes, he turned away.

"Who's your little friend, Pitt?" said a snickering, high-voiced man beside the brawler.

"This is the brat from Kurahaven that everyone's talking about," Pitt said.

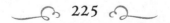

A voice called out from the front of the pack. It was a man with silver hair and a long, drooping mustache. He stood on a barrel with a trumpet in one hand, and the buzz of the crowd instantly died. "Contestants!" he bellowed. "You know the rules. Race to the top, and ring the bell. May the best runner triumph. The race begins when the king lowers his sword."

Hap peered between the shoulders of the men in front of him and saw King Brugador for the first time, at the top of the road. He was a hulking bear of a man with a forked beard and a bald head gleaming in the sun.

The silver-haired man raised the trumpet to his lips. For a moment the only sound came from the gulls coasting on the breezes overhead, and then the instrument moaned a long, low note. Every eye in the crowd turned toward the king as he raised his sword. The trumpet's mournful note echoed and died, and the sword slashed to the ground. The runners surged forward, and the crowd roared.

CHAPTER
19

Hap had a simple plan: drift along with the crowd, so that he didn't get run over from behind, and then slowly let the others pass him. But he didn't even make it off the dock.

Pitt, the brute beside him, stuck a leg in his path. Hap felt a searing jolt in his shin and tumbled hard onto the planks. His palms flared with pain as splinters pierced the skin.

"Oops!" shouted Pitt. Hap looked up and cried out. Pitt staggered over him, pretending to lose his balance, and let his dead weight drop onto Hap's back. Hap felt all the wind forced from his lungs. He heard noise from the spectators: shocked gasps, empathetic groans, bellowing laughter.

Pitt laughed. "Sorry, didn't see you down there!" He put

a hand on the side of Hap's head and used it to push off, grinding Hap's cheek into the planks. Then he let himself fall again. Sharp pain stabbed at Hap's ribs.

"Now I've slipped again," Pitt cried. "Dear me, I hope I'm not hurting you!"

All Hap could do was whimper. With his head pinned sideways, he could see the rest of the pack flying away. Magador was already five strides ahead of the next runner and had turned onto the steep road.

Hap drew in enough breath to squeak out some words: "Get off me!"

"Can't you see I'm trying?" Hap felt a knee press hard against the small of his back. "Whoops again!" Pitt shouted, and he let his full weight crash down for a third time. It was suddenly impossible for Hap to breathe, and a white panic flooded his brain.

The sound of the crowd changed abruptly. One minute it was laughter and catcalls. Then it was an astonished collective gasp. The crushing weight disappeared. Hap rolled on his side to look. He saw a bug-eyed Pitt pinwheel through the air and fall into the harbor, sending up a plume of water. The sailors on the ships howled and applauded.

Oates stood beside Hap with his jaw jutting and chest heaving. He lifted Hap by the arm and set him on his feet. Hap wobbled and steadied himself as pain flared in his chest and his back. "Thank you, Oates," he managed to wheeze.

"I've had enough of these people. How about you?" Oates said.

Hap nodded. Everyone was staring. He saw Umber push to the front of the crowd.

Oates snorted. "To be honest, I think you should win this bloody race."

Hap felt something like lightning course through his limbs. Umber nodded at him once, just a subtle jab of the chin. Hap saw the pack of runners spreading apart as the swiftest pulled ahead. Magador was on the third of seven switchbacks.

"Will you go already?" shouted Oates, and Hap was flying before the words were done.

He didn't run like other people. It was another one of the odd gifts he'd been given when some mysterious process had turned him into a Meddler. His legs were strangely powerful— when he sprinted and pushed off with all his might, he covered three times the length of an ordinary stride. The ground fell away and rushed under him, until he touched down and a single foot propelled him again, picking up speed.

Hap glanced up and saw Magador at the fourth switchback. Fifty strides behind the prince a cluster of five runners tussled as they ran. One man was hurled over the side, and he tumbled onto a pack of runners below, bringing them all down in a heap. Hap gritted his teeth and ran harder. He didn't head for where the road met the level of the harbor—he raced at the steep slope, bent his knees, and sprang high into the air, landing halfway up the first stretch of road. Shouts of surprise arose from the spectators.

A movement beside Hap caught his attention. It was the man with the high-pitched voice who'd spoken to Pitt—lying in wait, it seemed. The man rushed at him with wild, goggling eyes and spittle flying from his teeth. "Quit now if you know what's good for you!" he squealed. Hap sprang again and heard a yelp of dismay as the villain clawed vainly at the air that he had just occupied.

Hap touched down on the second level of the road, already thirty feet above the harbor and amid the slower runners. Men rushed by, and a denser swarm threatened to trample him. Hap sprang again and soared to the third level. Magador was sprinting hard, two levels above, with his arms pumping and nose flaring like a bull's. The prince looked down at his competition, and his face twisted with fury when he saw Hap. He called to someone behind him and stabbed toward Hap with his finger.

Just as he prepared to leap again, Hap heard a voice beside him. "It ain't worth it, kid." A man was lying nearby, clutching a broken arm. Hap ignored him and dropped to a crouch with muscles coiled. The road above was crowded with runners. Hap spotted a gap and timed his leap to land inside it. But he hung in the air too long. The moment he landed, a shocked runner collided with him, and they both fell.

"Where'd *you* come from?" demanded the runner, grabbing a bloodied knee.

"Sorry!" cried Hap. He scrambled to his feet and looked up. Magador was around the sixth of seven turns. Directly above, a man stood and stared at him, shaking his head is if to say, *Don't even try*.

It was easy enough to avoid the man. Hap leaped at an angle, coming down several strides away. And when the man rushed at him, Hap sprang out of reach. Cheers came from below, and from people lining the top of the hill above. He landed off balance and stumbled forward to avoid a dozen men sprinting past. They were red-faced, panting, and exchanging punches as they ran. When they passed, Hap stepped into the middle of the road again.

Magador was rounding the last turn, with a straight sprint to the bell. He looked down as Hap looked up. Their eyes met, and Magador laughed.

Hap jumped. Without pause he touched down and soared again, landing in front of Magador. He leaped a final time, with all the force his legs could muster, and heard the wind in his ears. When he finally landed, the bell was before him, with an astounded King Brugador standing beside it. The king of Sarnica was the size of a bear and looked twice as savage. "What foul magic is this?" he growled.

Magador was nearly there, slowing as he arrived. His smile had turned to a snarl, and his breath hissed between his bared teeth.

Hap froze. The bell was within reach. All he had to do was pull its dangling cord, but he hesitated. He glanced around and saw, behind the king, a woman in a gold-trimmed gown leaning forward in a chair. She had a small face dominated by large dark eyes, framed by cascades of curling brown hair, and topped by a golden crown with glittering red gems. *She's lovely,* thought Hap. Both she and the girl beside her gaped at Hap—whether it was because of his green eyes, his enormous leaps, or his reckless behavior Hap was not sure.

Magador arrived, looking ready to murder. The crowd that wreathed them fell strangely silent. The prince scowled at the woman and then growled at Hap, keeping his voice low even as his eyes bulged with fury. "Well? Do it already! Ring the bell!"

Hap sensed the king glowering down, and he looked into the merciless eyes of the prince. "I do this for Sophie," he said, and he grabbed the cord and yanked. A clear, piercing note rang out. There were more gasps than cheers from the crowd.

A servant came to drop a cloth over Magador's shoulders, but the prince shoved the poor fellow away and took a step toward Hap. "You're not even breathing hard," he snarled. Magador's chest was heaving, and perspiration rained from his brow. Behind them other runners dashed up and touched the bell.

Hap gulped. He couldn't think of a thing to say. Seconds passed that felt like years, as Magador loomed with his jaw grinding. Behind him the king's breath sounded like a giant bellows.

A hand came down on Hap's shoulder, and he nearly yelped aloud. It was Bertram, thrusting a cup into his hands. "You must be parched," Bertram said, stepping between Hap and the prince. "Drink, Happenstance."

Thank you, Hap thought, grateful for the timely intervention. He guzzled the water. Magador glared at a group of other runners who loitered at a safe distance from the prince. Hap understood why Magador was furious: It was their job to ensure the prince's victory, and they had failed. But how could they have known that Hap would barely use the road at all, except as a springboard to the top?

"Your Highness! Your Highness!" shouted a voice from

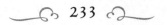

below. It was the silver-haired man who had started the race at the docks. He was riding a horse up the same road. The horse clattered to a stop beside the bell, and the man dismounted. He hurried to where the king stood, and bowed to the enormous man. They exchanged muttered words, and the king nodded. The silver-haired man went to the bell and tugged on the cord so that the bell pealed out loud and long, quieting the crowd.

"There has been an infraction of the rules," shouted the silver-haired man.

"I thought there weren't any rules," Hap said quietly.

Bertram nudged him. *"Shhh,"* he whispered.

"At the start of the race the contestant from Kurahaven received assistance from a spectator," the silver-haired man continued. "This is forbidden, and by rule that contestant is disqualified. The victory therefore goes to Prince Magador." The crowd responded with halfhearted cheers, which soon fell to a gossipy buzz.

The prince's men gathered around him, whooping and laughing. If the prince was happy with his victory, he did not let it show. He scowled at Hap with a look that sent chills through Hap's bones.

The woman in the chair watched Hap as well. When Hap looked her way, he thought her mouth turned slightly up at the corner. The girl had retreated to hide behind her shoulder, but she peered out, staring at Hap with a curious expression.

Bertram tugged at Hap's arm and whispered, "Let's get you out of here. Magador is sure to punch someone, and I don't want it to be you."

They hustled through the streets, back to the friendly Hare and Hedgehog. Umber struggled mightily to keep the grin off his face. He leaned forward and whispered to Hap across the table. "Did you really say, 'I do this for Sophie'?"

Hap blushed. "It just came out of me. I wasn't thinking."

"He said it, all right," Bertram said, laughing.

Oates honked into a handkerchief. A tear rolled down his cheek, and he reached over and squeezed Hap's shoulder. It was meant to be a gesture of appreciation, but Oates clamped down so hard that Hap dropped his spoon into his stew.

A stranger walked by the other side of the table. He leaned over Umber's shoulder and looked directly at Hap, after glancing around to see if he was being watched. "Wonderful!" he whispered, barely moving his lips. He moved off without another word.

Bertram watched him go. He clasped his hands together on the table before him and leaned toward Hap. "Well, Happenstance. Despite officially losing the race, you have managed to embarrass both the king and the prince in one stroke. And in front of the prince's wife, too!"

"His *wife*?" Hap shrank into his seat.

Bertram nodded. "That was Fay. The princess. She was stolen in a raid on another island, by the way. Yes, losing in front of her did not make Magador a happy man, I'm sure."

Hap couldn't stand to meet anyone's eyes. "I'm terribly sorry."

Bertram grinned. "Sorry? Most of the people in this land would shake your hand, Happenstance, if they weren't scared to death of being seen doing it."

Umber's smile faded a little. "It's that bad, isn't it?"

"You have no idea how cruel those two are," Bertram said over the rim of his cup. He turned to Oates and Hap. "This kingdom was taken twenty years ago by force. Brugador holds it by the throat, with a loyal army to defend him. Those who speak against him are dead, or suffering in the Midnight Dungeons."

"And diplomacy has failed?"

"Utterly," Bertram said. "There is nothing more I can do here, Umber. I'm leaving after these games." He brooded for a moment, tracing the rim of his cup with his finger. "You know me. It's not my way to surrender in the pursuit of peace. But when I speak to Brugador and Magador, and look into their eyes, I see something terribly familiar. It's the same sort of grasping ambition and thirst for blood that I encountered firsthand long ago." Bertram rubbed his temple and glanced at Hap. "Umber, does your ward know my history?"

Umber shook his head. "That should come only from you."

"But you've chronicled the story?"

Umber nodded. "Only for my private collection."

Hap straightened in his seat as Bertram leaned closer.

"How old are you, Happenstance?" Bertram asked.

Hap looked at Umber with his mouth ajar. It was a good question, now that he thought of it. He was born some eighteen years ago, but many of those years had somehow passed in the blink of an eye.

Umber answered for him. "Let's say twelve."

Bertram squinted and blinked, pondering the vague reply. "Twelve, you say. All right. When I was about your age, Hap, I had a terrible ordeal. I fell under the spell of a wicked spirit that lurked inside a mirror. In those days I dreamed of inheriting my father's barony, and of the battles I'd win against my kingdom's enemies. The mirror had a long history of corrupting the people who fell under its spell. It saw the thirst for war and glory that was in my heart, and it twisted my mind, bringing out the worst in me. I became evil, Happenstance, and I plotted unspeakable things. But I was lucky, because I was saved by the people who cared for me. Parley was one of them, in fact."

Bertram rubbed a hand across his chest and arms, as if soothing old wounds. "And that is how I came to know evil when I see it. But there is no terrible mirror at work this time—just a legacy of violence, passed from father to son. Brugador and Magador have only themselves to blame. And they are beyond redemption."

Umber lowered his voice. "And there is no other . . . recourse?"

Bertram leaned closer, so that only Umber, Hap, and Oates could hear. "Do you speak of rebellion? No, Umber. Not on this isle. You know me—I am a peacemaker, not a warrior. Still, if any kingdom deserved to be taken down, it is this one. But the people are too afraid, and Brugador is too strong. I've even reached out to foreign parties, but none are willing to help. There will be no uprising, and no invasion."

"We should get out of this stinking place," said Oates. Hap nodded vigorously.

"After we see the dragons," Umber said.

Oates snorted. "Who cares about the dragons? Why don't we just—"

Umber's brow furrowed, and his voice rose. "*I care* about the dragons, Oates. We came all this way to see them, and we'll stay until we do."

Umber's temper didn't flare very often. Hap shrank in his seat. Oates stood so quickly that his chair clattered to the floor behind him. "I'm taking a walk," Oates said. "In fact I think I'm going back to our ship. I'd rather hang around with those spider monsters than these disgusting royals."

Umber shook his head. "You're staying right here."

The veins in Oates's neck bulged. "I don't want to."

Umber stood and put his fists on the table. "You work for me, Oates. We need you here."

"Need me for what?" Oates said, crossing his burly arms.

Umber sighed. "You saw what Hap did in that race. And you know what happened the last time a young person bested Magador. Despite the prince's so-called victory, his pride is wounded, and he's savage enough to seek revenge. I need you to keep Hap safe, Oates. Please." Umber put a hand on Hap's shoulder. Hap didn't know how to feel about it. The only expression he could manage was a wincing smile.

"It's important, Mister Oates," said Bertram.

Oates's angry expression melted a bit. "Fine. For Hap."

"Excellent," Umber said. "Now, let us keep a low profile for the rest of the day and give Magador time to cool down. Then it's the Dragon Games tomorrow."

Their room was large, with curtained beds in the four corners. Oates snored like thunder, while Umber, who could sleep through a volcanic eruption, drifted off to sleep after washing his healing wound and wrapping a new bandage around his head.

Hap, as always, was awake, and he was afflicted with an overwhelming boredom. He wished he were back at the Aerie, where he could wander freely while the rest of the household slept, and poke into all of the interesting books and artifacts of that strange place. Here he could not leave the room. Umber had told him to stay put, and Hap hardly needed to be told as much. Not for a million gems would he step outside and risk an encounter with the cruel prince.

He passed the time thinking about the people he knew. He hoped Prince Galbus was still sober and determined to assume the throne. Sophie, he figured, was busy with her works of art, or practicing with her bow. Thimble would be prowling the dark corners of the Aerie, searching for rodents to slay. Balfour would be home by now, seeking a way to save Caspar from the bidmis. Smudge would dive into the same problem with all his manic energy, because it was his brother who needed saving.

The notion of brothers brought Eldon Penny to mind. What was Eldon doing now? Umber had promised to find him a good position so he could earn a decent living. Hap wondered if he would ever see his brother again. Maybe he would tell him the bizarre truth some day. Or maybe it would be better if he never knew. After all, why would Eldon be happy to find his lost brother, if it wasn't the same boy he'd once known?

The thought panged his heart, which only added to his catalog of aches. Hap poked at his torso, bruised in a dozen places at the start of the race. He stood and stretched, and strolled over to the room's sole window, which overlooked a castle courtyard. Most of the other windows surrounding the open space were dark. A few glowed with a dim light, as their room did, with its single narrow candle burning on a table by the door.

A shiver ran down his arms, like wind across wheat. He folded his arms against the sudden chill. Seconds later a fever swept through his body. His eyes felt on the verge of boiling. "What now?" he whispered, though he knew what it meant. He saw a filament in the air, emerging from his chest.

There was something odd about this thread. It was short, for one thing—only a foot or two long, and slanting to the floor. And the color was strange—ugly, gray and purple, like a bruise. He put his hand through it, knowing that it would make a sound that only he could hear. And it did, but the sound was dim and unpleasant.

Near his foot a beetle crawled across the floor. As Hap watched it, a strange glow surrounded the bug, and an impulse seized him. It was suddenly very important that he touch the beetle and perhaps hold it in his hand. He bent low to reach for it, and he saw the color of the thread change as he moved. At the same instant he heard a whistling sound just above his head, and a *thunk* and a *twang* across the room.

An arrow was embedded in the door, its feathered end still vibrating.

Hap pressed his back to the wall beside the window. *I should be dead,* he thought. He risked a quick peek at the courtyard. It was empty. He slid down the wall until he was sitting and dropped his head into his hands. *Was the archer Magador, or one of his minions?* He supposed he'd better wake Umber and Oates and let them know, once his heart stopped thumping so fast.

It occurred to him that the green-eyed man that he'd come to think of as Willy Nilly would be pleased by what just happened. It was *derring-do or duly die,* and while ducking to pick up a beetle wasn't very courageous, at least he hadn't died. His powers had saved him.

"I don't care," he whispered. "I just want to go home."

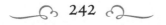

to the Aerie today... curious specimen he is... strength defies belief. He can uproot a good-sized tree and lift a stone as big as himself. But he suffers from a remarkable curse: He can speak only the truth. Thank heavens I don't share the same affliction. This fellow wants me to cure the he... I will try, but it has occurred to me that such a man would be extremely useful. Even if I find the cure, will...

CHAPTER
20

"Oates, I realize we're trying to keep Hap safe. But please stop looking like you're going to crush the first person who gets too close," Umber said as they walked down the crowded street.

"You told me to look for trouble," Oates said. His fists were bunched, and he scowled at every person who looked their way.

"Yes, look *for* trouble. Not look *like* trouble," replied Umber. "Anyway, Hap, it occurred to me: I believe you had a breakthrough last night."

"Do you mean with the filaments?" asked Hap.

"Exactly. You've started to understand what they mean. That thread told you that you were in mortal danger and showed you how to avoid it. Some strange instinct illuminated the object that would save your life. You actually meddled with fate, Hap. How exciting!" When he saw the expression on Hap's face, Umber added: "At least it would be exciting if someone hadn't tried to put an arrow in you."

"Where are we going, anyway?" grumbled Oates. "I thought the Dragon Games were at the archery field."

"No, there is a special arena. Someplace we haven't seen yet. Ah, that must be it there."

The crowd streamed into a building that resembled an enormous half-barrel. It was made of dark stone, nearly windowless, and seemed ancient. A wagon rolled into view, pulled by horses and surrounded by men with axes. A heavy wooden crate was on the wagon, with a man standing on top with a spear. Hap heard a squeal as the crate shook. The man on top grinned and jabbed his spear between the slats of wood. A louder squeal followed.

The color left Umber's face. His eyes narrowed as the wagon rolled into the arena through a large archway, and a second wagon with another crate followed.

"What's going to happen in there?" Hap asked.

"I don't know," Umber replied.

A cry pealed from the crowd ahead. "Umber! There you are! Umber!" It was Hameron, dressed in clothes so ornate that they were almost a parody of fine dress. He was waving a red cane over his head. They could hardly avoid him, since he stood in the entrance they had to take.

Umber didn't bother to smile. "Hello, Hameron."

The head of Hameron's cane was a tiny skull with a reptilian look. He put both hands atop it and grinned at Umber. "Good news! The king wants you near him during the show."

"Is that so," said Umber.

"It is," said Hameron. "Word of your reputation has reached his royal ear, my friend. He knows of your interest in the magical beasts of the world and would like you to be with him when the dragons are at last unveiled."

Umber looked at Hap and Oates and shrugged. "Well. We can hardly turn down a royal invitation."

"Huh. Bigger on the inside," Umber said, blinking to help his eyes adjust to the dim light inside the arena. It seemed that way to Hap as well, because the wide oval floor was hollowed out deep below. It felt like a place that had been there for a thousand years, primitive and austere, built of dirt and mortar and stone. Flaming pots ringed the flat oval. There was a dark tunnel at the far end, barred by a gate where a pair of guards stood, hugging shields to their chests and crossing spears. The air inside was warm and heavy and tainted by greasy smoke that stung Hap's eyes.

Hameron led them down between rows of stone seats, all filled with spectators, half of whom seemed to be the king's warriors. Just above the arena floor was a wide platform with gilded chairs and a throne that was barely wide enough to contain the bulk of King Brugador. Magador was beside the king, and then Fay, Magador's bride. The same girl stood behind the princess. She looked directly at Hap and then leaned forward to whisper in Fay's ear. The princess peered at them from the corner of her eye.

The king grunted when he saw Umber and Hameron coming, and gestured to the empty seat at his right hand. Hameron moved toward the chair, but Brugador put a hand to his chest and pushed him back. "Not you. The visitor sits there."

Hameron's face turned the shade of a beet, but he forced a smile and bowed. "Your wish is all that matters, Your Majesty."

Umber cleared his throat, made a bow of his own, and sat by the king, while Hameron took the next seat down. Umber leaned forward to look past the king and nod to the prince. Magador, who slouched in his chair and looked half asleep, barely moved his fingers in response. The prince's gaze shifted to Hap, and Hap shivered at the malice under the half-closed lids. Before he looked away, Hap noticed the strange way

Magador was dressed, with light armor on his chest and chain mail on his arms and legs.

A dozen soldiers surrounded the king. Their presence, and the swords and spears they held, made Hap feel like a sheep inside a den of wolves. When Oates sat in an unoccupied chair, Hap hurried into the seat beside him.

They were close enough to hear the rumbling voice of the king. "So, Umber. Hameron tells me you travel the world in search of monstrous creatures."

Umber nodded. "True, Your Highness, but not all are monstrous. I find many beautiful."

The king snorted. "But you've never seen a living dragon?"

"I have not, Your Highness."

Brugador leaned forward and sneered toward Hameron. "Umber, that little toad is quite pleased with his triumph. Thinks he's bested you at last." Hameron smiled weakly under the disdainful glare of the king.

Umber kept an even expression. "It was a daring feat, taking those eggs from under the dragon's watchful eyes."

The king chuckled and sat back in his throne. He scratched at his beard, and a crumb of bread tumbled out. "But you would not have taken the eggs at all, would you?"

Umber crossed his legs and folded his hands on one knee.

"No, Your Highness, I would have observed what I could and left them there."

Brugador stared. He seemed to be waiting for Umber to lose his nerve and look away, but Umber met his eyes with the patience of a cat.

"Well," the king finally said, smacking his lips. "If you object to the theft of the eggs, I wonder if what happens next will offend you."

Umber's gaze did not waver. "I imagine that depends on what happens next."

Oates prodded Hap's leg and pointed. At the far end of the arena a flickering light appeared in the tunnel. The guards pulled the barred gate open. There was an unpleasant rusty screech as it swung inward, and the buzz of the crowd fell to a hush.

Prince Magador stood, suddenly alert, and the armed men behind him thumped their spears on the floor. There was a halfhearted scattering of cheers among the crowd as Magador loped down the steps and vaulted the low wall that surrounded the arena floor.

"Where is he going?" muttered Oates. Hap shrugged and pressed his arms against his roiling stomach. He stole another glance at the princess, who watched without expression as her husband strutted across the arena floor. Hap noticed the girl looking at him and turned quickly away, feeling a blush in his cheeks.

One of the wagons, drawn now by four men hauling ropes, rolled out of the tunnel. More men followed, armed with long spears. The gate swung shut behind them. A man mounted the wagon and climbed onto the box. Umber was struggling to remain impassive, but Hap saw his fingernails sink into the arms of his chair.

Magador stepped to the center of the arena. Attendants brought him a jeweled helmet and armed him with a double-bladed battle-ax and a shield with a spike at its center. The prince widened his stance and crouched and then banged the shield twice with his ax. At that signal the man atop the box threw a latch. The front of the box fell open. The crowd inhaled.

Nothing happened. The men on either side stuck their spears between the slats, prodding. There was a squeal, and the box shook, and finally the beast inside scrambled into the torchlight.

The exclamation came from a thousand mouths at once: "Ooh!" Time crawled and perception sharpened as Hap beheld the dragon. The creature looked dangerous and lovely at the same time, with a sleek body and a spiny sail that ran down its back. The head and feet were oversized, in the manner of any baby animal. It seemed to be made entirely of precious materials: gold and copper scales, silver claws, and sapphire eyes.

"Look what they've done to it," muttered Oates. Hap groaned when he saw what Oates meant. The dragon's legs were chained, so the creature could only shuffle. Wire wrapped around its jaw clamped its mouth shut. Cloth was bound on the end of its tail; Hap supposed the tail was barbed or clubbed and posed a threat. But he was sickened most by what they'd done to the wings. They were underdeveloped, and too small for flight. But still they were damaged, with raw scars still visible, and they could only flap uselessly at the dragon's sides.

"They've cut its wings, the filthy cowards," Oates fumed under his breath.

The chains binding its feet rattled as the dragon tried to back under the wagon. But the men wouldn't let it hide. They jabbed with their spears, forcing it into the open, where Magador waited, twirling his ax.

Hap turned away, unable to watch the dragon's fate. Umber watched with his palm across his mouth. Fay pressed her lips together so tightly that the color was drained from them, while the girl behind her hid her face in the princess's tumbling brown hair. Sounds rippled through the crowd: shouts, laughter, moans of dismay. Hap stuck his thumbs in his ears and squeezed his eyes shut.

When a cheer arose, he opened his eyes for a moment, then shut them again. But an unwelcome image still pried into his brain: Magador with his helmet pushed back from his grinning face, holding a bloody prize high for the crowd to see.

Hap heard the awful, animal roar of the king: "I slew the first myself, Umber, did you know? Now my son is a dragon slayer with me! Brugador Dragon Slayer! Magador Dragon Slayer!"

Wagon wheels rumbled again, and the doors screeched open. Hap kept his eyes closed until he felt a tap on his knee. Umber was hunched before him, speaking softly. "Are you all right?"

Hap shook his head. "Can we leave?"

Umber glanced back toward the king and shook his head. "Sorry, Hap. That's impossible. We've already done enough to offend Brugador and his son. You have to be strong, until this is over."

A sour taste bubbled up Hap's throat. "How much longer? How many more are they going to kill?"

"Two, I think," Umber whispered back.

"How can you stand this?" Hap asked. "You of all people."

Umber straightened, taken aback. "Sometimes there's nothing you can do." He returned to his seat by the king. Before long another wagon rolled out of the tunnel, bearing another dragon, and other warriors gathered around to face it. Hap covered his eyes. Once a gasp from the crowd made him look. The dragon had knocked one of its adversaries to the ground, wounding the man. But others rushed in, prodding with spears and keeping the creature at bay. Minutes later the king's roar told Hap that another dragon had died.

By the time a third dragon had been cruelly slaughtered, he felt nauseous and weary. And just when he thought the ordeals of the day were through, he heard the booming growl of the king: "Umber! You and your party will join me for dinner."

Oates paced their room, slamming the stone wall with one fist at each turn. "This makes me sick. You're a powerful man, Umber. There must be something you can do."

Umber rubbed his brow with his fingertips. "Don't you both understand? I have no leverage here. And believe me, we must not anger this king any more than we already have."

Hap felt a twinge in his heart. Umber had always seemed an extraordinary man, infinitely resourceful and quick to act when he perceived cruelty or injustice. For the first time since meeting Umber, Hap felt disappointed.

"I'm not going to this dinner," Oates said, folding his arms.

"Yes, you are," Umber snapped. "Brugador may be one of the foulest swine to ever walk the earth, but you will dine with him tonight. I'm serious, Oates. You too, Happenstance. One does not snub a king."

There were three dozen or more at the dinner, at a rambling table cluttered with bowls, candles, pitchers, and platters. Hap found it hard to enjoy the food, since he was sickened by the presence of so many at the table. King Brugador sat at one end. There was a roaring fire in the hearth at his back, giving his vast bulk a halo of orange. Hameron was near the king, and a bored-looking Magador was at the opposite end.

Around the table were guests from other island kingdoms that were allies or conquests of Sarnica. Some shared the cruel nature of Brugador, while others suffered in his presence. Bertram sat across from Hap and offered a tight smile whenever their eyes met.

There were no women at the table. Hap wished that the princess were there. Something about Fay's grace and beauty would have made the occasion easier to endure. And if she had been there, the girl might have been with her too. Hap was suddenly aware that he wanted to see her again, to catch her staring his way another time. He wondered what her name was.

Hap's body tensed as Hameron stood and wandered toward them with his eye on Umber. "What did you think of my dragons, Umber?"

Umber sipped his wine. "As magnificent as I dreamed they'd be. Too wonderful for the fate you've given them."

One of Hameron's eyes twitched. He leaned closer and spoke softly. "Umber . . . I . . . actually did not realize what my patron would do with them. Those duels . . . would not have been my choice."

Umber's expression hardened. "Nevertheless." Hameron wilted under his stern glare, and Umber drummed his fingers on the table. "But let's put that aside for a moment, Hameron. I have a question for you. With your knowledge of the strange and magical, you might know the answer."

Hameron straightened and put a hand over his heart. "It would please me if I did."

"Good. What do you know about the bidmis?"

"The bidmis?" Hameron's brow lifted. "Don't tell me you've found them."

Umber waved the question away. "It's for my chronicles. I just want to know if you're familiar with their legend, and their curse."

Hameron puffed his chest. "In fact I have done my share of research into that tale. The man who awakens them is

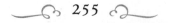

their master for life. They will do whatever the master bids, and are capable of almost anything. Tempting, isn't it? Although the materials that I have seen hint at a dark side to their obedience. It wouldn't be a curse without a dark side, would it?"

"True enough," Umber said. "But I've always wondered— is there a way out for the master? If he wants to end the 'curse,' such as it is."

"Of course there is," Hameron said, grinning.

Umber waited for the answer.

Hameron chuckled. "Death!"

"And nothing else? No other escape?"

"Not to my knowledge." For a moment Hameron's arrogance faded. "Getting what you desire often comes at a price, doesn't it, Umber? That's the lesson of the bidmis, I suppose." His shoulders jerked, and his smug demeanor returned. "But really, I doubt they even exist."

Umber shrugged. "You're probably right."

Hameron extended his hand. "I enjoy these talks, Umber. We have so much to share."

Umber looked at the hand for an uncomfortable moment before finally taking it. Hameron noticed the hesitation. He nodded curtly and returned to sulk in his seat near the king. A few minutes later Hap saw him whisper into the king's ear.

Brugador guzzled the last of his wine and slammed the goblet down. A trembling servant rushed to refill it, as the king leaned forward to peer down the length of the table.

"Umber," he growled. "What is the name of your bodyguard?"

Oates was hunched over his plate, gnawing on a meaty bone. He froze in mid-bite and looked sideways.

"Bodyguard, Your Highness? I think you mean Oates," Umber replied.

"Oates," sneered the king. He had a voice like thunder, and when he spoke, the room fell silent. "You're the fellow who tossed a man into the harbor."

Oates dropped the bone onto his plate and put his hands flat on the table. "Right. I did that."

Brugador used his dinner knife to pry dirt from under his thumbnail. "A man as powerful as you could serve me well. I pay my private guard handsomely. Perhaps I could be your employer, instead of Umber. Would you like that?"

Oates kept his eyes lowered. "I would not."

The king's beard twitched. "Why not?"

"Because I don't like you."

There were gulps from the other guests. The guards that surrounded the table broadened their stances. Brugador grinned fiercely, and his brow shadowed his dark eyes. He

257

turned to Hameron. "You were right, Hameron. This man *is* compelled to speak the truth."

Hameron looked at Umber, flicking his eyebrows. Oates turned toward Umber as well, silently pleading. Umber raised the fingers of one hand and mouthed silent words: *It's all right.*

"So, Oates, you don't care for me," the king said. "I wonder if you are the only one. Tell us, has Umber spoken ill of me?"

Oates groaned. "Yes." He dug his hand into a pocket inside his vest.

Silence smothered the room. Hap could barely breathe as Brugador, clearly enjoying this unusual game, went on with his questions. "Really? What did—hold on, what are you doing there?"

From his pocket Oates had pulled his muzzle—a piece of leather that covered his mouth and tied around the back of his head. He worked frantically to knot the strings. "I'm putting this on," he answered, his voice already muffled.

The king slammed his fist on the table, upending the goblet and spilling a dark pool of wine. "Take it off! Put it away!" The king's soldiers leveled their weapons.

"Do as he says, Oates," Umber said.

Oates's shoulders slumped. He stuffed the muzzle back in his pocket. "Why did you bring me here?" he said to Umber. The rims of his eyes had begun to redden.

The prince leaned forward, baring his teeth. "What did Umber say against my father, you great oaf?"

As Oates fought the irresistible urge to reply, it seemed to induce a terrible pain. He groaned, and spittle flew from the gaps in his gritted teeth. When he answered, it was a hoarse mutter. "He said Brugador is one of the foulest swine to walk the earth."

"What else?" said the king.

"He said you murdered your way to the throne, and you smell like bad meat."

Hap looked at a circle of shocked faces around the table. Three of the guards had crept behind Oates, eager to strike. Beside him Hap heard Umber whisper, "Didn't know his memory was that good."

"Another question for you, Oates," Brugador said.

"Please, no more," Oates said. He covered his face with his hands.

Brugador looked like a beast closing in for the kill. "Hameron told me that Umber would be offended by my Dragon Games and would try to put a stop to them. Does Umber intend anything of the sort?"

"No," Oates muttered, shaking his head. "He says it is not our place to interfere."

The king nodded. He thrust a dirty finger toward Bertram.

"Furthermore, Oates, you and Umber have been seen in the company of that man there: Bertram Charmaigne. The so-called peacemaker who came here to tame my son and me. Some suspect that Bertram might be in touch with my enemies inside and outside my kingdom, plotting to overthrow my rule. Is that true, Oates?"

Oates thumped the table with his fists. A tear trickled down his face. He turned to glare at the king. "No. Bertram said there can be no rebellion and no invasion. Your army is too strong, and your enemies are too afraid. So your foul kingdom is safe." Oates's chair scraped as he stood up. "That's enough. I'm leaving. And I'll thump anyone who tries to stop me."

The guards behind Oates exchanged nervous glances, and their swords quivered in the air. Magador stood up, with a knife in his hand that flashed in the torchlight.

Brugador's enormous chair groaned as he leaned back and laughed. "Ha! Let the truth teller go! He's done me a great favor."

Umber prodded Hap's arm, and they both stood. "My ward and I will take our leave as well, Your Majesty," Umber said. "And I must apologize, of course, for those unkind words."

Bertram got to his feet and bowed toward both ends of the table. "If you will pardon me, it's best if I leave as well.

For good, I think. My efforts here have clearly amounted to nothing. Perhaps time will soften your heart, Your Majesty, and we might speak again. In the meantime I will leave with the morning tide."

As they left the room, Hap heard a muttered joke and a burst of laughter behind them.

They walked at a brisk pace through the castle halls. Hap was sure the king's men would spring from every corner with swords stabbing and axes flying. Normally, the presence of Oates would reassure him, but the big fellow trudged along in a daze, sniffling and staring at the floor.

When they reached their room, Umber eased the door shut. While Oates stood with his great shoulders heaving, Umber did a curious thing: He lit three candles and placed them on the windowsill. "Take a seat, Oates," he said when he turned around.

"Right," said Oates. He seized a chair and flung it down with such violence that its shattered pieces clattered off every wall as Hap and Umber danced to avoid the flying debris. Oates crumpled to his knees and clutched his hair. "Umber," he said with a moan. "I could not help it. Oh, why did you let me come with you? Why do you say anything at all when I am around? Look what I have done. They'll try to kill us before we leave. You know they will. But they'll have to take me first, I promise you."

Umber knelt by Oates's side. "Oates, my friend. Put your mind at rest. I'm the one who must apologize to you."

Oates looked up. His lip trembled. "What? Why?"

A sly grin teased the corner of Umber's mouth. "I've been using you. You've been manipulated, by me and Bertram. But it's for a good cause, I assure you."

Oates stared, wagging his head from side to side.

The skin between Hap's eyebrows furrowed. "What do you mean, Lord Umber?"

The sly grin blossomed into a wide smile. "Oates told the truth as he knew it. But he was really passing along a lie. There will be an uprising after all. I've been corresponding with Bertram for months, my friends. Brugador's enemies are going to attack from many fronts, with foreign assistance. It will happen before dawn this very night, in fact. And during the confusion we're going to get away with the dragon's eggs."

Hap gaped at Umber, feeling dizzy. "We're going to take the eggs?"

"Steal them, actually!" Umber nodded happily, and then his eyes widened with alarm as Oates sprang up, gripped the front of his shirt, and lifted him until his legs dangled off the floor.

"You *used* me?" Oates cried, shaking Umber.

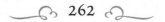

"Not so loud," Umber said, patting Oates's forearm. "I had to, Oates. Bertram said the king was growing wary and thinking about calling all of his forces back to the city. That would have doomed the rebellion. So we used you to throw him off the scent, you see? Tonight they'll celebrate far too much, and the timing of the attack will be perfect."

Oates lowered Umber to the floor with a dazed look in his eye. Then the big fellow started to hum to himself and began the oddest jig Hap had ever seen, grinning, twirling his arms, and kicking his legs. "Ha!" Oates sang. "I told a lie! I told a lie! Can you believe it, Hap? I actually told a lie!"

The dance and song were so absurd that Hap had to laugh along with him. "But Lord Umber," Hap finally said. "How are we going we steal the eggs?"

"We'll need some help, of course," Umber replied. There was a scratching sound at the window. Just beyond the three candles Hap saw a familiar head and multilegged body, dangling outside at the end of a thin strand of silk.

"That was quick," Umber said. "Hello again, Arabell!"

CHAPTER
21

"Are you sure nobody but me can see the *Silkship?"* Hap asked. He braced himself against the sill and held his breath, because Arabell was climbing up his leg and onto his shoulder, cooing with delight at the sight of him.

"Not in this darkness," Umber replied. "Just you, and Arabell, perhaps. I believe the spider-folk can see pretty well in the dark."

Through the window Hap watched the ship rise into the night sky, hundreds of feet above the castle. The oval shape was perfectly apparent to him. In fact the ink between the stars above was the only true darkness he ever perceived. "Did Pilot know you planned to steal the eggs?"

"I told him during our journey. And I used Bertram's

courier. Parley to send him a note this morning. Pilot's been hovering overhead since dark, waiting for my signal."

The sight of Arabell had wiped the delighted expression from Oates's face. "Why is that creature here?"

Umber rubbed his palms together. "With her help this ought to be as easy as a walk in the park."

Hap frowned. He could only imagine the obstacles in their way. The halls of the castle were patrolled. The door to the chambers below was guarded. The eggs were locked in a crate, and only Hameron had the key. And the city was surrounded by walls and gates. Besides that, some assassin, most likely Magador, had tried to kill him once and was probably still lurking about.

"Hold on," said Oates. "If there's going to be a rebellion, why do we have to steal them? We can just wait for this pig of a king to be dethroned and ask the rebels for the eggs."

"Rebellions are messy, unpredictable things," Umber replied. "In the chaos of battle anything could happen to those precious eggs. Besides, we can help the cause with this burglary. The king will be distracted and unbalanced before the attack even starts. Let's hope it all succeeds, my friends. This is a place ruled by barbarians, and you can't even get a decent cup of coffee." He clapped his hands. "Let's begin! Oates, snuff those candles and put out the lantern. Hap, see if anyone is lurking in the courtyard who might notice us. Arabell, darling, can you weave us a ladder?"

Hap thought they would climb down from their window. Instead Arabell went up to the roof of the castle, unspooling silk behind her. Within a minute they were climbing the ladder she had woven. Umber bore a pack on his back, into which he'd placed some of the strange bottles he employed in his adventures, and Oates had an empty sack that was meant for the dragon eggs.

They ducked into a shadowy corner on the roof. Umber pointed. "There—that's where we have to go."

Oates responded in the same low whisper. "To those three little towers?"

"They're not towers. They're chimneys," Umber said.

Hap felt a flash of understanding. "Those are the chimneys above the Dragon Incubator—where Hameron is heating up the eggs!"

Umber nodded. "And fortunately for us only one of them is being used."

"We're going down there?" asked Hap, clutching his shirt.

"I am," Umber said. "On Arabell's thread. Oates will haul me and the eggs back up. Your job is to be our lookout, with those wonderful eyes of yours. Now, is it safe to move?"

Hap looked over the roof of the castle. There were tall

watchtowers around it, but no watchmen visible in them. "Yes, it's safe."

We must make a strange sight, Hap thought as they scuttled across the roof: two men, a boy, and a monstrous spider with a human head. They moved as swiftly as they dared, slowed by the dangerous angle of the roof. A slip might send one of them tumbling into the courtyard far below.

Hap saw hot air shimmering out of the central chimney. Somewhere below, a crystal dragon egg sat on a heap of orange coals. But how far below? It had to be a long way, because the incubator was beneath the castle.

Umber tried to peer down the working chimney, but he pulled his face away, squinting and coughing. "Not my brightest move," he said. He stepped to an unused chimney and peered down. Then he moved his hand around the mouth of the chimney and frowned. "Oh, dear," he said.

"What's wrong, Lord Umber?" asked Hap.

Umber tugged at his cheeks. "I may have miscalculated."

Oates rolled his eyes. "You mean you've messed up."

Umber squatted beside the chimney and lowered his head. "I thought the chimney was bigger. I don't think I can fit."

Hap squeezed his eyes closed. He filled his lungs with air and let it whistle out slowly, through his nose. "I can do it," he said. "I'll go."

Umber looked up at him. He smiled, and the corners of his eyes wrinkled. "That's brave of you, Hap. But it's a lot to ask."

While his eyes were closed, Hap was haunted by visions of the poor infant dragons in the arena and finally Magador holding the severed head of a creature that never should have been stolen from its home. "I want to do this."

Hap thought he saw a tear in the corner of Umber's eye. Umber dug into his pack and produced one of his bottles. It was red with dark liquid sloshing inside. "Now, Hameron is a paranoid sort. He didn't allow a lot of people in that chamber, in case someone decided to steal an egg. So it may be empty, or there may be one or two people down there at the most. And so . . ." He held the bottle carefully over the center of the shaft and let it drop. There was a brief silence, and then the tinkle of glass far below.

Hap looked at Umber, questioning.

"That was one of my *sleeper* bottles. A cloud will billow out from that broken vessel and knock out anyone in the vicinity," Umber said. He sat on the roof and crossed his legs. "Wait a few minutes, and it'll be safe to go down. Arabell, can you weave a rope for us while we wait? Not too thin—Oates needs to hold it without cutting himself. And put a loop at the end for Hap's foot, if you don't mind."

Arabell seemed to understand every word he said. Hap watched, fascinated, as she quickly spun a cord.

"That should do it," Umber said. "Oates—would you step away from us for a moment?"

"There's something you don't want me to know," Oates said. He shrugged and walked a few paces away.

Umber drew close to Hap and handed him a key on a silver chain. "This will open the lock on the crate of eggs."

Hap looked at the key. "How did you get this from Hameron?"

"I didn't. But it will work. Take care of this key, Happenstance. It's one of the most precious things I own. It used to belong to Turiana." Hap nodded as he put the chain over his head. It clanked against the other object he wore around his neck: the locket with the enormous pearl that Nima had given him, on a day that felt a hundred years in the past.

Oates returned when Umber waved to him, and he curled most of the cord around his arm. Hap perched on the edge of the chimney, put his foot into the loop, and gripped the rope tight. Umber gave him a sack for the eggs, which Hap slung over one shoulder.

"All right," Hap said, feeling a little light-headed. Before Oates could begin to lower him, Arabell bounded over and perched on his shoulder. Her little claws clutched his shirt tight.

Umber pursed his lips. "Looks like she wants to go with you. But I promised Pilot she'd come to no harm."

"We'll be careful," Hap said. He was glad for some company, even if it was this strange creature. Arabell trilled in reply.

"Don't take any chances," Umber said as Oates began to lower Hap one arm's length at a time. "Give up on the eggs if you have to. Tell us when you're ready to come up—we'll hear you just fine at this end of the shaft. Or yank on the cord to signal us if you can't talk."

Hap's pulse pounded in his ears as he dropped slowly down the chimney. By the time he was halfway down, his clothes were blackened wherever he'd touched the sooty sides, and he had to struggle to keep from coughing. Below he could see the broken glass of the bottle, bathed in a dim orange glow.

Hap knew everyone ought to have been knocked out by Umber's bottle, but he still tensed as his feet touched down. He squatted in the hearth and looked around him. Arabell climbed down from his shoulder. Judging from the devilish grin on her face, she was enjoying the adventure.

There were two men, both slumped on the floor. One was near a table in the center of the room, next to an overturned chair. Hap recognized him at once. "Hameron," he whispered in disgust. The other was a guard, sprawled near the hearth where the stack of coals burned orange-hot. One of the guard's hands was dangerously close to the fire. Hap took a moment to push it out of harm's way.

"Let's not waste any more time," he told Arabell. He hurried to the chest and pulled Umber's key out from inside his shirt. A strange thing happened as he reached for the lock. The key transformed before his eyes. Notches appeared, pegs sprouted, and the key grew shorter and fatter. *No wonder it's precious,* Hap thought. *It can open anything.* He slid the key into the heavy padlock and turned it. The lock sprang open. Beside him Arabell cooed. He tucked the key back down his shirt and lifted the lid. Inside was a heap of the crystal eggs, gently glimmering from within.

Hap was as nervous as a bird. He looked behind him to make sure nobody was approaching before stuffing the eggs into the sack, counting them as he went: . . . *nine, ten, eleven.* "Now we just have to get the one that's cooking," he whispered to Arabell.

But when he looked at the burning pile of coal, there was no egg on top.

"Where did it go?" Hap said. Arabell tapped his knee and pointed. Hap bit the bottom of his lip. "Oh, no. Not good."

The egg had already hatched. A baby dragon, the size of a cat, was in a small cage on the table where Hameron had been sitting. The creature lay on its side with its chest gently rising and falling, knocked out by Umber's bottle.

Hap lugged the bag and the caged dragon to where the silk rope dangled at the bottom of the chimney. He peered up and saw Oates and Umber high above, looking down anxiously. "Almost ready," he said as loudly as he dared. Umber saluted.

Before he could attempt to knot the rope around the neck of the bag, Arabell scuttled forward. She spooled out gluey silk and bound the bag and the cage to the rope. "Nicely done," he told Arabell. Hap was beginning to get used to her strange appearance. "You're very useful to have—"

He clamped his mouth shut. A sound was coming from behind him. Not immediately behind him—somewhere farther back, beyond the chamber where he stood. A man coughed and groaned.

Hap remembered when Hameron had led them down to these underground chambers, and what he'd glimpsed down the hallway. Prisoners kept in eternal darkness: the enemies of the king. The effects of Umber's bottle probably hadn't reached all the way down there, Hap figured.

His hand wandered to the front of his shirt, and he felt Umber's key under the fabric. There was a tug at his ankle.

Arabell stared up at him. She tipped her head toward the hearth where the silk rope dangled, ready to lift them out.

"Hold on, Arabell," Hap said. He looked at the instruments of pain cluttered along one wall. They had been pushed aside so the place could serve as the incubator. If the attempt to overthrow Brugador failed, this room would soon return to its usual purpose. *Torture chamber,* Hap thought. There was a pain in his jaw from his teeth pressing together. He didn't need the filaments to predict the fate of those prisoners.

Umber's voice rappelled down the chimney. "Hurry, Happenstance!"

Hap stuck his head into the hearth. "Back in a moment!" Without waiting for an answer he pulled the key from his shirt and ran toward the dungeon. Arabell protested with a squeak.

It was a short sprint down the hall that connected the incubator to the dungeon. Despite the pitch blackness, he could easily make out the crowd of prisoners behind the bars. *So many,* he thought. Dozens of men were locked in four cells. Half were dozing in the filthy straw on the floor. The rest milled around, groping at the darkness or passing their hands across the stone walls or iron bars. They were shirtless or dressed in rags, and their skin was marked with wounds old and new. There were groans, sniffs, coughs, and whispers.

Better do this quietly, Hap decided. The prisoners would

have no idea who he was. They might mistake him for a guard and throttle him in the dark. He crept forward to the farthest cells.

The key squirmed in his hand, assuming a new longer form. He slipped it into the keyhole and turned it. There was a hint of a rusty squeal, but none of the prisoners seemed to notice. Hap moved on to the next door, stepping softly. There a prisoner was standing by the lock with his hands wrapped around the bars, not a foot away from the keyhole. The fellow had a shaggy black beard with a strip of gray. The flesh of his bare chest was striped with scars. He stared blindly into the corridor. The eyes looked right through Hap, but it still gave him chills.

Hap put the key into the lock and turned it. It made only the softest click, but in the dark silence it was like a crack of thunder. The prisoner's head jolted, and he stepped back. Hap moved swiftly to the next door.

Whispers came from the first two cells as he unlocked the third. "Do you hear something?" "Is someone out there?" Hap heard metal screech. The man with the striped beard was pushing his cell door open. There was an almost comical look on his face, half astonished and half wary.

The whispers grew as Hap finished his work. "Our cell is open!" "Close it—you know what they'll do to us!" "I'm not closing it; this is our chance!" "Don't go—it's a trick!"

Hap took a chance and spoke aloud. "It's not a trick. I set you free. Good luck!" He ran toward the incubator, then scraped to a halt as he passed the stairs. A light was visible, shining from around the curve of the steps. A voice called: "Hameron, the king wants to know if another one's hatched. Hameron?"

Hap looked behind him. A horde of prisoners was creeping forward on their toes, blinking at the darkness. He heard footsteps descending the stairs, and the man called out again, very close. "Hameron! Answer me! What, is everyone asleep down there?" Two shadows appeared.

Oh, bloody bells, Hap said to himself. He rushed into the dim light of the Dragon Incubator and bit off a scream. The guard who'd been knocked out by the bottle was staggering to his feet, rubbing his eyes. Hameron still lay senseless on the ground.

The guard shook his head. His gaze focused on Hap and his expression darkened. "What are *you* up to?" He drew his sword and stepped forward, before tripping and crashing to the floor.

A sticky length of silk bound his feet together. Behind him Arabell nipped at his ankle and then sprang back, away from the sword that clashed on the floor inches from her legs.

Fear and indecision paralyzed Hap for a moment. The

two guards who'd come down the stairs rushed in, alerted by the sounds of the struggle. They paused to assess the situation and saw Hap standing dumbstruck. Their fellow guard hacked at the silk around his legs, screaming. "I can't feel my foot! What did you do to me, monster? I've been poisoned!"

The two newcomers looked at each other and then drew swords together. But before they could take a step, they were engulfed from behind by dozens of half-naked, bedraggled prisoners unleashing their pent-up rage and squinting at the dim light as if it were the burning rays of the sun.

Only seconds had passed, but to Hap it was like an hour. He sprang for the hearth. As he gripped the rope with both hands, Arabell climbed up beside him, bouncing on her many legs with excitement.

"Ready!" Hap cried. As Oates began to haul them up, Hap took a final look at the room. The guards could not be seen under the swarm of raging prisoners. Hameron's eyes fluttered open, and he stared dumbly at the bag, the boy, and the spidery creature vanishing up the chimney and out of sight.

"Ow!" cried Hap. Oates was pulling him up so fast that his shoulders scraped against the sooty stone. When he reached the top, Umber grabbed him under the arms and hauled him onto the roof.

"What happened down there?" Umber cried.

"I let the prisoners go," Hap said.

Umber's face cycled through a rush of emotions—surprise, fear, doubt, disbelief—before settling into a delighted pride that swelled his chest. "Well, that will just add to the confusion! I should have thought of it myself." One of his eyebrows rose. "Were you *meddling* just now?"

Hap shook his head. "I just thought . . . it was the right thing to do."

Oates cleared his throat. "Umber, shouldn't we signal Pilot?"

"Right you are!" Umber said. He dug into his pack and pulled out another, smaller bottle. He pried off the wax around its neck and pulled the cork. Instantly the bottle glowed with a bright blue light.

"Did you hear that, just now?" said Oates.

Hap *had* heard something. A thin whooshing sound, like a reed being whipped through the air, just over their heads. Far below something clattered against stone, perhaps in the courtyard.

"Is someone *shooting* at us?" Umber said.

Hap turned to look at the nearest watchtower. It had

been unoccupied before. Now there was a trio of men leaning out, armed with bows. "Look out!" he cried. A second arrow struck the chimney, angled off, and rolled away.

Hap looked up. The *Silkship* was coming down but still hundreds of feet above. A thin strand of silk dangled from the gondola, so long that it almost reached them. Arabell squealed up into the night.

"Get behind the chimneys!" Umber cried. Hap leaped, and Oates followed toward the little safety the chimneys would offer. Umber stopped to lift Arabell up toward the strand of silk. "Go, Arabell!" he shouted. She clutched the silk and started to climb.

As Umber raced for the chimney, Hap saw the arrow leave the archer's bow, and his heart froze as he watched it fly. He shouted, "Watch out!" but the arrow struck before the words were out. Umber stumbled forward a few more steps and fell onto his chest, with the feathered end of the arrow sticking up behind him.

"Is he hit?" cried Oates.

"Who, me?" replied Umber, lifting his head. "I felt something, all right!" Hap saw, with blissful relief, that the arrow had stuck in Umber's pack. But the relief vanished just as quickly, because a thick vapor was billowing from the pack.

"Did you have another sleeper bottle in there?" said Oates, coughing.

"That's some awful luck right there," Umber said. "Quick, hold your . . . hold your . . . hold . . ." His eyes rolled up and his head slumped down. At the same moment Hap felt a great wooziness overcome him, like water flooding his brain. A darkness his eyes could not penetrate descended. The last thing he heard was Oates's heavy body thump down beside him.

than

ately poor folk suddenly

g of gold dropped on

their doorstep, attached to a

strange line of severed thread. A

man unjustly imprisoned is

whisked away from his tower-top

prison cell. These things happen

nly in the darkness, or when a

covers the land. Pilot won't

admit to any of this, of course;

CHAPTER
22

Have I been sleeping? Hap wondered, as consciousness returned. His brain felt muddy, and his limbs couldn't move. *Is that how it feels? I don't think I like it.* At first he couldn't recall where he was. In the Aerie? On the *Bounder*? The *Silkship*? And then he remembered stealing the eggs, and the bottle filled with sleeping potion, shattered by the arrow.

His mind cleared, but his limbs still wouldn't move. There were footsteps by his ears, and he realized he was lying on stone. He forced his eyelids open.

"They're startin' to wake up," a gruff voice announced.

Umber was next to him, lying on his side. The bandage was gone from his head, and fresh blood had trickled from his half-healed wound. His arms were in manacles, and his legs as well.

Hap looked down and saw the same restraints on him. Oates was there as well, but with a great heap of inch-thick chains coiled around his body from shoulders to knees. Surrounding them were two dozen soldiers, all with axes, swords, bows, spears, and torches that cast a flickering underworld glow on the castle's great hall. *They must have dragged us down off the roof,* Hap thought.

"Let's get on with this," said a familiar voice. It was Brugador, the king. Magador was beside him. The prince picked up a bucket and tipped it over Umber's head, spilling filthy gray water.

Umber sputtered to life and blinked the water from his eyes. "Why, hello, Your Majesty," he said, sounding groggy.

Oates groaned and tried to sit up. A large man with a spear stood over him and kicked Oates in the side, between the coils of chain. "Remember me?" the man said. Hap recognized him at once—it was Pitt, the man who'd bullied him at the start of the race.

Oates stared up, squinting. Bruises covered his face, and blood trickled from one side of his nose. "Yes, I remember you. You're the pig of a man I threw into the harbor." This remark earned Oates another kick, which the big fellow absorbed without so much as a grunt.

"Where is Hameron?" bellowed the king. "Why hasn't he

been fetched yet? I want to know if he was in on this!" Hap saw the sack of dragon eggs and Umber's pack at the king's feet. The baby dragon was there, curled and trembling in a corner of its cage.

One of the soldiers stepped forward and bowed his head. "The men you sent haven't returned from the Dragon Incubator, your highness."

Magador was there. He hurled the empty bucket, barely missing the soldier. "Then you go find them, idiot!"

Good luck, Hap thought, thinking of the prisoners he'd freed. Apparently, their escape had not yet been detected. He wondered where they were.

Magador strode forward and kneeled beside Umber. "What will it be, Father?" Magador said. His eyes bulged and gleamed, and he licked his lips. "He's the first citizen of Kurahaven. Do we kill him, or save him for ransom?"

"I care nothing for ransom," Brugador said. He walked to his throne and lifted a weapon that leaned there: a club with a fat spiked head. "I want them dead."

"You are wise, Father," Magador said. He pulled a long knife from the sheath at his side. Hap tried to keep the moan from escaping his lips, but it came out anyway. Magador chuckled when he heard it.

"A favor, Your Majesty?" Umber said.

"A favor!" cried the king, swinging the club at his side. "Are you my jester now?"

"Listen to me, for just a moment," Umber said. "You invited me here for a reason, Your Highness. You wanted me, a man of renown from a country you envy, to witness your growing might and report to my people that you are a formidable man. In return I tried to steal something that was precious to you. I admit I was outraged by what I saw in the arena. I found your treatment of the dragons barbaric and ghastly. So I tried to stop it. And look at me now: shackled and defeated, at the mercy of a man who shows none. You have won, Brugador, king of Sarnica. You were better than me."

Magador spat on the ground. "What is this flattery? What do you want, Umber?"

Umber ignored the prince and kept his gaze fixed on the king. "As you savor this victory, I ask one simple favor." He craned his neck to look at Hap. "You'll have to do it without me, Happenstance. I know you can." Umber took a deep breath and faced the king again. "I ask that you spare the boy."

Hap's mind whirled. A choking sound was all his throat could produce.

Brugador sneered. "Spare the boy?"

"I don't expect you to understand, Your Highness. But the

boy is more important than you could ever believe. Not to you or to anyone in this world. You'll think I'm mad if I try to explain. But millions upon millions of lives are at stake. The boy must live. Let him go, Your Highness. Put him on the next boat to leave your kingdom—any boat. He will never trouble you again, I promise you."

Brugador stared down at Umber, and then took a long look at Hap.

"Oates," Umber said. "I don't mean that I don't care what happens to you—I—"

"I understand," Oates said.

Brugador threw his head back and guffawed. "What an entertaining fellow you are, Umber!"

"He's a liar," Magador said. "And he's wasting our time."

"I'll leave it to you, my son," Brugador said. "Shall we spare this green-eyed pup?"

Hap's blood chilled when he saw the look on Magador's face. The prince's lips pulled back, baring every tooth. He pressed his thumb into the blade of his knife, so eager for blood that he had begun, unaware, to spill his own.

More words spilled from Umber. His voice quaked. "I consider myself a good man, King Brugador. But I can imagine myself doing cruel and terrible things. Isn't the opposite true for you? You can imagine being good and merciful. If you've ever felt that impulse, to do one good and just thing in your life, let this be your moment. Spare the boy!"

"Never," Magador said. "And you will watch the life flow from his veins." The prince flipped the knife and caught it by the handle. Hap tucked his neck between his shoulders. Oates grunted and tried to flex his arms. The chains shifted and clanked but would not break.

"Disappear, Hap!" Umber cried. "Meddlers can do it! You can do it!"

"I don't know how," Hap croaked.

He heard the king's mocking laughter. "They're all mad. Better off dead!"

A door clattered at the end of the great hall. Hap opened his eyes to see one of the king's soldiers. "Your Highness!" he cried, rushing forward.

"Not now!" bellowed the king.

The breathless man could barely wheeze out words as his chest heaved. "Enemies . . . invading . . ."

"What?" Brugador's eyes nearly disappeared as his brow descended. "Where?"

"They attacked . . . the gate . . . from inside and out! More streaming in. Fires in the city. The people . . . our people . . ."

Brugador seized the front of the man's shirt. "What about the people?"

The man's eyes bulged. His voice broke as he forced out the answer. "Some of them—most of them—they're helping the enemy!"

The king shoved the man, who stumbled back and was caught by other soldiers. For a moment Hap dared to hope for a reprieve. But the king lifted the mace with both hands. "Finish them with me, son."

Hap, unable to watch, turned his face away in time to see dozens of men burst out from a shadowy corridor. They were the prisoners he'd freed, armed with clubs, spears, knives, candlesticks, pieces of furniture, and anything else they'd been able to find on their journey up from the chambers below. Once they were seen, they shouted in a chorus of rage, with all their fury focused on the king and prince who had masterminded their torment.

Pitt was closest to the mob. In his surprise he stepped back, too close to Oates. Oates coiled his chained legs and unleashed a kick of astonishing violence. Pitt was a blur in the air until he struck Brugador an instant later. Their skulls cracked together, and both men fell limp. The king hit the floor facing up, and Hap cried out in disgust when he saw the nose crushed flat.

Is he dead? Hap wondered. But it hardly mattered. The prisoners leaped over Hap and Umber and fell upon their oppressor like wild dogs, wreaking terrible violence on the still form. Soldiers and prisoners clashed, and the noise was like an avalanche.

Hap barely heard Umber's cry. "Hap! Turn yourself so I can reach the key!"

The key! Hap thought. He rolled and wriggled until Umber's manacled hands found the loop and pulled the key over his neck. Umber slid the key into Hap's manacles first, and then Hap undid Umber's locks and sprang to Oates's side. The chaos of battle was only a stride away. Men screamed in mortal agony, and then a triumphant shout arose.

Oates stood up, seething with anger. He shrugged off the heavy chains and then picked them up at one end, ready to swing them as a weapon. "Where is Magador? Where's that filthy prince?"

The prisoner with the white stripe in his black beard was there—he seemed to have emerged as their leader. "I think you mean *King* Magador. Brugador is dead. But the new king ran like a frightened dog, and the rest followed."

Umber glanced at the dead king. His face paled, and he covered his mouth with his hands.

"You're the boy who freed us, aren't you?" the prisoner said to Hap. He pointed with his sword. "I saw you in the chamber below. You went up the chimney."

Hap nodded.

"If you'll excuse us, gentlemen," Umber said, "we really have to go. Oates, grab the sack."

"Where are you going?" the prisoner asked. Hap took a closer look at the man. When he looked past the shaggy striped beard and dirty face, Hap realized something about him: He was like a lion, with a coiled strength and an air of authority.

"Off this island, any way we can," Umber replied.

The prisoner nodded. "The boy saved us. And that big fellow slew the king. You helped us; we will help you. To the harbor!"

Umber looked at Hap and Oates and shrugged. "Right. To the harbor, then."

Hap tugged Umber's sleeve and whispered. "Lord Umber, what about the *Silkship*? Can't Pilot get us out of here?"

"We missed our rendezvous on the roof," Umber said out of the corner of his mouth. "And I have no way to signal Pilot now. Things could get messy here—we'd better just hightail it and hope the *Silkship* finds us later."

With a small, bedraggled army as their escort, they ran through the dark halls. Hap carried the dragon's cage and Umber took the eggs, so that Oates could keep the chains as a weapon. Shouts echoed, inside the castle and out. They heard the thump of feet and the clatter of armor, and they hid in shadows once to let a group of soldiers rush by. Hap held his breath until the footsteps had died away.

"I am Umber, from Kurahaven. Who are you, sir?" Umber asked the man with the striped beard.

"Tolliver," he replied. "Save your questions, friend, until we get you out of here." Tolliver waved them along and led the way into another corridor. As they rounded another corner, they came upon two people, huddling together and terrified. It was a girl and a young woman, dressed in nightclothes. The girl stepped in front of the woman and spread her arms wide, scowling at the gang of prisoners.

It's the princess, thought Hap. *And that girl.*

"Don't scream, Your Highness," threatened Tolliver. The men stared and looked at each other. It was clear from their shock that they knew who they'd blundered into.

Fay put her hands on the girl's shoulders. She spotted Umber and Hap among the men and widened her eyes. "Please, sirs," she said. "Take us with you."

With the princess and the girl among them they rushed at the door that led to the top of the harbor road. Hap recognized the spot: It was where he'd finished his race. A dozen soldiers stood, halfheartedly guarding the way, but they bolted when they saw Oates charging with twenty feet of chain whirling over his head.

Tolliver grinned at the sight. "We could use a man like that!"

They poured down the harbor road. The former prisoners were limping and gasping, and some of their wounds had begun to bleed anew. The exhilaration of sudden freedom had taken them this far, but Hap wondered how much longer they could maintain their strength. Umber huffed beside Hap as he ran, clutching the sack of eggs close to his chest. Behind them a fiery glow blossomed over the castle. The wharves below were in chaos as people rushed toward the ships. Despite the darkness, sails were unfurling, and one ship was already underway.

When they reached the bottom of the road, Tolliver stopped the group and turned to Umber. "What ship . . . is yours, sir?" he shouted, panting, over the din.

"None of them," Umber replied. "We'll have to commandeer one."

"Which would you like?"

A light dawned in Umber's eyes. "Ah. Why not? That one, Tolliver! Can we take it?"

Tolliver's shoulders drooped when he saw where Umber pointed. "The *Eel*?" It was the long, slender galley, a vessel of war rowed by slaves.

Umber smiled. "Some other men inside that ship would cherish their freedom too, don't you think?"

Tolliver nodded but looked doubtful. "Those guards will put up a fight." Thirty armed men, the ship's night guard, prowled the deck of the *Eel*. They lined the rail, watching the mayhem around them. Half were gathered at the top of the gangplank, ready to defend the *Eel*. "But if that colossus of yours is with us . . ."

"I'm with you," Oates said. There was a stack of barrels on the wharf. He lifted one over his head with two hands and hurled it at the deck of the *Eel*. The men on the ship carried torches, which made them easy to see. But the barrel must have appeared out of the gloom with no warning, because the men near the gangplank didn't move to avoid it. Five of them fell like bowling pins. The girl stared at Oates with her jaw hanging.

Oates seized another barrel. "What are you waiting for?"

Tolliver nodded, laughing, and his men charged up the ramp. By the time they reached the deck, Oates had knocked down seven more of the crew, and the others started to leap over the sides.

As Hap ran, he felt a hand clasp his. He saw the girl beside him, with the princess holding her other hand. It was an awkward way to run, especially with the dragon's cage tucked under his other arm, but he didn't shake his hand free. Hap felt the ramp bounce as Oates followed them onto the ship. The prisoners hurried to throw off the ropes that kept the *Eel* tied to the dock.

Once aboard, the girl dropped Hap's hand and clutched the princess around the waist. Fay stared at the castle with a grim, tight-lipped smile. Flames slithered from its windows. The sounds of battle drifted down: distant shouts and the clang of steel. Then came a deep, thunderous rumble. Two hundred men on horses clattered into sight at the top of the road. Hap saw a familiar figure leading them. "It's Magador!" he said. At the sound of the name the girl clutched the princess tighter, and Fay's lip curled in a gesture of pure disgust.

Magador leaned forward in his saddle, peering down at the harbor. It seemed to Hap that his gaze was fixed on the deck of the ship where they stood. Hap looked with alarm at the prisoner standing next to them with a torch in his hand, illuminating the princess. He could only imagine how recognizable she was, and the rest of them too, even from that distance.

Umber had the same thought. "Douse that light!" he cried. The prisoner tossed it overboard, and it hissed in the harbor.

Arrows sipped at the air. The baby dragon squealed in its cage.

"Get downstairs!" shouted Umber. "They're shooting at us from the other warship!"

The other ship, the enormous sailing vessel that was painted blood-red like the *Eel*, was moored nearby. Archers lined its deck. Arrows struck all around, pinging off the boards and lodging in the rail. On the harbor road the sound of hooves grew and deepened in pitch. Umber ran beside Fay, shielding her from harm, and Hap and Oates followed them through the open hatch.

Tolliver met them at the bottom of the stairs. "The guards are all gone, Umber. And they took the keys with them. We can't free the slaves!"

"Perhaps we still can," Umber said, touching the front of his shirt, where the key hung out of sight.

Hap looked at the vast room that ran the length of the ship. Benches lined the sides, with an open aisle running down the spine of the craft. Oars were stowed under the benches. And along the sides of the ship, men sat against the walls on straw mats. There were manacles on their legs, each connected to long chains. *This was their life,* Hap thought. *They ate, slept, and rowed, right here.*

The men stared at the newcomers, frightened and uncertain.

"You have rowed for a tyrant," Umber said. "Will you row now for freedom?"

The men whispered to each other, daring to hope. Heads nodded.

Umber walked to the locks that secured one end of the four chains. "King Brugador is dead," he began, and paused while a loud cheer rang out. Using his body to obscure the key from sight, he opened the four enormous padlocks. "But Magador lives. And he is riding toward us now with a sizable force. We need to get out of this harbor as fast as we can. But first unchain yourselves!"

Grins appeared as the men realized what was happening. They seized the chain and pulled it through the rings on their manacles, slipping free one by one. A man sprang up and raced for the stairs, eager to flee the ship that had long been his prison. Umber cried, "Come back!" but the fellow disappeared—only to leap back down the stairs an instant later.

"It's raining arrows out there!" the man cried. A murmur ran down the rows of freed slaves.

"Trust the man who has freed you! It's row or die!" shouted Tolliver. The oarsmen hurried to their places, passing the oars through the slots on the sides of the boat. One of them ran toward the stern and began to pound the great drum mounted there, and the oarsmen soon fell into rhythm.

The ship began to creep through the water. There was a splash outside—the gangplank falling into the sea. Tolliver ran to the hatch and risked a look. "That was close," he said. "Magador's cavalry had just made it to the wharf." His face brightened. "Magador riding to the harbor—do you realize what this means, Umber?"

Fay answered the question for him. "It means he's given up. If he was going to fight for his kingdom, he'd have been in the city. Now he'll scurry away like the rat that he is."

"Pardon me for suggesting, Your Highness," one of the oarsmen said, grunting as he pulled on his oar. "But somebody ought to go up and steer this crate before we crash into something."

CHAPTER
23

Tolliver took the ship's wheel. Hap and Oates flanked Umber at the stern, and they watched the harbor, trying to see what had become of Magador and his cavalry. The eggs and the dragon, for the moment, were stowed below in the captain's cabin. On either side of the ship the oars stabbed at the water, circled, and rose again, in practiced rhythm. The drum below sounded like the ship's thumping heart. Hap peered into the dark sky for a sign of the *Silkship* but saw none. On the horizon ahead there was no glimmer of daylight yet, but the rising sun couldn't have been more than an hour or two away.

"Pardon me," a clear, high voice said behind them. It was Fay. She wore the same expression, Hap noticed, as the prisoners he'd freed: happy and wary together.

"Hello, Princess," Umber said.

Her brow knitted. "Please, Lord Umber. Never call me that again. I renounce that title now as I always have done in my heart. I am merely Fay now."

"And more noble for it," Umber said, bowing his head and sweeping his hand. Fay's dark eyes crinkled at the corners. The girl was at Fay's side. When Hap looked at her, she turned away. He waited a moment and looked her way again, and once more she averted her eyes. Hap felt the oddest sensation, as if a feather had tickled his heart.

"The men say it is you I should thank for my freedom," Fay said to Umber. "And for the end of that tyrant, Brugador."

Umber stuck his thumbs in his vest and bounced on the balls of his feet. "In fact I am the last person you should thank. It was my ward, Happenstance, who freed Tolliver and the prisoners and made your escape possible." Hap glanced again at the girl. She was gazing at him once more, but this time her eyes looked twice as big.

"And," Umber continued, "it was Oates here who slew the king. Although that might have been an accident."

"It wasn't," said Oates.

Fay nodded. "I am grateful beyond words, Happenstance and Oates. If there is anything I can do to thank you, please tell me."

Oates replied instantly, "I would like a kiss." A look of horrified regret transformed his face, and he clamped his hand over his mouth. But Fay took no offense. She stepped in front of Oates and pulled his hand down. Oates lowered his head, and she turned his face to one side and kissed him, brushing the corner of his lips with hers. Oates stared at her, blinking, and then drifted away in a daze. Umber looked sideways at Hap and puffed out a breath of air, as if to say, *He could have said worse.*

"I think you had a friend in Faldran," Fay said to Umber. "Bertram Charmaigne, the peacemaker. Are you worried about him?"

Umber looked back at the strife-filled city. "Bertram knew this attack was coming. He chose to stay, to help restore order if it succeeds. I think it will."

She nodded. "And where will you go now, Lord Umber?"

Umber considered the question. "Kurahaven, eventually. But this ship isn't made for a long journey over open sea. I suppose we'll head for the nearest friendly island. Ornast, maybe—there will be merchant ships there, maybe even one of mine. From there I'll arrange transportation for these men, and for you, my lady. You can go home, if you like, wherever that is."

The girl wrapped her arms around Fay's waist again and

hid her face. Fay stared at the sea. "Do you know how I came to be Magador's wife?"

Umber cleared his throat. "I was told that he kidnapped you from a village."

Her jaw tensed. "Yes. And then he burned the village. There is nobody left except for me and Sable. She is my sister's daughter." She closed her eyes and rested her cheek on Sable's head.

Umber raised his hand, perhaps to touch her shoulder, but he paused, uncertain.

"I have always wanted to see Kurahaven," Fay said without looking at him.

Umber used the hand to tug at his nose. "Then we will take you there."

There was a smaller boat mounted upside down on the deck of the *Eel*. As some of the freed prisoners loosened its ropes, Tolliver approached Umber. "The men and I are going back. The ones who are well enough, anyway. Some will have to stay on this ship."

Umber looked at the ghastly scars on Tolliver's shoulders. "You have suffered enough. Nobody would blame you if you didn't return."

Tolliver shook his head. "That's our home back there. We want to fight for it if we're needed."

Umber held a hand out, which Tolliver grasped. "When you get back, look for a good man named Bertram Charmaigne," Umber told him. "He's there to help. And don't worry; we'll take care of your wounded friends."

In their brief acquaintance Oates had attained a mythic status among the prisoners, and each of them insisted on shaking his hand and clapping his shoulder. A few begged him to join them, but Oates declined. Soon the small craft was packed with men and rowing back toward Faldran.

"Good man, that Tolliver," Umber said.

Umber and Hap rummaged through the captain's cabin and found maps to help them navigate. Before Umber could unroll a parchment, they heard Oates calling from above. "Umber! Get up here!"

The oarsmen watched with sudden concern as Hap and Umber ran up the stairs. Oates stood by the stern rail, pointing in the dim light of dawn. Far behind them columns of smoke snaked high over Faldran. "See it?" said Oates.

Hap nodded. Umber squinted into the gloom. "What is it, Hap?"

"Another ship," Hap said. It was following the same course.

"My spyglass is in my pack," Umber said. "Hap, would you mind?"

Hap was three steps away before the request was completed. He flew down the stairs, grabbed the pack, and rushed back to Umber's side. Fay and Sable had joined them at the rail.

"You look," Umber said when Hap tried to hand the spyglass over.

Hap peered into the brass tube and aimed the spyglass until the distant ship was inside its circle, leaping suddenly closer. A familiar figure stood at its prow. Hap's shoulders twitched, and he lowered the spyglass. "It's the big red ship that was next to the *Eel*. And I think Magador is on it," he said quietly.

Sable trembled, and Fay stroked her hair.

"Fay, what do you know about that ship?" Umber asked.

"It is the *Shark*. A sailing vessel, and a fast one," Fay replied. "The most feared ship in these waters, besides this one. There might be two or three hundred aboard, fighting men and sailors."

A sailing vessel, thought Hap. He felt a breeze across his face. It was coming from behind them, filling the *Shark*'s sails.

The *Shark* suddenly changed its course, and archers gathered along one of its rails. Hap raised the spyglass again and saw a much smaller craft in the water, just ahead of the *Shark*. It was the boat that Tolliver and the prisoners had taken. The lantern on the small ship must have drawn Magador's attention in the dark. The prisoners began to row furiously, trying to evade the

Shark as it bore down, but they could not move fast enough. The *Shark* crushed the boat under its enormous hull as Tolliver and the others leaped off the sides. The archers sent dozens of arrows into the water as the *Shark* swept past. And when that was done, the prow of the *Shark* turned again, pointing their way. Hap bowed his head and struggled not to cry out.

"What's happening out there?" Umber asked, leaning close.

"Tolliver's boat," Hap whispered, so only Umber could hear. "Magador ran it down." Umber shut his eyes and shook his head.

"They've seen us, haven't they?" Oates asked.

Umber rubbed his hand across his mouth. "It's still pretty dark. Put out all the lanterns. Oates, tell them to do the same below—in the stern cabin, especially. And ask the oarsmen if they can quicken our pace."

Hap stared at the ship in the distance. *He knows who's on this ship,* he thought. *And he's seen us, all right. Because he's coming straight for us.*

Fay bit her lip. "We should have known this would happen. Magador has lost his kingdom. There is only one thing left for him now. That is revenge."

Hap heard the drum below quicken its pace, matching the rhythm of his own heart.

"You, sir, at the helm," Umber called out. "Remind me, what is your name?"

"Barber," the man replied. He was one of the freed slaves, a former sailor who had been chosen by the others to steer the ship.

"Barber, I think we ought to turn south—this wind favors our pursuer."

Barber nodded and eased the wheel to the right.

Hap watched the *Shark* to see if her course would change as well. A shiver ran down his arms. For a moment he thought it was from the cool breeze picking up. But when the cold vanished, swept away by a sudden fever that pooled in his eyes, he knew he was about to see the filaments again.

This time there were many of them, all emerging from the people around him: Umber, Oates, Barber, Sable, and Fay. A dense tangle of the apparitions emerged from the narrow prow of the ship. *One for every person below,* Hap thought. They slithered like snakes, forward across the sea, skimming the waves. *Our paths. Our fates.*

He heard Sable's voice. "Look at his eyes!" Fay hushed her.

Hap ignored them. He found it hard to breathe. Every filament had a dismal, discolored look. He walked among them, letting his hand pass through the mysterious wisps of light, listening to their mournful song.

"Lord Umber, what is he doing?" Fay said. Umber didn't answer, but from the corner of his eye Hap saw him gesture, putting a finger to his lips.

Hap wandered to where the great tangle of filaments came together. When he stepped into their stream, they sang to him, more clearly than ever. The song was strange, and made of many sounds—faraway chimes, water gurgling over stones, crickets in the night, and other noises no words could possibly describe.

The filaments did not surrender their full meaning. *I'm not skilled enough yet,* Hap thought. But he knew in his heart it was a chorus of the doomed. *Everybody on this ship is going to die.* His legs weakened, and he fell to his knees.

Umber had followed him across the deck. He bent beside him, perhaps to steady Hap, but Hap warded him off with a raised palm. *There must be something I can do,* he said inwardly. Wasn't that the point of the filaments—to be able to steer fate? He remembered the beetle that had saved him from the arrow, and how a strange, hazy aura had surrounded it, and how dim everything had looked except the thing that mattered most.

"Where is it?" he whispered hoarsely. He raised his eyes, scanning the deck, and his heart nearly burst from his chest when he saw what he was looking for.

CHAPTER
24

The ship's helm.

What better tool to steer fate? Hap ran to it, so engrossed in his task that he pushed Barber aside and grabbed the wheel.

"What's the matter with you, boy?" Barber bellowed.

Umber stepped between them. "Stand back a moment, Barber, I beg you."

Hap was afraid to speak, to look anyone else in the eye, to do anything that might make the vision waver and disappear. The filaments had never appeared for long, so he didn't know how much time he had left.

He turned the wheel right. It was harder than he expected, and he grunted with the effort. Ahead of them the filaments began to turn, anticipating the new course. But their color still foretold destruction. Hap turned the wheel farther, but still only doom seemed to lie ahead.

Shifting his grip on the wheel, he spun it back to where he'd started and then slowly edged it in the other direction. The path still led to death. He turned the wheel another fraction. *More death.*

Barber struggled to get by Umber. "The boy is wasting time! They'll catch us all the sooner!"

And then, when Hap pushed the wheel a little farther, he saw the threads brighten. Not completely, but not the ugly gray they'd been. The color shifted, dimmer and lighter in turn. "What does that mean?" he muttered to himself. "A chance?" He pushed it farther, and the color improved by another small degree. A little farther and it dimmed again, more ominous than ever. He pulled it back, just as the threads vanished.

Hap looked over his shoulder. Umber, standing with his arms spread to keep Barber back, was half smiling at him with one eyebrow arched. The others stared as if he'd lost his mind.

"That's the only direction we can go," Hap said. "If we steer anywhere else, all of us will die."

Disbelief and suspicion hung in the air. Barber broke the silence. "We can't go this way, you fools! With this wind at her back, the *Shark* will be upon us in an hour." Hap looked

at the ship behind them. It seemed closer. The sky suddenly brightened, as the rim of the sun appeared in the east.

"This may not seem sensible, but you need to trust us," Umber said.

"Never mind sensible—this is lunacy," Barber shouted.

Other men were on deck, and they gathered in a circle around the helm, each with furrowed brows.

"Don't you see what's going to happen?" Barber cried. "We can keep our speed up for a while. But the oarsmen will lose their strength, and the ship will slow. But the *wind* won't tire. It will take the *Shark* right up our stern. And there's a mob of armed men on that ship, with arrows and javelins and axes, ready to make mincemeat out of every one of us. So we have to change our course!"

The small crowd of men murmured and closed their circle, frightened and angry. Barber tried to seize the wheel, but his feet were suddenly a foot off the deck, pawing at air. Oates had lifted him with a hand under each arm. He placed Barber gently down again on his other side, and then stepped in front of the helm and folded his arms. "Nobody is changing course." The crowd shuffled backward, murmuring.

Umber dug his compass from his pack. "Would someone get the maps from the captain's cabin? We might as well find out where we're going."

Barber shook his head. "I'll go," he muttered. "You're crazy, the lot of you."

"People say that about us all the time," Oates said.

"They do, don't they?" Umber said, wiping his hair back from his forehead. "Oates, will you take the helm?"

Umber pulled Hap aside and spoke quietly. "You saw the filaments again, obviously." Hap nodded. "Was it different this time?" Umber asked.

Hap squinted as he considered the question. "I felt like . . . I could understand them better. Not completely. Like a book with most of the words crossed out. Or a song where you can't hear the words, but you know it's happy or sad just from the melody." He pressed a hand against his forehead. It was still damp from the fever's sweat. "We have to stay on this course, Lord Umber. We still may not survive, but at least we have a chance."

Umber tugged at his lips and nodded.

Hap looked at Sable and Fay, standing amidships and watching the *Shark.* "When I was seeing the filaments . . . I heard the girl say something about my eyes."

Umber's eyebrows hopped. "Yes. They got brighter. Twinkling, like stars. Back to normal now, though."

I'm never normal, Hap thought, slumping against the ship's rail. He noticed Umber staring at the top of his head. "What is it, Lord Umber?"

"Hap, what did you say Willy Nilly's hair looked like?"

"Um . . . white. Like spun glass, almost. With bits of color."

Umber reached into Hap's scalp with a thumb and forefinger. Hap felt a tug and a dot of pain, and then he looked at the strand of hair that Umber was holding before his eyes. It glistened in the sun, like a crystal thread with rainbow flecks.

Hap put both hands atop his head and groaned. "No. Are there any more?"

"A few," Umber said.

At that moment Barber returned with an armful of maps and spread one wide across the angled table that stood beside the helm. The map showed Sarnica and hundreds of miles of surrounding sea. Umber placed his brass compass on the map, near their position. Hap stepped close to watch—anything to take his mind off that glassy strand of hair.

"Never seen one like that," Barber said, leaning down for a closer look at the compass.

"The latest model," Umber replied. He slid a fingertip across the map, projecting their path. "Oh," he said when his finger landed on something. His mouth shrank to a tiny puckered circle.

"You can't be serious," Barber said. "Not there."

"Afraid so," Umber replied.

Hap looked down at where Umber's finger rested on the

map. The mapmaker had drawn a circle of flames and written the words *Beware the Boiling Seas*.

"Listen, sir," Barber said. His anger was rising, but he had the sense to keep his voice low. "I've seen that place. No sane captain goes near it—they steer clear. And it's nearly a day away. Believe me, we'll be cut up like baitfish long before then. And besides, this ship was made for attacks along the coast, not voyages across the wide ocean. Think about all those oar holes lining the sides. In a stormy sea the waves rush right in. Can't you see the madness in this?"

"I understand, Barber," Umber said. "But this is our only chance to survive. And now I must ask you to hold your tongue, so the others don't lose hope."

Barber's face flushed red. He opened his mouth to protest, but Fay appeared beside him, sliding her arm under his elbow. "Sir, let us speak," she said, pulling him away.

Umber watched them go. "I hope she's on our side," he said.

"I could toss him overboard," Oates offered.

Umber laughed. "Just keep us on this heading." He turned back to look at the *Shark*. "Getting closer, isn't it?"

Hap nodded. His eyes went back to the map. "What are the Boiling Seas, Lord Umber?" He bit his lip, fearing the answer that he also expected.

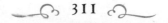

"That's another name for the Inferno, Hap. Where Desolas lies. We may see Caspar again after all. If he's still alive."

Hap shut his eyes and sighed. On each side of the ship he heard the slosh of oars in the water. And below he heard the incessant beating of the drum. It seemed to be telling their fortune:

Doom. Doom. Doom. Doom. Doom. Doom. Doom.

Hap saw Barber at the prow, staring at the far horizon. Fay strolled back to speak to Umber, followed by Sable.

"Our friend Barber will not interfere," she said.

Umber smiled at her. "It seems you have a gift for persuasion."

"I told Mister Barber what I know of you. You see, I have heard of some of your exploits, Lord Umber," she said. "Hameron told me. He was a loathsome man, but he admired you greatly and yearned for your respect."

"Hameron," Umber said. "I wonder if he's still alive."

The breeze stiffened, sweeping across the ship from stern to prow and sending Fay's hair fluttering like a pennant. She glanced at the *Shark*. "How long until we are caught?"

"A chase at sea is a drawn-out affair," Umber said. "It could be hours yet. Or not at all. But I should step downstairs and ask if we can pick up the pace a little."

Hap gnawed at a fingernail. *It won't be hours,* he thought. When they first spotted the *Shark*, he could hide it behind his thumb, extended at arm's length. Now his hand could not obscure the ship. And the wind, gaining strength under the sun, was pushing it faster still, while not helping the *Eel* at all.

A timid voice spoke from behind him. "I've never seen eyes like yours." Sable stood there, looking down at her feet.

Hap's face felt suddenly warm. He said the first thing that came to mind, and regretted it instantly. "Yes, I know they're weird."

Her bottom lip trembled. "I didn't mean . . . ," she began, and then she fled to the far end of the ship.

Hap rolled his eyes toward the dawn sky. "That was brilliant," he muttered. From below he heard the steady drumbeat, a little faster now: *Dumb dumb dumb dumb dumb.*

Oates spent an hour tossing anything they didn't need into the sea, but still the *Shark* drew closer. Standing at the stern rail, Hap didn't need a spyglass to see Magador pacing back and forth across the bow of his ship like a caged animal. A dozen men assembled behind him, and someone handed Magador an enormous bow that was nearly as tall as he was. He notched an arrow in the string, raised the bow, and fired.

The arrow arced high and fell, splashing into the water a hundred yards behind the *Eel*.

He's testing the distance, Hap thought. *Those arrows will reach us soon.*

One of the prisoners who was too injured to go back to Faldran hobbled up the stairs and limped toward Umber, who was speaking quietly with Fay. The man whispered in Umber's ear. Umber blanched, excused himself, and hurried below.

Hap followed, trying to ignore the fear that tweaked every nerve. As he went down the steps, he heard angry voices below.

"We'll never outrace the *Shark*!"

"This will get us all killed!"

"Maybe we should surrender—Magador will want this ship, and he'll spare us so we can row it!"

Hap reached the lower deck and stared down at the twin rows of oarsmen. He saw sweat-soaked faces, bared teeth, angry brows, and sinewy, muscled arms still circling in unison.

"Gentlemen, believe me—your only hope lies along the course we have set," Umber called out, raising both hands. "I promise you one other thing: You will be rewarded for this. There will be thirty pieces of gold for each of you. And I will use my fortune and influence to take every one of you back to your homes."

One oarsman stood up, dropping his oar. "What good

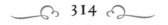

is gold if we're dead? Surrender now and he may show mercy!" The next oar in line struck his, and the disturbance in the rhythm rippled down the row in both directions. The muttering rose in pitch, with every man talking at once.

Fay brushed past Hap. She'd come down so quietly he hadn't noticed her. She walked past Umber and stared at the oarsman with her fists on her hips.

"Mercy?" she shouted. Something in her voice caught the attention of the men, and every head turned her way. Hap stared, struck likewise by her fierce beauty.

"You expect mercy from Magador?" she cried, staring from man to man. "Nobody spent more time in his company than me, his bride. I tell you there will be no mercy. And how do you think he will deal with me, the woman who fled from his clutches, if he catches us? Will you leave me to that fate, all of you?"

The men stared, their faces reddened by her words. The oars fell back into rhythm.

"But it is not me you should row for, brave men. It is for yourselves and your freedom. Haven't you chafed enough in your chains? Is it not a gift to have your limbs unfettered? There must be something each of you has to live for!"

A young man near Fay spoke, his face twisted with emotion. "I want to see my wife again. And my little son."

"And you will," Fay said. "I believe you will. But we have to trust the men who are guiding us now. Because of them the tyrant Brugador is dead and his foul son has fled the kingdom. Believe in these men, I tell you." She turned and looked at Umber. "Because I do."

Umber closed his eyes and bowed his head toward her.

The drummer kept his steady pace, but every thump was louder. "Come on, brothers!" he cried. "This is our ship now, and what is the wind against hearts like ours?"

Umber led Fay and Hap up the stairs, puffing out a great breath of air. He turned to Fay, shaking his head with admiration, and took one of her hands in his. He opened his mouth to speak, but Oates's voice came first. "Umber!" he called, standing by Barber at the helm. Barber was gaping up with his mouth hanging open. Oates jabbed his thumb at the sky.

"There you are," called a powerful voice from above. The *Silkship* was hovering a hundred feet over their heads.

The men on deck scrambled for spears, axes, gaffs, and anything else that might fend off the airborne invader. "Calm yourselves, gentlemen!" Umber shouted. "This is a friend."

Pilot leaned over the gondola rail and scowled back at the *Shark*, where archers were gathering at the bow. "Shall I drop a ladder, Umber? I think you ought to climb aboard. If you die, it'll be harder to get the rest of what I'm owed."

Fay's eyes widened, and Sable gasped. Umber smiled at them and called up to Pilot, "I'm afraid we can't desert our new companions."

Pilot frowned. "But where are you heading?"

"The Inferno," Umber replied. "Don't ask why; I don't have a decent explanation. But do you think you can do something about our pursuer?"

Pilot craned his neck to examine the *Shark*. "Dangerous to interfere," he said. "My vessel is no warship."

"The tyrant Brugador is dead, Pilot. His son is on that ship, and he's looking for vengeance. On me, and on his wife, who is aboard with us." Umber raised his hand toward Fay.

Pilot grimaced. "It'll cost extra."

"Of course it will," Umber said with a sigh.

Hap was startled by something that clattered, skidded across the deck, and spun to a stop. It was an arrow, and when its motion ceased, the arrowhead pointed at him.

"The sooner the better, Pilot," Umber added.

Fay watched the strange ship float up and away. "Lord Umber, you are a man with interesting acquaintances," she said. Hap wondered what she'd have thought if she'd glimpsed the spider-folk.

"The arrows can reach us now, Fay. You and Sable should get below," Umber said.

Fay shook her head. "I must see this."

The *Silkship* drifted back until her shadow was on the deck of the *Shark*. That caused a great commotion on her deck, as men scrambled and pointed at what must have seemed an impossible sight. Hap heard them shouting, until a furious voice rose above the others to restore order: Magador. But one man on the *Shark* could not contain his panic. He pointed and screamed at the flying ship, even after Magador struck his face with the back of one hand. Magador grabbed the front of the man's shirt and drove him backward, shoving him over the rail and into the sea. Hap shut his eyes and heard Fay gasp.

"Do you see what Pilot is doing?" Umber said to nobody in particular. "Coming at them out of the sun." It seemed as if every man on the *Shark* was extending a hand to block the sun and find the flying craft. Hap saw a thin column of black smoke rising from the *Shark*'s deck. *Is it on fire, perhaps?* he wondered.

"What can he do to stop them?" asked Sable. She had taken shelter behind Oates.

Hap saw lines of silk dangling from the *Silkship*, fluttering in the breeze as they grew longer. They were being spun by Arabell, Quellen, and Gossilen, who were spread along the side of the gondola. Pilot leaned over the gondola's side, peering down. He made a slashing gesture with his hands, and the threads were severed. They fluttered down and stuck fast wherever they fell, to the sails, masts, and spars. More of the sticky threads followed. The sails that once bulged with wind sagged and twisted. Spars bent and shook.

"That'll make a fine mess," Umber said.

Sable laughed and clapped her hands, and Hap allowed himself to smile, though he was beginning to think that Pilot had descended too low. His mouth flattened when he saw the archers lift their bows. The heads of their arrows were strangely fat and round.

Umber's face went gray. He bellowed up to Pilot, waving his hands and pointing. "Pilot! Get out of there!"

The archers dipped the arrows into something like a cauldron on the deck, which was the source of the smoke. When they brought the arrows up again, aiming at the *Silkship*, the heads were on fire.

CHAPTER
25

A dozen arrows flew up like fiery comets.
Four struck the belly of the gondola, and two snagged in the cocoon, while the rest fell short and hissed into the sea. Where the arrows burned, the silk skin melted away, opening ragged gaps. Hap saw Pilot turn the *Silkship*'s wheel, but before the ship responded, three more flaming arrows pierced her belly.

The *Silkship* drifted sideways as the flames spread. Hap saw the spider-folk creep onto the side of the cocoon. Arabell raced ahead of the others. She plucked the burning arrows out and dropped them, and the three of them hurried to patch the holes in the skin. But the fires continued to burn the gondola below.

The *Shark*'s crew roared over their victory, and the archers sent more burning missiles after the *Silkship*, though she was beyond reach. They hardly noticed that one of their own burning arrows had fallen into the crease of a twisted sail. Shouts of celebration turned to cries of alarm as men swarmed up the ship's rigging and hacked at the lines that held the sail, trying to cut the canvas loose.

Hap's fingertips dug into the tender skin below his eyes as he watched the *Silkship* struggle. The gondola smoldered, with pieces breaking away and splashing into the sea. Smoke billowed and hid the nose of the craft from view. Hap moaned as he saw the fire creep toward the cocoon, threatening to open up a hole far too big to patch. The ship plummeted toward the sea, spinning as it fell.

"He's crashing," Oates said.

Umber leaned over the rail, staring hard, even nodding, with his breath whistling fast through his nose. "No. Not crashing. He's dousing the flames, while he can."

Just as the flames crawled onto the cocoon, the *Silkship* touched the ocean. The gondola was half submerged, with the nose pointing up. Steam rose and the flames died. The cocoon began to lose its shape, wrinkling and sagging, as bubbles gurgled up from the sinking gondola.

"Lord Umber," cried Hap, "we have to go back and help them!"

Umber shook his head. "That'll be the end of all of us, Hap. I think Pilot and his friends will make it. But only if we lure the *Shark* away."

Hap stared back, biting his lip. Umber was right, he could see. Even though the *Silkship* was lying crippled and vulnerable in the water, the *Shark* never veered from its pursuit of the *Eel*. Magador's men finally cut away the burning sail, which fluttered across the waves in flames. The ship crept after them, falling farther behind with every stroke of the *Eel*'s oars. Magador roared orders, swatting at men with his bow, as they climbed the ropes to hack at the gooey strands of web that snarled their remaining sails.

On the *Silkship* the dark forms of the spider-folk scrambled across the skin of the cocoon, frantically spinning and repairing. Finally, just when Pilot's vessel was so distant that it was nearly out of sight, the ship rose hesitantly from the water, just above the waves, and drifted in the opposite direction. Before long it vanished, hidden beyond the curving horizon.

Umber lowered the spyglass he'd been pressing against one eye. "I guess Pilot has seen enough."

Hap went downstairs. The men at the oars breathed heavily, and the air stank from perspiration. The beat of the drum had slowed with their pursuer delayed.

An oarsman called out to Hap, wheezing. "You, there. Have we left the *Shark* behind?"

"It's far away but still chasing us," Hap replied.

The man shook his head. "Magador will never quit this chase. Never."

"Shut your mouth and row," the man beside him said.

Fay walked between the benches, holding a tin cup with a long handle. She passed it to the oarsmen on either side so they could drink. Hap watched her for a moment. The quiet words she offered to the men seemed to refresh them as much as the water.

Hap wandered to the captain's quarters at the stern, where they'd left the eggs and the cage. He froze at the door. Sable was there, sitting with her legs folded under her skirt. She had a piece of cord that she dangled into the cage. The coppery dragon inside snapped at the cord, finally catching it and tugging it from side to side until Sable giggled and released it. She sensed that someone was behind and turned.

"Oh, hello," she said, smiling.

"Hello, Sable," Hap said. For some reason his voice cracked.

She stared at Hap's eyes for a long while and then turned back to the dragon. "It's so beautiful. What is its name?"

Hap shrugged. "It doesn't have one."

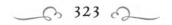

Sable wrinkled her nose. "It has to have a name! I'll think of one."

"All right," Hap said.

"Are you going to keep it? Will it be your pet?"

"I doubt it. It'll get big and dangerous. Umber wants to take it back where it belongs."

"Oh." Her lips formed a pout. "I suppose that's the right thing to do. And what were those creatures on the flying ship? I saw them—they looked horrible."

"They're not horrible at all," Hap said, crossing his arms.

Sable looked at him sideways, and then her mouth opened in a smile. "Jewel!"

"Excuse me?" Hap said.

"I will call the dragon Jewel. Her eyes are like gems. At least I'm going to say it's a girl dragon."

"Oh. Yes, Jewel is a good name."

"So are yours," she said.

"Mine?"

"Your eyes. They're like gems." She stood and faced him. "The dragon's eyes look like sapphires. Yours are like peridot."

Hap's face felt like he was too close to the sun. He could summon only single-word replies. "Uh . . . peridot?"

Sable stepped closer. "I've seen lots of gems. Magador gave

them to Fay. He was horrible to her most of the time. He hurt her and screamed at her. And he thought jewels would make it better, even though they didn't. He gave her diamonds, and rubies, and opals, and sapphires. But I think I liked the peridot the best." She was standing quite close now, looking into Hap's eyes.

"Oh. Um . . . oh." Hap wondered why his brain had turned to oatmeal. "I wonder . . . I'm going to see . . . Bye, now." He left the cabin and went back upstairs, where the ocean air might help him breathe.

The pursuit was a strange, almost tedious thing. The *Shark* had no replacement for its fallen sail and so could not regain all its speed. As the sun crossed overhead, Hap thought the *Eel* might even be pulling away. But as the afternoon wore on, the oarsmen tired. The former prisoners who were healthy enough to assist took turns at the oars. Umber joined them. Fay tried to row, but the men would not allow it, and she went back to toting water. She and Sable found the ship's provisions and brought biscuits and salted fish to the men.

Oates broke down the walls of the cabins and hurled them into the sea. Everything that could be spared, he tossed. And then he went down and rowed with the others.

Hap took his turn as well, rowing beside Umber, who

leaned closer to speak. "Hap, have you ever noticed that on some women, the tip of their nose moves ever so slightly as they talk? Just the tiniest wiggle, barely perceptible?"

Hap looked sideways at Umber. "I have never noticed that."

"Ah. Well, it's quite enchanting," Umber said, smiling to himself.

The limits of Hap's endurance had never been fully tested until those countless pulls on the oar. *My legs are stronger than my arms,* he thought, as his muscles were seared with pain. The skin on his palms blistered and tore, so that Fay had to wrap strips of cloth around his hands. An oarsman finally tapped him on the shoulder, taking his place, and Hap blundered up onto the deck to see how near the *Shark* had drawn.

His heart sagged. *So close again.* Magador was at the prow, easy to recognize. Soon he would test the range of their arrows once more. And the cauldron on the deck of the *Shark* was smoldering anew.

Doubt and regret gnawed at Hap's gut. They had taken this course across the open sea based on his vision. What if he'd been wrong? What if they were no longer on the right heading? He'd been secretly hoping that a friendly ship would cross their path and offer help. But there were no vessels in sight. If the *Shark* caught them, they were defenseless, and most of them would be too exhausted to fight. Even Oates with all his might could not hold off two hundred warriors.

Hap walked to the prow of the ship and leaned forward, staring at the horizon. Something was there. He squinted but could not bring it into focus. It was a blur of white, rising into the sky, tiny from this distance but surely enormous. *Smoke and steam,* he realized. The Inferno was ahead. He dashed down the stairs.

Umber was still at the oars, in the middle of telling a story to the rest of the men. As the oarsmen pulled, they tilted their heads to hear it better. And strangely, they all listened with expectant smiles. "And so, after that scolding, the messenger boy went back to the palace. A few days later he returned to the prince's country estate," Umber said, shouting over the drum. "And the prince asked him again, 'What news do you bring from the palace?' And the messenger boy said, 'The queen is on the roof and we can't get her down!'"

There was a pause, and a few puzzled glances, and an intake of breath, and then the men burst into raucous, howling laughter, so hard that tears rolled from their eyes. Amid the agony of exertion and the fear of annihilation it seemed to Hap that they welcomed any excuse to laugh.

Umber grinned widely. "Where I come from, gentlemen, that's the oldest joke in the book. How nice to find untainted ears!" He saw Hap looking at him and noted the urgent expression. "Yes, Hap?"

Hap stood beside him and spoke quietly. "The Inferno. I can see it."

"And how close is the *Shark*?"

"The arrows will reach us soon."

Umber called out to the men resting at the front of the room. "Can someone spell me?" One of the prisoners got wearily to his feet and limped down the aisle, still chuckling over the joke. Hap heard men repeating its final words—"The queen is on the roof and we can't get her down!"—and the laughter that rippled anew each time.

"Not much longer now, my friends," Umber said to the others. He went up the stairs, and Hap followed.

Umber rubbed his forearms and rolled his aching shoulders as he looked ahead of the ship, and behind. He called out to the helm. "Barber, do you see that column of smoke ahead?"

"I wish I didn't," Barber replied.

"Make straight for it."

"Oh, that's a grand idea," Barber replied. "And what will we do when we get there? Shall I rub spices all over myself, as long as I'm going to be roasted?"

Umber grinned. "I'm partial to rosemary myself." He turned to Hap and spoke quietly. "Find every bucket on the ship and fill them with seawater. If those arrows land, we'll put out the fires." He tapped his chin with his fist. "This is a pretty narrow ship, don't you think?"

Hap looked from rail to rail. It was a long craft, but slender indeed: at the widest less than ten strides across. When he guessed why Umber had asked, his stomach somersaulted. "No . . . No! Lord Umber, that's madness!"

Umber smiled on one side of his face. "Letting Magador catch us in open water is madness. Yes, Hap, we're going to take this ship right through the gap in the Inferno. As fast as we can, because those fissures will scorch her sides. The *Shark* is too wide to follow. This is the chance you gave us, Hap. The chance to live! It's some very fine meddling, in my opinion." He pinched his chin between his thumb and finger, turning something over in his mind. "We have to live, Happenstance. You and I. For more reasons than you know."

Hap squinted up at Umber. He was already being asked to someday save a world he'd never seen. How could there be more? He watched as Umber dug his hand into his vest pocket and pulled out the note from Prince Galbus. Umber unfolded it, perused it once more, and handed it to Hap. "I meant to keep this to myself. But if the worst happens today, I would like to know that somebody else has seen it. Go on, Hap. Read it."

Hap clutched the note between his cramped, aching fingers, and read it in silence.

My dear Lord Umber,

I have been immersed to my ears in preparation for the inevitable ascension to the throne. My poor father has his good days and bad, and I can hardly tell if he will be with us for another year or merely another day. He seems both astonished and pleased by my sudden sober nature. I spend as much time as I can by his side, assaulting him with questions about kingly things. There is nothing an aged person likes better than to find his knowledge sought and treasured, I have discovered.

There is one thing I wish you to know, Umber. I trust it will make you happy. Do you recall the paper you presented to my brothers and me a few years ago? A humble proposal, you named it. You suggested the formation of an advisory council, comprised of commoners from the four corners of the kingdom. Furthermore, you suggested that the members of that council be elected by a vote of their peers. Commoners choosing commoners, to offer advice to the king! I assume you recall how Argent nearly threw you bodily from the palace. He found your document dangerous, preposterous, and practically treasonous. I think you frightened him, really. After all, the power of a monarchy rests on the notion that only nobility has the right to rule. To Argent, the idea of extending any sort of power—even the advisory, symbolic power you suggested—to the common folk was to set a dangerous precedent that would ultimately lead to violent dissent.

Argent crumpled your proposal, threw it into the fire, and stormed out of the room. It might surprise you to know that I rescued the papers before they were consumed, and have kept them to this day. I perused them from time to time in my less drunken moments, and your ideas seeped into my consciousness. They stirred something in me, those words of yours. I could feel an awesome power within your proposal, and how it might lead to something wonderful, but it was beyond my blunted intellect to grasp.

With your words in mind and pocket, I did a reckless thing. I had my driver take me in a plain carriage far into the countryside, to a town where nobody would know my face.

And I went into an inn to seek a commoner—the sort of
man you think should be given a voice in our palace.

The very first person I met was the fellow who tended
the bar. This ordinary man, who could neither read
nor write, was in fact the most fascinating fount of
information and opinion, having served so many
travelers who ride in and out of that town. He knew
things, Umber. We talked of taxes and treaties, foreign
lands and domestic decrees. The barkeep had an agile
mind, and good sense as well. Believe me, I have met far
greater fools among our counts and barons.

I began to realize that you are even more clever than
we give you credit for, Umber. You knew what would
happen. Those ordinary people would prove their
worth, and in doing so, would finally understand their
worth. Once granted a voice they would not be muzzled.
And this would inevitably lead to . . . what? It is not that
the ordinary man would aspire to be a king. But still, the
course you set might one day mean the end of kings, for
the betterment of all men. That strikes me as glorious
somehow. I can begin to understand, but for my brain it
is like staring into the sun, and I have to look away.

Umber, I will make you no promises except this. When the time comes and the full weight of the crown rests on my unworthy head, you and I will talk at length about your humble proposal. I both dread that day, for my father's sake, and look forward to it, for men like the barkeep and his brethren.

Until then,
Yours in friendship,
Galbus
Prince of Celador

A sudden gust of wind tore the note from Hap's weakened grip. Umber clutched at the paper, but it slipped through his fingers, flew over the rail, and fluttered into the sea. He clapped his hands to his cheeks, but then lifted his face to the sky and guffawed, even as Hap cried, "I'm sorry!"

Umber tousled Hap's hair. "Ha! What does it matter. It's the ideas that count, not the paper they're written on. Besides, I've read it so many times, I know every word."

The vast column of smoke and steam was still miles away when the first arrow landed on the stern of the ship. The archers gathered at the prow of the *Shark*, and the cauldron of flame was brought forward. Magador waited, foremost among them, confident that the *Shark* was inching closer by the minute.

Hap looked over the side of the *Eel*. The oars wobbled as the strength of the oarsmen waned. On the *Shark* the arrows were dipped into flame and raised high.

"Take cover," Umber said. He and Oates and Hap, the only men on deck besides Barber at the wheel, ducked behind the short wall that protected the helm. Hap held his breath, and he heard arrows clatter on the deck.

Umber peeked over the wall. "We have seconds—put out the flames and get back here!"

They ran out, Umber and Hap with buckets of seawater and Oates with a barrel. A score of arrows had been launched, and half were blazing in the wooden planks. Hap put three of the fires out and then glanced at their pursuers. The archers were preparing a second volley. He dashed water on another flame and then hurried back for cover as Umber shouted, "Back to the helm, *now!*"

Hap pressed his back to the wall. The flaming arrows struck again, more hitting the mark by the sound of it. "This is bad," Oates said.

They hurried out a second time, doing what they could. At the prow of the *Shark* Magador raised a speaking trumpet to his lips. They could just make out his words across the distance. "Stow your oars and surrender now! It is your last chance for mercy."

"Mercy," growled Oates as he splashed water onto more flames. "Like he showed to Sophie. I know a lie when I hear it, Umber!"

Umber's eyes popped. "Look out!"

The archers had changed their tactics. Half of them had waited to fire until Oates, Umber and Hap had emerged from hiding, and now more streaks of feathered death rained down. Hap leaped aside, but from the corner of his eye he saw one heading straight for Oates. Just before it struck, Oates raised the barrel to his chest, and the arrow struck it, humming after it landed.

They rushed back to hiding again. Umber's chest heaved. "Let the fires burn—we'll douse them after we're inside."

"Inside what?" cried Barber. "Inside *that?*" He pointed at the Inferno. It was enormous before them, blotting out half of the sky. The flares of molten rock could be seen churning at the foot of the raging column of steam.

"We can do this," Umber said. He peered forward. "Hap, our gap was on this side. Do you see it?"

Hap stared at the fissures. "To the left," he said. "Next to the very tall plume of fire."

"You want me to take *this* ship through *that* gap?" cried Barber, when he realized where Hap was pointing.

"It'll be a close shave, Barber, but we can do it!" Umber waited with an openmouthed smile, but Barber failed to appreciate the pun.

Barber released the ship's wheel and stepped back, shaking his head. "No. It won't be me that dooms us. I won't."

"Allow me," Umber said, grabbing the wheel. "I've always wanted to steer a ship. Barber, get downstairs, and tell the men that this is the fateful moment. Speed the drum! One more pull and we'll slip through where the *Shark* cannot follow. Hurry, man—but don't get killed on your way."

Arrows rained down, reaching beyond the helm this time. The smell of burning wood stung Hap's nose. Barber gulped, peered over the wall, and then dashed for the stairs. Hap heard his voice below, exhorting the others. The drumbeat hastened: *Doomdoomdoomdoomdoom*. Men screamed as their muscles protested, pushed beyond the limits of endurance. But the splashing of the oars beside the ship was weak and out of rhythm, and paddles struck paddles.

Hap looked behind them, through a notch in the wall. He groaned aloud when he took in the scene. Small fires dotted the deck. The *Shark* had closed the distance faster than he could have imagined. She was nearly on top of them, and she had angled in her pursuit, preparing to draw up alongside. Near her rail stood a crowd of warriors with spears, swords, and axes. In front of them stood the archers, ready to let death fly toward anyone who presented a target. And in front of the archers, leaning over the rail, there were men with hooks on the ends of long lines, ready to swing and toss them.

"What's going on now?" asked Oates.

"They have ropes with claws on them."

"Grappling hooks," Umber said, always the educator. He kept his eye on the gap, easing the wheel to aim the ship carefully. "They'll use them to pull us close and board us. How much time do we have?"

Hap peeked again. The prow of the *Shark* was just yards behind their ship. But the men on her looked alarmed as they gaped first at the Inferno and then back at their helm, wondering if they would ever turn aside. Magador screamed an order, and the men with grappling hooks began to swing the ropes over their heads. "No time at all!" Hap cried.

Oates snatched up an empty barrel, then stood and flung it at the prow of the *Shark*. Hap watched through the notch as a flock of arrows was unleashed instantly. The men with the ropes ducked to avoid the barrel as it splintered. By the time they stood up again, the *Shark*'s prow had overtaken the stern of the *Eel*.

"Hold on!" Umber cried, making a final turn of the wheel. It brought them closer to the *Shark*, and the hulls squealed and the *Eel* rocked as they rubbed together. Hap felt a gust of heat wash across his face. The Inferno was directly ahead, a boiling, billowing wall of steam soaring a thousand feet high. Lava spewed from craggy vents to the right and left. The *Shark* was right beside them, crushing the rearmost oars. Magador dropped his bow and seized a battle-ax, and he roared as he stepped onto his ship's rail, ready to leap onto the *Eel*. But his fury turned to puzzlement, and then rage renewed, because the helmsman of the *Shark* altered her course, turning hard to keep from slamming into the fissures that lay ahead. Magador swung the ax, planting it in the *Shark*'s rail, and screamed at his helmsman.

The *Eel* entered the gap. Umber whooped and laughed with his face lit red by the fountains of molten rock. Hap could only wonder how a man could feel such joy with violent extinction so close at hand.

encountered our
warlords and cruel
tyrants, their deeds cannot
compare with the most brutal
and destructive forms of hatred
and conflict that plagued
my world. Could the monstrous
creatures and wicked beings that
dwell here be the reason, I
wonder? Perhaps when there
are ogres and trolls and goblins
to menace a people, they are
less inclined to turn their

CHAPTER
26

The first time they'd made this trip,
in a boat a third as wide, they had timed their passage to take
advantage of the ebb and flow of the eruptions. Now the fissures
raged on either side. Hap heard howls of protest and woe as
the men below glimpsed the brilliant, orange-hot spectacle
through their oar holes. Blobs of molten rock rained down
on the sides of the deck, where they smoldered and ate into
the planks. Oates raised a barrel for protection, and Hap and
Umber huddled underneath. The *Eel* shuddered and groaned as
if the ship could feel the pain, and a terrible wrenching sound
came from the starboard side as it scraped on submerged stone.
Oars snapped like twigs, the ship shuddered, and their progress
slowed. For a terrible moment Hap thought they might stop

altogether and be burned alive, but they crawled forward again as the remaining oars plunged in a sudden burst of energy fueled by panic.

Umber crowed like a rooster and threw his hands toward the sky as they cleared the fiery gauntlet. He shouted toward the hatch: "We're in! We've done it!" There were weak shouts from below, and dozens of thumps as men slid off their seats and collapsed on the floor, utterly spent.

"Bear in mind, the ship's on fire," Oates said.

"Ha, ha! We should put those out," Umber said.

The few men with any remaining strength staggered upstairs to help extinguish the fires, splashing them with buckets of seawater and smothering them with wet cloth. Hunks of lava cracked and hissed as they were doused.

A warm mist surrounded the ship, as the curtain of steam was pushed into the Inferno by the following breeze. But as the boat drifted forward, the mist cleared, and the island of the bidmis came into view. Barber dropped to his knees as he beheld it. His voice fell to a frightened, reverent whisper. "What is this place?"

"Desolas lies ahead," Umber said.

Hap stared. The great, glassy obsidian palace was still there, with its soaring tower that pierced the sky. The hundred-foot statue was complete and the scaffolding removed to reveal a perfect likeness of Caspar. More remarkable still, the bidmis had somehow found the pigments needed to paint the figure, and they had achieved such perfect color that the figure looked ready to step off its stone pedestal and wade into the sea.

The great pyramid of glass was gone, as if it had never existed. In its place a new structure rose: a giant staircase, spiraling upward and around in ever tighter circles. When it was done, Hap could see, it would be the tallest thing on the island yet, vaulting even higher than the lofty tower.

Fay stood beside Hap, and Sable beside her. "There are . . . little *people* on that island," Sable said.

"They are the bidmis," Hap said. And to himself he added, *Perhaps Caspar is still alive after all.*

Most of the oarsmen were on the deck now, and when they saw the island their words grew from a buzz to a roar. Umber stepped up to the helm and cupped his hands beside his mouth. "My friends, my friends—lower your voices and listen!" Every head turned his way. "We're safe for the moment, but it might be best for us to take this ship back into the mist. As you can see, there are some unusual creatures dwelling on that island."

"They're goblins, is what they are!" an oarsman shouted. "Millions of them!"

"Quiet, please. Not goblins," Umber replied. "And you

exaggerate their numbers. There can't be more than fifty thousand."

That statement did nothing to calm the crowd. Umber waved his hands downward, asking for silence. "But please, my friends, some of you get back downstairs and help us turn this ship around. We're drifting closer by the second, and I don't want a certain fellow on that island to see us."

The men muttered, but two dozen trudged down the stairs. In the near silence that followed, a chilling sound rolled across the water. It was a voice: thin, weak, utterly desperate, and on the brink of insanity. "Umber! I see you on that ship, Umber! Are you back to save me? For your sake I hope so! Come here this instant or I'll send them after you, you hear me? *You hear me?*"

Umber sighed and rapped his head with his knuckles. "A bit of bad luck there, my friends." He shouted across the waves. "On my way, Caspar!"

The reply was a mad cackle. Hap saw Caspar on the balcony of his obsidian palace, dancing and waving his hands in the air before falling to his knees and crawling down the stairs.

The *Eel* drew closer to the island, and the men raised their heads to take in the vast, bizarre structures that loomed over them.

"Listen carefully," Umber told them from the prow. "Do not make the slightest threatening gesture toward that man or those creatures. They will destroy any attackers. And nobody should set foot on that place. As long as your feet are in the water, you are safe."

"Our feet aren't leaving this boat," Barber said, and every man's head nodded in agreement.

Caspar stood at the shore, waving them closer with trembling hands. Exhaustion was etched deep into his face, with his eyes sunken, bloodshot, and constantly blinking. He teetered from side to side, on the verge of falling over, and pinched the flesh of his own arms to stay awake.

Umber looked down at the water below their prow, and called back. "Stop rowing. We'll drift the rest of the way." Barber relayed the order to the men below, and the oars rose dripping from the water. A moment later the hull ground against the bottom.

"Hello, Caspar," Umber said. "We are here because our lives were in—"

"Get off the ship! Stand in the water before me!" cried Caspar. Spittle flew from his mouth as he screamed.

One of the smallest bidmis appeared at Caspar's side. "What do you bid me, master?"

Caspar stared down at the thing with goggling eyes. "Must

you trouble me now, you miserable thing? Curse you all. . . . Play your drums and dance for me, then!" The bidmi bowed and trotted away, and Caspar whirled back to snarl at Umber. "Did you hear me? Come off that ship and stand before me! And bring that little Meddler with you!"

Umber looked at Hap, wincing. "Sorry, my friend."

Boards were quickly hammered across four barrels to make a crude raft, which was lowered to the water. Hap and Umber scrambled down ropes and climbed onto the raft, using a pair of oars to row it closer to shore. A deep, low drumming had begun, and the whole island seemed to vibrate. Every bidmi on the island ceased in its labor and began a strange dance. They dropped into a low crouch, waved their arms and hopped from side to side. They clacked their teeth to the rhythm as well, and the sound sent jagged chills across Hap's every nerve.

"Can you save me, Umber? Do you know the way?" Caspar's hands shook so badly that it took an effort to clasp them together and raise them.

"Caspar, I realize you are close to the breaking point," Umber said. "I sent Balfour back to Kurahaven to search for an answer. And I have made my own inquiries during my recent journey. I wish I could offer hope, but in truth I don't know if there is a way out of your predicament."

Caspar's face lost its last trace of color. He slumped to the ground and whined. "No way at all?"

Umber shook his head. "I beg you, do not harm the people that are with me because I did not return with a solution. They came here only to save themselves from a terrible fate. But Caspar, there is still a chance that Balfour may turn something up."

Caspar's shoulders shook, and his face contorted. "But what of your little Meddler, Umber? Surely he can steer fate in my favor! Can't you, boy?"

Hap couldn't look at Caspar. He stared at the waves. "I am sorry, sir. I can't control these powers of mine yet. I truly wish I could."

"Balfour may be on his way here now, for all we know," Umber said.

Caspar waved his hand in the air. "No, Umber. There is no more time. I can't hang on any longer. No sleep. No rest. My mind . . . I'm losing my grip, Umber. Soon those horrible, hairless things will ask my bidding, and my muddled thoughts will have no answer. Or I will not be able to wake from my slumber. I will be devoured, and do you know what? I welcome death, and the release it brings. That winding stair they are building? I mean to walk off its top step when it is done. And then these cursed creatures can return to their chambers, and heaven help the next fool who knocks on their door. It's true, Umber. I've known it all along. Death is the only release from this curse. Only death."

Umber stood a little straighter. Hap looked at him and could almost see the thought sparking in Umber's brain. Umber mouthed some words and scratched at the air with a finger. "Caspar," he said. "There is a chance. It will take more nerve than you can imagine. If you are willing to try . . ."

Caspar raised his head and pushed the tangles of hair out of his red-streaked eyes. "A chance? Tell me, Umber. I will try anything!"

Umber swept a hand across his mouth, hesitating. "It's true—death is the only escape. So you must die."

Caspar's head wobbled, neither shaking nor nodding. "Do you jest, Umber?"

Umber looked right and left to see if any bidmis were near. "This is hard to explain. In the place I came from, there were ways to revive the dead—but only if they weren't dead for long. Minutes, I mean. You must *die*, Caspar. By drowning yourself somehow, or cutting off your own air. Your heart will stop, and your breath will cease. Caspar, I don't know if this will work! Will such a death make the bidmis return to their slumber? Will they leave soon enough, so that I may revive you? It's a terrible chance to take—I can't even say for sure that I can bring you back." Umber squeezed his eyes shut tight. "I can't believe I'm suggesting this."

"Tell me . . . tell me what . . . ," Caspar said, slurring his words. His mouth sagged open and his eyelids fluttered, and he toppled onto his side. His head thumped against the stone, and the pain jolted him back to consciousness. He cried out and pushed himself up again, first to his knees and then unsteadily to his feet. Tears tumbled from his eyes. "Tell me what to do! How to die!" he howled.

"All right . . . all right. Let me think . . ." Umber gulped and pulled at his chin, searching his mind for the answer.

Hap heard voices on the ship behind them—many of them together, crying out in alarm. The words were lost amid the drumming of the bidmis. He turned to see what was happening, and time slowed to a snail's pace as he comprehended.

He saw the oarsmen peering from the oar holes, and the former prisoners lining the rail of the upper deck with Fay and Sable among them. But they weren't staring at the island anymore. They were pointing at the small boat that had crept up behind them—a vessel that must have been kept aboard the *Shark*. Eight men rowed it, and Magador stood at its prow with his bow raised before him.

The bow was empty, the arrow already in flight. Hap barely perceived it passing, like the shadow of a bird. It missed

Umber's ear by the narrowest of margins, and his hair even fluttered as it passed. There was a sound, sharp and soft at the same time, like a bite from an apple. Hap heard a grunt; when he turned he saw Caspar stumbling back with the shaft of the arrow lodged deep in his chest.

Somehow Caspar stayed on his feet, caught his balance, and stepped awkwardly forward again. He gazed down at the arrow and did the most curious thing: He laughed.

The drumming, the clacking of teeth, and the dancing stopped in the same instant. The silence was total and stunning. Every bidmi, from the tiny one nearby to the last one working atop the winding stair, turned toward Caspar, freezing in place.

Caspar took another awkward step forward. He blinked, and his eyes focused on the small boat and the man with the bow. He raised a finger and pointed. "I bid you . . . ," he tried to say, but his voice wheezed and failed. He gurgled, toppled, and fell into the sand.

The clacking of teeth began again, in a perfect, terrible, and deafening rhythm. The bidmis swarmed forward, down from the structures and out of the holes that riddled the island. They came at them like an avalanche, unstoppable. Hap heard the men on the *Eel* screaming, and even the piercing cry of Sable. Umber cried, "I'm sorry, Happenstance!" and wrapped his arms around him.

Hap shut his eyes, hoping that whatever happened would be swift. He heard water splashing before them . . . and then churning beside them. Umber's mouth was at his ear, shouting. "They know! They know it wasn't us, Hap! *They know!*"

Hap opened his eyes and saw the horde of creatures swimming past them, parting around the raft. The sea was so thick with bidmis that there was hardly any water to be seen at all, just pale bodies with arms whipping at blinding speed.

Magador strung another arrow in his bow. He raised it again, pointing it at the multitudes. Behind him the poor men who'd rowed him into the Inferno gaped, bug-eyed and howling with fear, at the approaching creatures. There was no time to turn their boat and flee. Some had weapons with them, and they lifted swords and axes, as if the onslaught could be deterred. Magador swept the bow right and left and finally let the futile arrow fly into the center of the mass before throwing the bow after it.

The boat rocked upward, and Hap heard wood crunching as the gnashing jaws of the swiftest bidmis chewed the hull. The full mass of the creatures slammed into the boat. They tipped it higher, with its prow pointing straight up. A shrieking Magador tried to climb onto the peak. Then the craft toppled, spilling the screaming men into the sea, and Hap shoved his face into Umber's chest and plugged his ears with his fingers.

There was near silence again a moment later. The clacking of teeth had ended—when there was nothing left to gnash, it seemed. Hap opened his eyes to see the waters growing calm again. The bidmis were returning to the island.

"Umber," came a croaking voice from the island. It was Caspar, lying on his back, with his ashen face turned toward them. One fist was wrapped around the arrow. His breath rasped, and he could only manage a few words at a time. "Not the . . . sort of death you . . . meant for me . . . is it?"

Umber rubbed the heel of his hand against his cheek. His mouth quivered. "Caspar. I truly wanted to save you."

The bidmis began to emerge from the water. They gathered around Caspar, with the smallest of them standing closest, staring silently down.

"Umber . . . ," Caspar said. "The archives I stole . . . about the Meddlers . . . You can find them . . ."

Umber sniffed. "Where, Caspar?"

Caspar's voice was only a whisper. "Not here. Left them . . . hid them . . . strongbox . . . you must find them . . ." The voice faded to nothing. Caspar's eyes closed, and his mouth went on moving, shaping but not sounding words. And then his lips fell still.

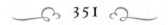

The crowd of bidmis that surrounded Caspar had grown, swelling to thousands and tens of thousands. They waited, staring, still and silent. Hap held his breath, wondering if the creatures would devour their dying master. Instead they turned as one and marched to the center of the island. They swarmed toward a great gaping hole beside the obsidian palace, flowing into it like water. Within minutes they had vanished, and the island was deserted except for Caspar.

Umber leaped off the raft into waist-deep water and rushed toward the shore.

"Umber, no!" shouted Fay from the rail of the *Eel*.

Umber ran onto the sand and kneeled by Caspar's side. He placed his hands on Caspar's chest, beside the arrow, and pressed down over and over again. He put his mouth to Caspar's and blew air into his lungs. All the while, Hap's gaze darted toward the hole where the bidmis had gone, but none of the awful creatures reappeared. Umber finally put his fingers to Caspar's neck, just below the ear, and again on Caspar's wrist. Finally, he straightened Caspar's legs and folded his arms, arranging him in a position of sad dignity. Umber stood and bowed his head for a moment, and then walked back to the raft.

He looked at Hap and sighed. "Oh, how I dread telling Smudge."

CHAPTER
27

Umber looked into the tunnel at the center of Desolas, holding a lamp shoulder-high.

"You want to go *in* there?" asked Oates.

Umber nodded. "You think I can resist? Just a quick peek. Come on, my friends."

They had decided to wait inside the Inferno for a day, hoping that the crew of the *Shark* would give up on Magador's return and decide to move on. In the meantime, to Hap's chagrin, Umber had insisted on this final exploration.

The tunnel wound like a staircase into the heart of the island. The air grew thicker and warmer with every step, and when Hap let his fingertips brush the rock walls, they were hot to the touch.

They came to the door that Caspar had described when they first met him on Desolas. It was barely as tall as Hap, but twice as wide, and made of ancient dark metal. A thick oval iron ring, big enough to fit one's head through, hung from its center. Words were etched into the door. The language was ancient and arcane, Hap knew, but he could still translate it aloud: "Knock thrice and master you shall be."

"Fancy that," Umber said. "All it takes to condemn yourself is to rap on this door." He pressed an ear against the door and listened for a while, then stepped back. Hap's heart shimmied up his throat as he saw Umber's hand rise toward the knocker. Oates reached out to seize him, but Umber opened his hand to show the stub of charcoal that he was holding. "Oh, did I frighten you again? Relax, my friends. Even I have more sense than to knock on this door. But with your permission I'll scrawl a warning for the next poor soul to read."

Hap's spirits lifted when, upon leaving the tunnel, they were greeted by a most welcome sight: the *Silkship* hovering over Desolas. When he saw Umber on the shore, Pilot brought the ship down.

The ship was battered and scorched. The floor of the gondola was just a lattice of threads. Hap's mouth turned dry when he counted only two of the spider-folk—one on the outside of the cocoon and one at the rail. His mind vividly replayed for him the memory of flames spreading across the ship and the spider-folk battling to save it. When he realized which of the creatures was missing, a frenzied shout exploded from his lips: "Arabell! Pilot, where is Arabell?"

Pilot leaned over the rail, and to Hap's great relief Arabell clambered up to his shoulder. She squealed a greeting, and Hap laughed and waved, surprised to feel a tear tumbling down his cheek.

"I never would have believed you could take that ship into the Inferno," Pilot said when the *Silkship* was nearly touching the shore.

"Now we're wondering when we can take her out," Umber replied. "Did you see that ship lurking outside?"

"I saw her sailing away as I approached," Pilot said. "She left corpses in her wake, just outside this ring of fire. So we can imagine what happened."

Umber nodded, grimacing. He turned to Hap and Oates with an explanation. "A mutiny, obviously. Magador left men in charge with orders to wait for him. The crew of the ship got other ideas when Magador did not return quickly." Umber pressed a hand against his stomach and shook his head. "I know those people meant us harm . . . but the loss of life these days. It's terrible. Terrible."

Sable gripped Hap's hand with such force that Hap wondered if even Oates could pry him free. "You're really getting on that ship with those horrible spider things?" she asked.

"They're nice when you get to know them," Hap replied.

"I wish you could come with us," Sable said quietly.

Hap shrugged. He wanted to answer her, but it was still hard to think when she was near. Something about the way she looked at him befogged his mind.

Umber and Fay were beside them on the sand. "You'll be fine," Umber told Fay. "Pilot said the weather is favorable for your journey. Barber is a good sailor—he'll get you to the island where my shipping company has a port. And then my letter of instructions will deliver you comfortably to Kurahaven, and we will meet you there."

"You have been more than kind, Umber. None of us will forget what you have—" Fay stopped and covered her face with one hand. "Is there something wrong with my nose?"

Umber's face turned pink.

"You were staring at it just now," Fay added.

"What? No! No, my lady. I didn't . . . uh . . . aah . . ." Umber fumbled for and finally recovered his wits. "As I was about to say, we have a quick mission to accomplish before we head back to Kurahaven. If you arrive before me, allow my man Balfour to show you around our grand city. But it's not time for farewells yet. We'll join you on the *Eel* and help you out of the Inferno before we part company."

With the oarsmen rested and the eruptions better timed, the *Eel* prepared to leave the Inferno through the gap. The *Silkship* dropped a line from above that Oates secured to the prow of the *Eel*, and when the oarsmen started to row, the flying ship pulled from above, adding to their speed. They passed through the gap with only a few more scorch marks to show for it.

The Silkship dropped a ladder onto the deck of the *Eel*. Umber asked every man on the ship to assemble on the deck, and he stood on a barrel, where all could see and hear him. "Gentlemen. The lady Fay carries a letter from me, bearing my seal. At the port where you are heading, she will present my letter to my associates. And if she and Sable have been delivered safely across these seas, each of you will receive your thirty pieces of gold." This pronouncement drew cheers from the men and a quiet smile from Fay.

Hap stepped close to Fay and Sable and spoke quietly. "I would like to give you something." With his body shielding the sight from others, he uncurled his fist and showed them the object he held. It was the locket that Nima had given him, opened to reveal the enormous pearl inside. Sable gasped and covered her mouth. "You might need this on your journey. To buy your safety, or even your comfort. Please take it." He closed the locket, took Fay's wrist, and pressed it into her hand.

Fay smiled and pushed her fingers through his hair. "This is far too generous, Happenstance. I will take it for safekeeping, but only so that I can return it when we see you again in Kurahaven."

"But you'll use it if you need it?" Hap asked, stealing a glance at Sable. Her mouth was hanging open, and her eyes were enormous.

"We will," Fay answered, and she kissed his cheek.

After long good-byes Oates climbed up to the *Silkship*, followed by Hap and finally Umber, and the vessels parted ways.

The sack of dragon eggs had been brought aboard, and the cage with the baby dragon as well. Oates stared at something at the other end of the gondola: a long, lumpy object wrapped in canvas. "Ugh. Why didn't we just bury him, Umber?"

Umber clasped his hands behind his back and cleared his throat. "Oates. Happenstance. We need to talk."

Hap sat up straight. When Umber called him Happenstance and not Hap, the topic was usually turning serious. Pilot, who was consulting charts at the wheel, looked over his shoulder.

Even the three spider-folk, who were still busy repairing the damaged gondola, stopped and watched.

Umber pressed his lips together, hesitating before he spoke. "We know that there is a great destiny in store for Happenstance. Oates, I have not told you everything, but you must understand that the stakes are extraordinarily high, and a billion lives may be at stake."

Oates began to cry out, but Umber raised a hand. "Nobody you know, Oates; nobody you know. And if I tried to explain how I know this is true, I'm not sure you'd believe me. But it *is* true. And only Hap can save them."

Hap shuddered. He hated the thought of this, and the crushing weight it brought down on his spirit.

Umber put a hand on Hap's shoulder. "That is why we need to discover everything we can about what the Meddlers are and what they are capable of. We must learn about Willy Nilly, the man who gave Hap his special abilities. Caspar had at least some of the answers we seek, in the documents he stole from my archives. Those documents are now in a strongbox that Caspar has hidden elsewhere. We must find it and retrieve it. And we will do whatever it takes."

Hap looked again at the still form wrapped in canvas. The spider-folk had wound their thread around it at the ankles,

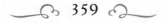

knees, waist, chest, and neck, binding it tight. "But there's nothing we can do, Lord Umber. Only Caspar knew where the strongbox is. And now he's dead."

Umber's mouth shrank and tightened. "Like I said, Hap. We will do *whatever it takes*."

Hap scrunched his eyebrows. He couldn't imagine what Umber meant.

"I don't like this, and I don't imagine you will either," Umber said. He turned his back to them and lowered his head. "I have asked Pilot to take us to the soul crabs."

Hap's stomach churned. He pushed himself to his feet, leaned over the side of the gondola, and vomited into the sea.

CHAPTER
28

Hap didn't want to, but he kept looking at the shrouded body. Every time he did, he lowered his face between his knees and clasped his hands behind his neck. Umber must have noticed, because while Hap's face was buried, he whispered something to Pilot. Hap heard the chatter of the spider-folk, and then the sounds of claws scrabbling and cloth scraping. The next time he looked up, Caspar's body was nowhere in sight. Hap found it a while later when he peered through the gaps in the newly repaired floor. The body was dangling under the gondola, suspended by thin lines of silk.

Umber sat beside the cage with the baby dragon, feeding it pieces of fish that the spider-folk had caught. The dragon swallowed the pieces with gusto, then opened its mouth and squealed for more.

"How is Jewel?" Hap said, kneeling beside him.

"Jewel? You've named her?" Umber said.

Hap shrugged. "Sable did."

"Ah, *Sable*," Umber said, with a sly emphasis. He bumped Hap's shoulder with his fist. "Well, Jewel is an excellent name for this dazzling creature. After all the excitement this is my first chance to study her at length. I think it is a she, after all. Look at those limbs . . . almost catlike. And do you see the fluff at the edges of the wings, and in a ring around the base of the neck? Those might be feathers when the dragon is grown."

"Lord Umber," Hap said. "Do we really have to do this?"

Umber's lips formed a pout. "Study the dragon?"

Hap shook his head and pointed down, where Caspar's body dangled. "Maybe we don't need to learn more about the Meddlers after all. I mean, maybe Willy Nilly doesn't want us to know."

Umber drummed on his kneecaps. "Hap, if he didn't want us to try to find out, he wouldn't have left you with me for a guardian. Finding out is what I do, for heaven's sake. I can't resist."

Hap squeezed his eyes shut. "But to bring Caspar to that island . . . with those crabs . . . it's not right. . . ."

"It's my decision, Hap. You don't have to bear the guilt." Umber slipped another piece of fish between the bars of the cage, and the dragon snapped it up.

When they finally arrived at the islet of the soul crabs, Hap could not watch it happen. He went to the far side of the *Silkship* and stared at the horizon. Only once did he glimpse down, to see hundreds of the soul crabs pouring out of the cracks and caves on the little spit of land. They jabbered in all their voices and languages, and they raised their pincers high when they saw the ship floating above them and the shrouded form being lowered. After that Hap kept his eyes closed for a long time. And when he heard the noises begin, he jammed his thumbs into his ears and hummed to himself.

After some time he heard a commotion behind him, and Umber's voice shouting.

"That's it! Haul it aboard! Mind the pincers, Arabell! Watch yourself. . . . Nicely done, Gossilen!"

Hap opened his eyes to see one of the awful soul crabs lying upside down on the floor of the gondola. The spider-folk had wound their silk around its claws and legs, so the thing could barely move except for twitching. The eyestalks turned in every direction, and ugly gray spittle flowed from its wide mouth as a series of voices emerged. An old woman said, "Who are ye people, and what do ye think yer doing?" A man said, "What year is it, man? Do you know the year?" A child said in a strange language, "I'm still hungry; have you got any more?"

Umber leaned over the crab and shouted into its face. "Quiet, all of you! I want to talk to Caspar! Caspar, are you there?"

"I don't feel well," said the crab, in the voice of a young girl.

Umber scratched his head and frowned. He tapped the crab's shell with his foot, and the nearest claw snapped in vain. "I need to talk to Caspar! I've got some nice fish for you if you cooperate."

"We don't eat fish," said an old man's voice. "It's castaways we like."

"Listen, you," Umber said, wagging a finger. "We'll make a chowder out of *you* if you don't let us talk to Caspar. I know he's in there somewhere. Let him speak!"

The crab fell silent for a moment, and then a new voice rose up, different from any other so far. It was as low as distant thunder, echoing itself, and the words were in a tongue that Hap sensed was very old, perhaps the oldest of all. The sound crawled under his skin and jangled his nerves.

"What was *that*?" said Pilot.

"Hap," Umber said, gaping at the crab. "By any chance . . . ?"

"I understand him," Hap answered, after he took his hand off his mouth. "He said we don't have to kill him. He'll die anyway if we don't put him back on the island soon."

Umber crept closer to the crab again, and crouched beside it. "You there . . . who are you?"

The voice spoke again, and Hap shivered as he translated the words. "He said, 'I was the first. Long, long ago.'" From the corner of his eye Hap saw a white-faced Oates back away until his hips were at the railing.

Umber's eyes blinked madly. "The first . . . the first to get shipwrecked on that island?"

Hap's mouth was so dry it was hard to translate the next words aloud. "The first to wash ashore dead. But somehow not dead at all . . . because he awoke after death, and his mind was . . . as one with the crabs. And he was lonely . . . until more ships were wrecked . . . more bodies washed ashore over time . . . and he was glad for the company. . . ." Hap clapped a hand over his mouth. He wished the crab would stop talking so he wouldn't have to translate.

"What did he mean, he'll die if we don't put him back?"

The crab answered in that frightening voice. Hap relayed the message: "The island is special . . . if the crabs leave, they die. . . . He hasn't much time."

"Then let Caspar speak!" Umber cried.

The ancient voice murmured and fell silent. All they heard for a while was the snipping of hundreds of claws far below, and the hollow clatter of jostling shells. And then Hap's legs weakened when he heard a familiar voice coming from the crab's mouth. "Umber . . . Umber, is that you? I am here . . . but what has happened to me? I feel so odd. My vision is strange . . . you're hard to see."

"Caspar!" Umber cried, leaning closer. The stalks twisted, turning the eyes toward him. "Quickly, we don't have much time. You said you needed to tell me where you hid the stolen archives. The Meddler archives, Caspar! Where is the strongbox?"

The stalks quivered. "Have I escaped, Umber? From the bidmis?"

"You are gone from Desolas, Caspar. But what about the strongbox?"

"Why do my arms feel so strange? And my legs . . ." The stalks twisted, and the eyes looked down at the crustacean body. "What is this? What magic is this? Wait, I remember now—the arrow. It killed me. I know I died! *And what has become of me now?*" The legs writhed, but with failing strength.

"Caspar, there's no time. You must tell me about the strongbox!"

The ancient voice returned, deep and terrifying: *"Tell him,"* it said.

Caspar's voice whimpered and sobbed. The sound made Hap's throat constrict. "The strongbox . . . the strongbox. There's an inn south of Kurahaven, Umber. In Humble Hill. A cousin of mine runs the place. He's keeping it safe for me. Oh, Umber. What has become of me? And now I feel so weak. . . ." The voice trailed off. The eyes sagged on their stalks.

"Let it go," Umber said, getting to his feet. He bit his bottom lip. "That's what I had to know."

The spider-folk tugged on the lines of silk, dragging the crab up and over the side of the gondola. They lowered the crab to the sand thirty feet below, amid the horde. The others crowded close and snipped away the threads that bound the captured crab, tasting it and then spitting it out. Soon the crab that they'd captured could not be told apart from the rest of the awful creatures.

"I suppose we could snag another one and learn more," Umber said.

"No," said Pilot. He crossed his arms. "No more. These are abominations, and this is a foul, accursed place."

"I suppose it is," Umber said, nodding. "And I truly hope that's not really Caspar's soul in there. For the sake of mine." He wiped his hands down the front of his shirt, as if to clean them. "Let's not tell Smudge about this, all right?"

"And how am I supposed to keep that secret?" grumbled Oates.

"Good point," Umber replied. "Just stay away from him until I find a way to break the news."

"Fine with me," Oates said. "He reeks anyway."

Umber sighed. His next words made Hap want to shout with joy. "It's time we went home, my friends. The lair of the dragons is beyond Kurahaven, so we might as well rest at the Aerie for a while. Then we'll figure out the best way to take the eggs and the baby back where they belong."

They flew over the sea through day and night. The spider-folk kept mending and reinforcing the damaged floor of the gondola, spinning thread across the gaps, and tugging the crumpled cocoon back into its oval shape.

Hap leaned on the rail under a black sky salted with stars. Arabell spun a web between the rail and the cocoon and clung to it, right by Hap's shoulder. Hap scratched her behind the ears. She closed her eyes and made a soft trilling noise like a cricket. Hap wasn't sure why, but the image of Sable's face kept flashing in his mind. And curiously, he would see Sophie's fragile features nearly as often, and one face would displace the other, like two sides of a coin tossed in the air.

Pilot loomed over Hap's shoulder and pointed far below. "Those lights."

Hap stared at the spot, where tall arms of land embraced a calm bay, and a city stood by the shore on a rambling slope. A palace, stately and beautiful even from this great distance, rose above all. "We're home," Hap said.

"Wake your companions," Pilot said.

CHAPTER
29

Not a single light could be seen in the windows of the Aerie as they descended. Hap's heart warmed at the familiar sights: Umber's round tower rising from the square rooftop garden, and his own room at the corner of the Aerie, inside the great carved face. Umber chattered as they approached. "Gentlemen, this was an eventful journey. If we could have saved Caspar, I'd have deemed it a complete success. Think of all the good, though. A tyrant has fallen—and the tyrant who would take his place, as well. A kingdom and its people are free. We have the dragon eggs, and a baby dragon to boot. And we are close to unraveling Hap's mysteries.

"I'm starting to think that everything is turning our way, my friends. Even here in Kurahaven, Prince Galbus could soon be king—a man who, despite his flaws, understands the power of freedom and the voice of common folk. It's almost too much to ask for. I think I will celebrate by making myself an enormous pot of coffee. Better yet, Balfour can make it, if he is here. I will rouse him at once, and tell him, 'Eggs, Balfour! Omelets, bacon, toast, and coffee, as fast as you can produce it!'"

Hap smiled as the gondola touched the terrace beside Umber's tower. It seemed like a thousand years had passed since Umber had nearly woken the sea-giants, and they'd seen the death-boar in the forest, and Prince Argent had fallen.

But he was finally home again, and he couldn't wait to see Sophie and Balfour. Even surly Thimble and dour Lady Truden would be welcome sights. The only encounter he dreaded was with Smudge, because of the terrible news they would deliver.

"Moorings, girls," Pilot called to the spider-folk. Arabell, Quellen, and Gossilen scrambled over the sides, trailing lines of silk, and tied the ship down so it floated inches above the terrace.

Pilot opened the door in the side, and Hap leaped out first, delighted to feel the rock of the Aerie under his feet once more.

"I'm hungry too," Oates said, stomping toward the stairs. "I'll get Balfour."

"Wake him gently," Umber called after him. He yawned and arched his back, and then bent down and touched his toes.

"My payment, Umber," Pilot said.

"Oh, yes," Umber replied. "It's in my tower. Will you join us for breakfast before you leave?"

"I want to go before dawn," Pilot said.

"Always shy to be seen," Umber said. "I must say, though, you revealed yourself and your ship more than once on this journey."

"Only when necessary to save you, so I might be paid."

Umber chuckled. "Fair enough." He unlocked his tower door with his remarkable key. Just as he emerged again with a bulging, lumpy sack in one hand, a bleary-eyed Balfour came up the steps. Sophie rushed past him, padding on bare feet, still tying a robe over her sleeping gown. She flew to Hap and wrapped her arms tight around him. "We thought you were gone forever, lost at sea," she said, weeping.

"Balfour!" Umber cried, spreading his arms wide. "Yes, Hap is alive and well. And how good to see you! First, I'm sorry to say that you don't need to bother researching the bidmis anymore. Poor Caspar has met his demise."

"Umber," Balfour said quietly. It was almost a croak.

Umber didn't notice. "But we will tell you about everything, the whole amazing adventure. We got 'em, Balfour! The dragon eggs, and an infant dragon too! But before the tale I have an urgent need of coffee. A bucket of coffee. A barrel of coffee!"

"Umber," Balfour said again, louder.

The somber tone finally caught Umber's attention. His smile vanished. "What . . . what is it? Is something wrong?"

Balfour's face turned toward the stones at his feet. "It's Galbus. Prince Galbus."

Sophie's arms tightened around Hap. He felt her tears on his neck. Balfour raised his head and met Umber's questioning stare.

"He's dead, Lord Umber. The good prince is dead."

...on my latest episode of despair. This was particularly brutal, Balfour. I can hardly communicate how deep and dark is the pit into which I tumble. While I am afflicted, I spend hours pondering the